Romans 15:13

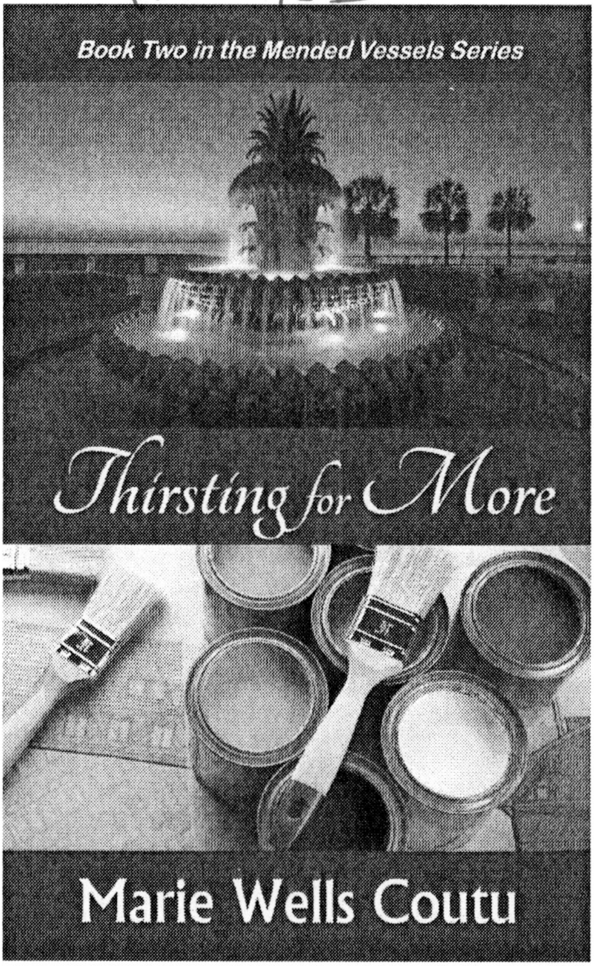

Marie Wells Coutu

Thirsting for More

ISBN-13: 978-1-938092-80-0
ISBN-10: 1938092805

This book is a work of fiction. Names, characters, places, and incidents are either products of the author's imagination or used fictitiously. Any similarity to actual people and/or events is purely coincidental.

Published by Write Integrity Press, 2631 Holly Springs Pkwy Box 35, Holly Springs, GA 30142.

www.WriteIntegrity.com

Printed in the United States of America.

Dedication

To my best friend and husband of forty-three years, who encourages me to write the stories God has placed on my heart, even when it means he has to share me with my characters and my readers. I have loved exploring Charleston and other places with him. From our beginning, he has shown me a love that many women never get to experience. Serving Jesus hand-in-hand with him makes my heart glad.

Acknowledgements

First, thank you to the readers of my first novel who have encouraged me and pestered me about when the next book would be done. Sorry it took so long!

And the many who helped shape this story and bring it to market (hope I don't forget anyone):

Susan May Warren and the "Toy Box" members of Deep Thinkers Retreat 2013 provided inspiration and gave me a better understanding of how to craft a novel with fully developed characters and beautiful writing. Most of all, Beth Vogt and Rachel Hauck, without your help, I would have floundered in the muddiness of a messy and superficial plot.

A special note of appreciation goes to my "first readers" for this book—Crystal Allen and her daughter. Your comments are always valuable and improve my stories, and I value your friendship.

C.L. Dyck helped me to finally understand MRUs and how to use them to keep the story flowing. Thanks also for your advice to "write with courage [and] let your storytelling sing with all your heart." I'm not there yet, but I'm trying.

Angie Arndt, fellow author, encourager, and dear friend. Our long-distance sessions are precious and help me to stay motivated. I look forward to seeing your books in print before long.

My incredible friend and editor, Jerri Menges. Thanks for making time to go over this book "one more time," in spite of your other deadlines and commitments, before I submitted it to my publisher.

Many people answered my questions about Charleston and the carriage tour business. I'm especially grateful to our friend Robert Fleming, as well as numerous carriage drivers and house tour guides whose names I did not record.

And, of course, thanks to my publisher, Tracy Ruckman, for your patience, and to the other Write Integrity Press and Pix-N-Pens authors for your help in getting the word out about all of our wonderful books. What a great team!

Author's Note

While this story is set in the beautiful port city of Charleston, South Carolina, in some cases I have used "creative license" for the purposes of the story. Certain locations, government processes, and community organizations, as well as all of the people, are products of my imagination. Thank you, Charlestonians, for understanding that any similarity or resemblance to real people or situations is entirely coincidental. And if you think you recognize a place or an event, but the details are not quite right, realize that I may have intentionally changed specifics for the sake of the book.

"But those who drink the water that I will give them will never become thirsty again. In fact, the water I will give them will become in them a spring that gushes up to eternal life."

The woman told Jesus, "Sir, give me this water! Then I won't get thirsty or have to come here to get water."

John 4:14-15
(God's Word translation)

Chapter One

If words could wound, could they also heal?

Victoria Russo had enough word arrows pierce her heart in the last fifteen years to kill an Amazon warrior. At an even five feet, she didn't compare in stature to those tall, powerful women, but on her first work day in South Carolina, she felt as out of place as they would.

Not that anyone would ever know. She would be as sugary as Scarlett O'Hara flirting with Ashley Wilkes. Her employees would have no reason to whisper behind her back this time.

She inhaled the history permeating the vast brick concourse of what had once been a railroad station but now housed the Charleston Tourism Bureau. The early February sun streamed through massive windows and threw its warmth across the various displays and brochure racks.

Victoria checked her watch. *7:45*. Despite the fact that the building would open to visitors in fifteen minutes, none of the workers seemed to be in a hurry, a sharp contrast to the energetic culture she'd grown up with. Just as the mild temperatures here in the South contrasted with the frosty Connecticut weather she had last seen in her rear view mirror three days ago.

Her four-inch heels echoing on the brick floor, Victoria forced her short legs to keep pace with Lauren Redmond's long stride as they headed across the concourse. The other woman, pale and naturally blond, oozed a model-like quality that she, with her Mediterranean coloring and jet black hair, could only envy. Victoria had liked Lauren from their first meeting when Lauren had been one of three people that interviewed her for the director's position.

They passed a nook where three wrinkle-faced black women were spreading out supplies for their all-day basket-weaving demonstration. Lauren led the way beyond them to the information counter that stretched across one side of the room. In the employees-only area behind the high counter, several of the staff—her staff—waited.

Lauren pushed through the wooden gate and the knot of employees grew silent. Victoria joined her, and Lauren introduced her to the group. As Victoria shook hands with each one, Lauren called off their first names.

Victoria struggled to understand their drawled greetings. But more than that, what had happened to that famous southern hospitality? The interview committee had wanted an outsider, but half of these people seemed as cold as the New England winter she had escaped.

"Nice to meet you, Ms. Russo." The voice of one of the customer service representatives—was her name Mary Beth or Marylou or Mari Lynn?—sang of southern breezes and honeysuckle. At least not everyone resented her being here.

Lauren introduced the last person as Amelia Wilson, the assistant director. The woman extended her hand to Victoria in slow motion but when their fingers brushed, she pulled away as if she had touched hot coals.

"Nice to meet you. Welcome to Charleston." Amelia's tone failed to match her words, and no smile cracked her heavy makeup. She stood a head taller than Victoria, and her brown hair with its blond highlights was arranged in a style that added several inches to her height. Did she always wear it piled high, or had she intended to make Victoria feel smaller?

The employees seemed to be waiting for her to make a speech, something she hadn't anticipated. But she could handle it. She drew her shoulders back. "I'm really glad to be here. Charleston is a beautiful city, and you guys have a very important job. You represent the city to every visitor who comes through here. I look forward to working with all you guys as we make Charleston a favorite travel destination."

Trite, perhaps, but it would do. A couple of the women began to clap, and most of the others joined in. The spotty applause ended abruptly when the wall clock began to chime. By the end of the eight chimes, the customer service representatives had taken their positions at the counter. A skinny man in his mid-twenties—his name might have been Jeff—hustled to unlock the heavy wood-and-glass doors.

Victoria swallowed hard. Despite his familiar eagerness, she reminded herself that he was not her ex-husband, Michael, and this was not Waterbury. She must not allow herself to find fault with an employee she didn't even know.

The electronic displays started up, sharing the history of the city's slave-holding era and Civil War heritage, and a few waiting visitors entered the building.

"Amelia, let's show Victoria to her office." Lauren led the way out of the information corral and headed toward the far end of the concourse. A gift shop and restrooms nestled under a lower ceiling. Next to the gift shop, worn oak beams created a massive staircase leading to a balcony and the second floor.

Lauren waited for Victoria and Amelia at the landing midway up. She indicated the room below with what almost seemed like a parade wave. "This stairway and the balcony give you a wonderful overlook of the activity down there." She smiled at Amelia. "Amelia's done a good job of holding down the fort, but I'm sure she's glad that you're here now."

Amelia appeared to be studying the ceiling far above them. At the mention of her name, she turned and stared at Victoria with the same frozen mask she'd worn downstairs.

Victoria had barely spoken four words to her, but the woman's angry vibes made her want to spit. She forced herself to smile. She had to be nice, to show that she would be the best boss anyone could hope for. "Amelia, I will really need your help as I learn how things are done here in Charleston."

Still no reaction.

Lauren pointed above them to the offices that fronted on the balcony. "The business offices are upstairs. You've got your office at the end, then Amelia's office, and a conference room. Down that hall are offices for the business manager, human resources, and a workroom." She proceeded up the stairs. "The HR manager will have some paperwork for you to do this morning. I'll introduce you to Tom, the business manager. Then I'll leave you with Amelia."

"Sure, I'll take care of her." Amelia nodded. Exactly how she would take care of her, Victoria didn't want to ask.

Below them, a family with four small children joined several other visitors waiting in line, and the hum of activity rose to follow the three women down the hallway. They entered the first office on the right.

An older man, whose stooped shoulders and receding hairline brought back images of her late father, rose and came out from behind his desk. He grasped Victoria's hand. His fingers were soft and smooth, and so was his voice. "Tom Peyton. Nice to meet you, Victoria."

The same words. This time, they dripped with a welcoming syrup that tasted like home. She blinked at the unexpected lump in her throat. In thirty-four years and three marriages, she had never before lived more than twenty minutes from her family.

He still held her hand in his. "If there's anything you need, you know where to find me."

She looked up at Tom Peyton. There was no going home. "Thank you. I'll want to review the budget with you in a few days, but I need to get my bearings first."

Back in the hallway, Lauren turned to her. "Sorry to leave you now, but I have to go open my store. Amelia can answer any questions but if something comes up that we haven't covered, feel free to call me."

Victoria wanted to grab her arm and handcuff her to keep her close. She inhaled Lauren's musky perfume, storing away the memory of it for later, when she might need a reminder that some people in Charleston did want her here.

"I'll be fine. I'm sure I'll have plenty to keep me busy." Like figuring out how to make friends with the employees. And break down Amelia's hostility.

Victoria followed Amelia along the balcony to the director's office. A metal bracket on the door held square wood blocks that spelled out her name—her former name. "V. Russo-Martinez." Not what she'd asked for. She didn't need that daily reminder of another failure.

Amelia unlocked the door and held out the key. "You might wanta keep it locked, even when you're in it." She nodded toward the concourse. "Sometimes visitors find their way up here, and you probably won't want to be disturbed. Here ya go." She pushed the wooden door wide open, causing it to bang against the wall.

Victoria crossed the threshold and gazed around the room, turning slowly to absorb the unexpected sight. Two waist-high windows stretched nearly to the ten-foot-high ceiling, providing at least daylight to the large, nearly empty space. White powder dusted the bare walls, and heavy paper covered the wood floor. The room was almost bare, furnished with only a green card table and a metal folding chair. A well-used beige telephone and an open laptop computer sat on the table, and cables snaked across the floor to a wall outlet.

So much for a welcoming, productive work environment. She'd gotten the call from Lauren offering her the position six weeks ago, just before Christmas. No way redecorating the office should have taken that long, holidays or not. Had she been wrong to believe the committee really wanted her?

"The painters didn't quite finish up yet but I figured you'd still want to use the office. They won't be back until the weekend." Amelia crossed to the window and pulled down a semi-transparent shade. "If it gets too hot for you, you might want to use this to block the light."

At least the shade worked. Victoria sat in the folding chair, which bore scars from years of abuse. Not quite the throne of power she had expected. She might as well be Cinderella, with the towering hairdo stepsister laughing at her. "What happened to the furniture?"

"It was in pretty bad shape. You can order some new stuff." Amelia didn't look at her.

Lack of eye contact had crushed her during the last six months at her previous job. She couldn't endure that kind of isolation again. Like her former co-workers, Amelia must be hiding something, although it couldn't be as bad as the secret that everyone in Waterbury had known except her. Whatever it was, she'd have to overcome Amelia's animosity with kindness.

She scooted the chair closer to the table, and the chair leg ripped the paper on the floor. Getting furniture purchased and delivered could take weeks. But complaining wouldn't do any good; she could see that.

Victoria eyed the blue cable trailing from the laptop, hoping it connected to a network. She adjusted the computer screen then tapped the space bar. "Is there a password?"

"Oh, shucks. The IT guys have to set you up with access to the network. Guess I'd better call and ask 'em to stop over." She moved to the table and punched a number into the phone, waited for the ring over the speaker, then lifted the receiver. "Hey, girlfriend. The new director started today. Can you send Jim Bob over to fix her up?"

Considering the way Amelia had treated her, Victoria couldn't help wondering if the name "Jim Bob" was a joke aimed at her.

Amelia paused, listening. "Yeah ... You got that right." She eyed Victoria. "Sure, that should work. I'll tell her."

She plopped the receiver down, jostling the unsteady table. She leaned against the table, pushing the edge into Victoria's midriff. "Jim Bob will come by this afternoon."

"This afternoon? I won't be able to use my computer until this afternoon?" Already the hard metal seat of the chair hurt her bottom. She pushed the chair back and stood, leaning over the table to look the other woman in the eye. Amelia might have height and hair, but Victoria had position. She'd been hired as the director, Amelia's boss. "What am I supposed to do until then?"

Amelia shrugged and started for the door.

Victoria sighed. Not even an hour had passed, and she'd almost lost her temper. She hadn't thought being nice would be so hard. "I don't suppose there's a cushion around here somewhere, is there? I can't sit on that chair very long."

Amelia scrunched her face into a thoughtful look, obviously fake. "Nope, not that I know of. You might find one over at the market."

Great. Her assistant director had shown a lack of respect from the minute they'd met. No doubt Amelia had planned this office of indignity and had intentionally failed to set up the computer network. Now she'd probably laugh about the situation with the other employees over lunch. No matter how far away Victoria moved, people would still be cruel. But this time, in this place, she would handle it differently.

She glanced at her black pumps, wishing she'd put comfortable shoes in her car. She couldn't even remember if Market Street was close enough to walk there and back. But apparently she would find out during her lunch hour.

A black woman wearing a flowered tent dress filled the doorway. She was as tall as Amelia but with a balloon face on top of an inflated body. "Morning." She squeezed through the door. "I guess you're Ms. Russo. I'm Jennetta, the admin assistant."

Victoria had begun to wonder if she would have any clerical help. She glanced at her watch. Nearly nine. She hoped Jennetta's office skills were an improvement over her punctuality.

"She's not late." Amelia crossed her arms. "Jennetta works reduced hours, nine to four."

"I see." Victoria offered her hand. "I didn't mean to be rude."

"That's okay. You didn't know." Jennetta gave her a limp handshake, while resting her other hand on her ample hip. Her mottled skin glistened with sweat where her bent elbow creased her fleshy rolls.

In spite of her first impression, Victoria wanted to like Jennetta. The woman accepted her apology without hesitation. Would she be an ally, or did her loyalty belong to Amelia?

Jennetta nodded to the door that Victoria had assumed to be a closet, on the side wall opposite the window. "I'm in there, in the office between you and Amelia, since I work for both of ya. I think you've got a couple appointments this morning. I'll just check." She waddled across the room and disappeared behind the paneled door.

Victoria hoped this wasn't the only entrance to that office. Had there been another door in the hallway? Surely the admin would be located so she could screen visitors.

Without another word, Amelia left, closing the door behind her.

Victoria shook her head then realized how strained every muscle of her body had become. She rolled her shoulders and her head to relieve the tension. Wanting to get started in her new role, she scanned the office, but she had nothing to do since she couldn't even use her computer. She strode to the window, hoping for a view of downtown.

No. She looked down at a parking lot and the blue-and-white top of the covered area where tour buses picked up and discharged their passengers. If she didn't have any appointments, she could spend her morning taking one of the two-hour tours. That would give her a chance to learn more about her adopted city. And would pass the time until she had computer access.

The door from Jennetta's office opened. "Ms. Russo, you got an appointment with Human Resources at ten thirty. And there's an owner of a carriage company here now to talk about his licenses."

Apparently Jennetta did have a door directly to her office. But carriage licenses, already? Victoria knew nothing about that process. And she had no one she could trust to advise her. Other than Amelia, who was clearly hostile, her staff seemed indifferent at best.

She looked around her bare office. Just what she needed—to meet with a prominent business owner in these conditions. "I need another chair."

"I put him in the conference room. Thought you'd be more comfortable there." Jennetta gave her a broad wink.

Maybe Victoria did have one person on her side. She nodded, smoothed her skirt and adjusted her matching blue jacket. "All right. What's his name?"

"Randy Lee Johnson. He owns Two Rivers Carriages." The way she spit out the words hinted at a dislike for the man or the company. Or both.

Victoria studied Jennetta, searching for a clue to her meaning.

But her assistant merely plodded to the main door and opened it, pointing along the balcony. "You know where it is?"

"I think so. Thanks."

Victoria found the conference room door open. Not much larger than her office, the room seemed like an afterthought. A massive wooden table surrounded by black chairs left little space to maneuver.

When she entered, the sole occupant rose and flashed her a smile that could have melted all of Connecticut. He wore Western-style boots and a bolo tie with his checked shirt and black jeans. A vague scent of saddle soap and straw reached her. He held a Stetson in one hand and smoothed his sandy-colored hair with the other before reaching out to shake her hand.

"Well, sugar," he drawled. "Nobody told me the new director of tourism was such a purty little thing."

Victoria had learned years ago to ignore compliments on her appearance, especially from a man who wanted something. So why did his words feel like aloe on the irritations she had already endured this morning?

Chapter Two

Victoria had come to Charleston to build a new life, and she had enough challenges with her new job. She refused to add another romantic relationship to the list. She would not surrender to the attraction she felt for the man in her conference room.

"You must be Mr. Johnson. I'm Victoria Russo." She gave him a firm handshake while searching his eyes for signs of deceit or manipulation. She saw neither. Only brown eyes, one of them half-hidden by a lazy eyelid that almost looked like he was winking.

She chose a place at the head of the long conference table, across the corner from the spot he had claimed. As she waited for him to fold himself back into his seat, she enjoyed the cushioned comfort of the rolling chair. Maybe she would borrow one of these to replace the metal seat of torture in her office until she could get new furniture. But first she had to learn the reason for this meeting.

"What can I do for you, Mr. Johnson?"

He slapped the table, startling her. "I'm not a formal man. Can we use first names? Mine's Randy Lee."

Two first names. Southern tradition, apparently. She smiled. "I suppose. I'm Victoria."

"No nickname? Vicky or…I knew a Victoria once who went by 'Tory.'"

Brian had called her 'Tory.' She leaned back in her chair, swallowing the sour thought. How had a business discussion taken this turn so quickly? "I prefer Victoria. But, Randy Lee, please tell me why you're here."

He lifted a tooled-leather briefcase and set it on the table, snapped open the latches, and produced a manila folder with several papers in it. "I'm adding some new carriages to my business. This here is the application for the licenses. We're a little behind schedule getting these approved. I thought maybe you could sign 'em now so I could get those blasted mules out on the street."

She opened the folder and scanned the form, uncertain what to look for. Two Rivers Carriages. Randy Lee Johnson, owner-operator. The usual information on location of business, phone number, liability insurance. Names of employees, total assets. Her eyes widened at that number. Apparently running carriage tours had been profitable for him. Page three listed four carriages, with a blank line for the license numbers. Was she supposed to provide those?

"I'm sorry, but as you know, today is my first day on the job. We, uh, didn't have carriages to license in Waterbury. I'll need some time to look this over."

"Well, sure you do. You just take your time. I don't mind waiting." He leaned forward and gave her a toe-curling smile.

How was she supposed to concentrate with him watching her like that, so close she could almost taste his outdoorsy cologne? She lifted the document and studied it, trying to forget about his lazy grin and the crow's feet around his dark eyes. She needed to finish this and get him out of here. She read each line slowly, forcing herself to concentrate on the words in front of her.

After several minutes, she reached the bottom of the last page, where a blank signature line was labeled "Tourism Director." She looked up at him and smiled, hoping her uncertainty didn't show. "Everything appears to be in order. If you'll excuse me, I'll get a pen." She started to rise.

"I've got one right here." He pulled a pen from his chest pocket in a quick-draw and offered it to her.

No chance to escape from his presence. Or to check with

someone else about protocol for these licenses. But how complicated could it be? The paperwork seemed straightforward. All she needed to do was sign the form.

When she had signed the paper, she handed the pen back to him and pushed the folder across the table. "I guess you know where this goes now. I'm afraid I don't."

"I do. Yes, ma'am." With his hand on the folder, he paused and looked into her eyes. "Or is it *miss*?"

Victoria forced herself to stay calm. Just because a good-looking man was charming and rich didn't mean she was attracted to him. She did not want a relationship right now. She had come to Charleston for a new start. One that, for a change, did not include a man.

"Ms. will do. Or just Victoria." She pushed away from the table and stood. "Excuse me, Randy Lee. I really must go get settled in. It was nice to meet you."

He scrambled to his feet and towered over her. He tipped his hat. "Real nice meeting you, Victoria."

Did he have to emphasize "real nice" that way? She hurried from the room before his rugged aroma sent her pulse into gallop mode again. She had been in town less than twenty-four hours and already temptation threatened. But she would resist.

Back in her office, she sighed at the sight of the folding table and chair. How could she 'get settled' when she had no furniture? She stepped into Jennetta's office. "Where are the files from the previous director? I'd like to look through them to get a feel for the job."

Jennetta pushed herself out of her chair. "They're in the file room. Anything in particular you want to see?"

"Let's start with events. The Lowcountry Fall Festival is the big one, right? Let me see everything you've got for last year's festival as well as what's been done for this year."

Jennetta nodded. "You got it. I'll be right back."

Victoria returned to her own office and moved the chair, sat in it, and adjusted herself to find a comfortable position. Impossible.

She stood and strode down the hall to the conference room, where she snagged the chair she had used earlier and pushed it back to her office. She sat in it and wheeled up to the card table, which now hit her on the knees. That wouldn't do. She fiddled with the levers under the chair seat until she found the right one and lowered the seat as far as it would go. The table would still be too low for any serious work, but at least she could be comfortable.

Jennetta entered, her arms full of manila folders. She glanced at Victoria's chair and grinned. "See you're making yourself at home." She deposited the stack of files on the table next to the laptop. "Here's the files you wanted from last year. Amelia's got everything for this year in her office."

At least Jennetta seemed apologetic. Victoria could look over the records from last year then ask Amelia to brief her on the plans for this year. Might be a good way to show her assistant she had confidence in her. "That's fine. These will get me started."

Just as Jennetta reached the doorway, Victoria remembered the nameplate. "Umm, Jennetta?"

"Yes'm?"

"I'd like the nameplate on the door changed to Victoria Russo. Can you take care of that?"

She shook her head. "I thought that's what you wanted, but Amelia insisted. I'll get it fixed right away."

After the door closed, Victoria's body sagged in the chair. More evidence of Amelia's game-playing.

After studying the files Jennetta had brought her and meeting with Human Resources for an hour, Victoria decided to find Amelia and offer to buy her lunch. Perhaps a little generosity would begin to melt the ice.

Hip-hop music vibrated from the office on the other side of Jennetta's. She tapped her fist lightly on the open door but had to switch to a more vigorous knock to get her attention. "Hi, Amelia. I wondered if you could bring me up to speed on the Lowcountry Festival. Maybe over lunch? I'm buying."

Amelia looked up from her computer. "I have lunch plans."

Of course she did. Or would make some plans as soon as Victoria left her office.

"Okay. Well, maybe we can have lunch tomorrow."

"Maybe."

"So when can we talk about the festival plans? I've reviewed the files from last year, and I think I have a handle on what all is involved."

Amelia stared at her as if she had just invited her to go swim in the ocean. "I'm booked the rest of today."

"I see." Amelia wasn't going to make this easy, but Victoria wouldn't give up. "Then let's meet at eight thirty tomorrow. I want to hear your thoughts on how things went last year and what can be improved." She turned to go but stopped and looked at the comfortable furnishings, the small round conference table with padded chairs. "Let's meet in here instead of my office. I think we'll get more accomplished."

"Whatever you say."

Victoria strode out of the room before she could think of a suitable response. Better that way, since what she wanted to say would be less than professional. She hesitated on the balcony then headed downstairs to check out the employee break room.

She found it off the main concourse, tucked in beside the restrooms. Three women were eating lunch at one of the four small wooden tables. Cabinets and a counter stretched along one wall. A countertop microwave hummed on one side of the stainless steel sink. On the other side sat a commercial coffeemaker with a half-full pot of the black brew. She needed some of that.

"Hello." She greeted the employees as she strode to the counter. "Is this coffee any good?"

All three looked at her but no one smiled. Finally, the one on the right, an older woman with curly gray hair, answered. "It'll do. Unless you only drink Starbucks."

Ouch. Did they think she was that elitist, just because she came from up north? She smiled, hoping to turn the conversation friendlier. "I do enjoy Starbucks occasionally, but mostly I just need it strong." She opened the upper cabinets until she found several cups and selected a black one with "Charleston" printed in red on one side. She filled the cup and, holding it with both hands, turned to face the small group. They had gone back to eating their lunches. "What about you ladies? Do you prefer Starbucks?"

Gray-haired lady—what was her name?—looked up. "Too pricey, if you ask me. I don't need no five-dollar cuppa coffee when I can make it myself."

The other two kept their gazes focused on their food. When the speaker turned her attention back to her sandwich, Victoria knew she had been dismissed. They had no interest in chatting with the new boss, even about a mundane topic like coffee.

She returned to the concourse just as the clock began to strike. Noon. Victoria felt as though she had been run over by a tour bus. She hoped every day wouldn't be this hard.

Chapter Three

Saluki Franklin stared at the B-plus marked in red ink on her social studies paper. She cursed at herself, thinking words that would earn a slap from her mama if she spoke them within her hearing.

But she had earned more than a slap by not studying for this test. She knew better than to go out with her friends the night before a major test. She would never get a college scholarship if she kept this up.

The last bell of the day rang, and she began to gather her books as other students headed for the door. Like all the classrooms at East Cooper High School, the dingy room needed to be repainted five or six years ago.

"Saluki, could you hang back a moment?" Mr. Danicourt, her social studies teacher, didn't sound too happy. His gray hair and beard hid the fact that he was East Cooper's "coolest" teacher—at least, in Saluki's opinion—a man with a big heart who took time to get to know kids.

She knew what he was probably going to say. And he was right.

She hefted her backpack onto her left shoulder and turned to face him. "Hey, Mr. D. What's up?"

He crossed his arms and leaned back against his desk, almost knocking over the tower of empty soda cans he'd collected . "You tell me. You seemed to have a problem with Friday's test. That's not like you."

"No, I—" She wanted to defend herself, but she couldn't really. She focused on the worn toes of her Wal-Mart sneakers.

"So, how was it?" His voice had softened.

She jerked her head up. "How was what?"

"The new Tolkien movie. Didn't you and your friends go to the midnight showing?"

Saluki gulped. How did he know? "Yeah, we did. The movie's great."

His gray eyebrows formed an upside-down "v," and he seemed to be waiting for her to explain.

But she had no excuse to offer. Not really. "I know. I should have studied more Thursday night. Plus I was really tired Friday."

He pursed his lips. "That only partially explains it."

"Partially? What do you mean?"

He moved behind the desk, taking a seat in the wooden chair. The wheels on the chair squeaked as he rolled back and leaned against the chalkboard. "Saluki, you're a straight-A student, and not just because you study hard for tests. You're a smart young woman. If you'd been applying yourself all semester, you would have known this material whether you studied the night before or not."

She scuffed a foot across the faded linoleum tile.

He lowered his voice so much that she could barely hear him. "Want to tell me what's going on?"

She didn't want to admit to a teacher—even Mr. D.—that she had been distracted ever since she started dating Dustin Fisher just after Homecoming. That Dustin made her feel loved for the first time in ages. That they planned to go to the College of Charleston together after they graduated next year. All that seemed too personal to tell a teacher, especially a male teacher. She shrugged. "Not especially."

"Okay." He stood and placed a hand on her shoulder. "But listen. With your grades, you stand a good chance of being valedictorian next year. That would make it almost a sure thing that you'll get a scholarship to any college in the state. I don't want to see you blow that chance."

The disappointment in his eyes scorched her heart. "I

know, Mr. D. I'll work harder, I promise."

"Good." He let his hand drop. "And if you change your mind about talking, you know where to find me."

She nodded and rushed out of the classroom, stopping at the water fountain. The cool water trickled down her throat but did nothing to rinse away the taste of failure. She had given in when her friends asked her to the movie, even though she knew better. She deserved the low grade, but she couldn't let it happen again.

The long hall, bordered by aging blue lockers on each side, had emptied fast. Beyond the fourth classroom door, she found her friends waiting for her.

"Hey, girl, what took you so long?" Majesty Moore had been her best friend since third grade. If it weren't for Majesty's ebony skin where Saluki's was caramel colored, the two could pass for sisters. They were the same height—five-foot-nine; they both wore size ten clothes, meaning they were not too thin, but not too heavy; and they wore their dark, kinky hair in the same style—pulled back and fastened with a large comb.

Saluki edged between Majesty and Dustin. "Nothing. Mr. D. wanted to talk to me, that's all. I didn't do very well on Friday's test." She twirled the dial on her locker and popped it open.

"Oooh, did you get an A-minus instead of an A-plus?" Majesty had a solid B average, but she liked to tease Saluki about her straight As.

She tossed her head and pulled three books from her locker. "Thanks a lot. I only got a B-plus. And it's all y'all's fault for taking me to that movie Thursday night."

Dustin took the books from her arms. "Don't worry about it, babe. You'll make it up." His blond hair draped over one eye, and he winked the other eye at her.

"Thanks, Dustin. That's what I need to hear." She tipped

her head against his chest, and with his free hand, he stroked her hair. The warmth of his touch started her skin tingling.

TeeJay Joiner, the fourth member of their group, made a choking sound. "Come on, you two. Enough." But he put his arm around Majesty's waist. "Are we staying around here all night or what?"

Saluki checked the time on her cellphone. "Shoot, I've got to book it, or I'll be late for work. The new director started today, and I don't want to make a bad impression right off."

Her part-time job assembling displays and writing self-guided tour descriptions not only earned her spending money but also gave her the chance to immerse herself in history. From her viewpoint, it was the ideal job. She had gotten the internship at the Tourism Bureau, an opportunity that few high school students had, thanks to Mr. D. "I'll catch up with y'all after work, okay?"

Dustin pecked her cheek. "I'll call you after supper."

She grinned. Her heart still did somersaults when he looked at her like that. Her mama didn't approve of him, but the world had changed since Mama was young. Interracial couples didn't raise eyebrows anymore, even in Charleston.

Thirty minutes later, Saluki dropped off her book bag in the employee break room and punched the time clock. She had finished writing copy for the new Civil War display on Friday, so she headed to Amelia's office to get her next assignment. Now that the new director had started, would Amelia continue to supervise her? She hoped not. Amelia made her feel like an interruption rather than an asset.

When she found Amelia's office vacant, she poked her head into Jennetta's office. "Hey, Miss Jennetta. How're things today?"

"Hmmph." Jennetta glanced up from her computer. "Hey, Saluki. You have a good day at school?"

She entered the office and shrugged. "Kind of a bummer. I

got a B-plus on a social studies test I should have aced."

"Uh-oh." Jennetta always made time to ask her about school. "What happened?"

She plopped herself in the visitor's chair. "Went to a movie last week when I should have been studying."

Jennetta leaned back, her chair squeaking from the movement, and crossed her arms. "On a school night? What came over you?"

"I know. It was stupid. But …" She looked at her hands. "I just like spending time with Dustin. He makes me feel, like, important. Pretty. You know?"

"I know. Just be careful you don't get carried away and forget who you are."

Saluki jumped to her feet. She didn't need a lecture; she'd already given herself one. "I'd better get to work. Where's Miz Amelia?"

Jennetta shook her head. "Not sure. Why don't you go introduce yourself to the new director?" She nodded toward the door between the offices. "You can go on in."

Saluki opened the door into the adjoining office. The half-painted walls were bare, and the only furniture was a folding card table and two chairs. "Whoa, looks like it's under construction."

She saw the surprise on the new director's face. Oops. Not the best start. She closed the door behind her and stepped forward, the brown paper on the floor rustling under her feet. "Jennetta said it was okay to come on in. I'm Saluki Franklin, the student intern."

The petite woman rose out of the padded leather chair, which Saluki suspected she'd borrowed from the conference room. "I'm Victoria Russo, the new director. What can I do for you, Sa—Saluki, is it?" She stood a head shorter than Saluki, and she was pretty. Dark hair, creamy olive skin, piercing green eyes, and a welcoming smile. She smelled like lilacs, and

Saluki liked her immediately.

"Yes, ma'am. I usually get my work assignments from Miz Amelia, but she's not in her office, so I thought—"

Ms. Russo gestured to the metal chair next to the table she appeared to be using for a desk. "Of course. Please sit down and tell me what kinds of things you usually work on. I'm afraid Amelia hasn't filled me in yet."

They both sat, and Saluki understood at once why Ms. Russo had chosen to use a padded chair.

A catalog lay on the table, open to office furniture. Saluki nodded to it. "Miz Amelia's yanking your chain, huh?"

"What do you mean?"

"She moved the furniture out before you got here, right?"

"The painters didn't finish, so … But I prefer to order my own office furniture anyway."

Saluki grinned. She could see Ms. Russo didn't want to show any sign of weakness. "And how's that table working out for you as a desk?" She reached over and touched it, making it shake.

Victoria laughed. "It is a little unsteady. I worry about the laptop falling off and breaking."

"Miz Amelia wasn't too happy about you coming. She thought she would get the job."

"What are you trying to tell me?"

She could get in trouble with Ms. Amelia, but she took a chance anyway. "I understand you want your own furniture, but—wouldn't you like a real desk to use until the new stuff comes?"

"Of course. But I thought the old furniture had been disposed of."

Saluki shook her head. "I got a feeling Miz Amelia was trying to put you in your place. I've been working here almost six months, and I think I know where the old stuff is stored. Come on, I'll show you."

As they headed down the stairwell to the basement storage room, Saluki decided working here would be even better now. She liked conspiring with this woman to thwart Ms. Amelia's petty scheme.

Chapter Four

By the end of her first week, Victoria could think of only one way to describe the tiredness she felt. Mental and emotional exhaustion.

Stopping in the timeworn entry of her North Charleston apartment building Friday evening, she shuffled through the advertising mail and pulled out an envelope from the electric company. They didn't waste any time sending the first bill.

She dumped the promotional flyers in the recycling bin and dragged herself up the steps to her furnished apartment. As she stuck the key in the lock, the phone inside started ringing.

Mother.

Her cell phone was reserved for business use and, at this point, only her mother had her landline number. And Mother would not be disappointed to hear how discouraged Victoria felt right now.

When she opened the door, the musty smell and murky shadows repelled her as they did every day. Closing her ears to the shrill demand of the phone, she dropped the mail on the kitchen table, along with her keys and purse. She kicked off her shoes. Her feet sank onto the cold linoleum and signaled their gratefulness.

She padded to the bathroom and pulled open the mirrored door of the medicine cabinet. Not many items on the glass shelves. Deodorant. One bottle of cologne. Shampoo and rough paste for her hair. Toothpaste. Multi-vitamins. Three types of pain reliever.

She chose the medium strength one. "Please don't let it turn into a migraine," she said into the vacuum enveloping her. From the kitchen came the jangle announcing that Mother had left a long message.

Back in the kitchen, she grabbed a bottle of water from the refrigerator, gulped a mouthful, and took the two capsules. Now she could listen to what Mother had to say. She picked up the receiver and punched in the code for voicemail.

"Victoria, dear, aren't you ever there? Please call me. Tell me what you're doing and when you're coming home." From the background, the words of *Love the One You're With* drifted into the pause. "Well, I don't know when I'll get to talk to you. I just wanted to tell you I miss you. The house seems so empty now …" Another pause. "Sorry. I don't mean to play the guilt card. I hope everything is going well at work. Love you."

She plunked the cordless phone onto the faded laminate counter. Since Victoria's father had died five months ago, Mother did nothing but wander around the old house rearranging knickknacks. Now that she was no longer a full-time caregiver, Victoria thought she would resume her church activities. Sadly, she had not.

But Victoria had her own problems. The morning's *Post and Courier* lay where she had left it that morning, folded open to the real estate ads.

As director of the Charleston Tourism Bureau, she ought to live in the city, not in a suburb. And this shoebox apartment threatened to suffocate her. South of Broad would have been her first choice, but the million-dollar price tags in that neighborhood didn't fit her government salary.

She picked up the paper and sank onto the couch. After scouring the listings this morning, she doubted she'd ever find a house she could afford. But she had to keep looking.

In spite of what Mother hoped—or what Amelia wanted—Victoria would never move back to Connecticut. Too many reminders of her bad choices resided there.

If every tour guide in the city and every member of her staff had to know all there was to know about Charleston, then so did Victoria. But she thought her head would burst by the middle of the third day of historic house tours.

Too many words and facts about the houses, about Charleston, about the Civil War. Trying to cram all the tours into her first two weeks had not been the brightest idea. She wouldn't be able to remember which house had the flying staircase, which one George Washington had stayed in, and which one was built for whose daughter.

Pacing herself might be more important than impressing her staff with her enthusiasm to learn everything she could and take every available tour. Maybe she could give herself a couple of months. After all, the tourism board had hired her for her abilities, not for her knowledge of the area. There had been plenty of applicants with knowledge—Amelia, for one.

Victoria and twelve or so visitors were supposed to be admiring the main bedroom of—which house was this? Alford, Alston, something like that. The tour guide, a mid-fortyish woman with a ring on every finger, moved to Victoria's side.

"Aren't you Victoria Russo, the new tourism director?" She had abandoned her tour-guide volume and charm, instead sounding almost accusing.

Victoria wondered if she was about to face another verbal battle over the Civil War. "Yes, that's me."

"I thought I recognized you from your picture in today's paper." The woman's blue eyes had narrowed to slits, and she sniffed, the stereotypical gesture of dislike. "I'm Cecilia Calhoun. Amelia Wilson is my very best friend."

Victoria sensed several of the other visitors watching them. She needed to defuse the situation. "Well, I'm glad to meet you, Cecilia. This house is a wonderful example of why people should come to Charleston." She waved her hands to indicate the room.

"I read about the tourism awards you received in Connecticut." Cecilia crossed her arms. "I suppose you're going to do wonders for Charleston's tourism."

Victoria gave her best smile. The woman obviously shared Amelia's resentment of her. "I hope I can help, but so much has been done already. I'm sure Amelia had been working hard since the last director left."

Cecilia nodded. "We were doing just fine until the recession hit. No one's to blame. It's the economy. People just stopped traveling, what with gas prices so high. "

"I'm afraid I can't do much about that. But I'll do what I can to get those who do travel to come back to Charleston."

"We'll see." Cecilia raised her voice over the conversations around the room. "Let's move on to the children's rooms. They're being worked on, so you'll only be able to look in from the doorway." She hustled across the room and led the group to the hall.

Victoria held back as the others clustered behind a gold cord that blocked off the room. She wished she felt as confident as she tried to appear. Some of the business owners held extremely high expectations for what she could accomplish, while other people, like Amelia and Cecilia, seemed to hope she would run back to the North in disgrace.

A familiar pungency teased the edges of her brain. When the rest of the group moved on, she stepped forward to peer through the doorway, and she knew what she had smelled. Plaster.

A man wearing white coveralls and protective glasses stood on a plank spread across two sawhorses. Using a trowel, he applied plaster to a gap in the cornice then picked up a shaped tool and sculpted the area to match the rest of the cornice that ran around the room. Antonio had tried to teach her to make that type of repair, but her hands were never steady enough to suit him.

She turned away and realized the other visitors had already gone downstairs. She scurried to catch up with them in the foyer and stopped on the bottom step.

"Thank you for visiting today." Cecilia aimed her southern cordiality at the main group. "As you leave, don't forget to enjoy the gardens. They aren't historic, but the camellias are in bloom right now. You don't want to miss those." She opened the door and the visitors filed out.

She turned to Victoria. "I suppose you can wander around the house as much as you like. That's one of the perks of your job."

Victoria moved toward the door. "Perhaps I'll come back another time and do that." She held out her hand, searching for a way to thaw Cecilia's attitude. "I can tell how much you care about this house. And about Charleston."

The woman gave her a limp handshake. "This is just a house. It's the people I care about. The ones that used to live here had fascinating lives. And the ones who come through now—well, they're just as interesting."

Victoria scampered down the front steps and headed for her car, aware of Cecilia watching her. But then, the whole city seemed to be watching her, waiting for her to work a miracle—or to stumble and fall.

Chapter Five

Tight little groups of Charlestonians shared private jokes as Victoria stood by a large pillar clutching her plate of appetizers and glass of wine. No point in waiting for someone to include her in their group. Unless she took action, she might as well be watching a movie from the projection room.

Large portraits at one end of the Charleston Museum's board room kept watch over the gathering. The hollow laughter of long-time acquaintances echoed off the tiled walls and floor. An antique chandelier highlighted the shadows of the odd angles in the room.

Her first official society event, the annual fundraiser for the museum, included all the important people she needed to know. Johnny Phillips, chairman of the Tourism Board of Directors, had warned her this evening would be her most important test.

"Some southerners don't especially care for northerners. We warned you 'bout that when we hired you." He had visited her office three days ago, just before he left town for two weeks. One of the two people who could ease her way into this world of the privileged and powerful residents of her new city had retreated to his vacation home in the North Carolina mountains. "I never did like going to those formal things," he said, defending his escape. "I only went 'cause Ellie dragged me, God rest her soul. But don't worry. You can handle yourself."

So here she stood. Abandoned.

Johnny—Mister Johnny, she corrected herself mentally with a nod to southern custom—and Lauren Redmond, the sole woman on the board, appeared to be her only allies in the city.

The third board member, Smith Alexander, had been lukewarm toward her.

Finally she spotted Lauren in a small, serious group. She straightened her back and aimed her shoulders in their direction, urging the new Nine West silver pumps—her mild splurge for this party—to carry her toward them without slipping on the smooth brick floor.

Lauren shook her pointer finger at the three men. "You don't know what you're doing. The city needs more investment."

Moving in near Lauren's elbow, Victoria waited to be noticed. When Lauren stopped talking, she spoke, attempting to slow her speech to match the words that flowed around her. "Good evening, Lauren. Hoped I'd see you here."

Lauren turned. "Victoria, good to see you." She shifted her position to allow Victoria to move into the circle and introduced her to the men. A lawyer and two bankers.

"Ms. Russo." The lawyer, fifty-something with a shaved head, jerked a nod at her then held up his empty glass. "Excuse me, ladies. Gentlemen."

"Don't mind him, Victoria," Lauren muttered as he moved away. "He thinks if your family wasn't here before the war broke out, you're not good enough to breathe, much less live in Charleston."

"That would be the war of northern aggression," added one of the bankers with a challenge-me-on-this smile. "The one you northerners prefer to call the southern rebellion, or perhaps the Civil War."

"Gracious, Leonard. Ease up." Lauren kept her voice light, but a current rippled beneath the surface. "That was a hundred and fifty years ago. I doubt if Victoria's related to the Yankee who shot your great-grandfather."

"Absolutely right, Lauren." The other banker, a fleshy-faced man with a crown of cottony hair, offered his hand. His lips curved into a pleasant smile and his intense eyes studied her. "Ms. Russo's parents prob'ly didn't come over from Italy until after dubbya-dubbya one."

Victoria could feel the heat rising in her face. The tour guides joked about southerners who would smile as they served you poisoned tea.

"Actually, Mr. … Owens, was it? Two of my great-grandfathers fought in World War One. And an ancestor on my mother's side was a founder of the Daughters of the American Revolution."

She stopped to take a breath. She changed her approach, striving for silky and conciliatory. "But I think there are more important things to worry about in Charleston today than who fought who in what war."

"Exactly." Lauren rescued her. "And I, for one"—she looked pointedly at the two men—"can't wait to hear Victoria's ideas for shoring up tourism. I'm sure they'll be great."

"We're all waiting to hear those ideas." Leonard frowned and looked at his watch. "When exactly will that happen?"

Victoria nearly bit her tongue trying to halt the retort she wanted to spit out. She had been here less than two weeks. She sipped her drink and tried to remain calm and professional. "I expect to have the campaign ready to present at the meeting of the Old Town Business Owners Association next month. I do hope you'll be there." She needed to exit this conversation gracefully before it turned nasty again.

Lauren must have sensed her discomfort. "If you'll excuse us, gentlemen, I need to introduce Victoria to some of the others."

Lauren led her away toward the large windows overlooking the bay. "I'm so sorry, sweetie. They'll change once they see what you can do for this city. They're just being protective."

"Protective?" Victoria turned to face her. "Of what? Their traditions? Their culture? How are we supposed to get tourists to come visit if this is the way strangers are treated?"

The other woman chuckled. "Heavens, dear. They don't treat tourists that way. Only people who move here who are, you know, different …" Her voice trailed off, as if she realized how bigoted she sounded. "Don't worry. Create a fabulous campaign and they'll come crawling with their tails between their legs. But, sugar, try not to be so defensive. It's not personal."

Not personal? Victoria looked around the room. The other guests stood at least ten feet from them. "People don't exactly seem eager to talk to me, Lauren. I feel as if I have the plague."

"Yes, well, if you don't watch what you say, you might as well."

"Was I supposed to stand there and ignore their comments?"

"Wouldn't hurt anything, honey." She looked Victoria in the eyes. "Let them say what they will. Your work will speak for itself."

Victoria looked away, unable to stand Lauren's gaze. She wasn't sure she deserved her confidence. She knew so little about this strange, wonderful city. Instead of Waterbury's industrialized atmosphere, the culture here seemed more focused on status and heritage. How was she supposed to create a campaign that would bring tourists back in this economy, when those who knew the city had tried and failed?

She cleared her throat and looked out the windows. "I'll try," she croaked. "To hold my tongue, that is."

"Okay, then, I'll introduce you to the mayor."

She followed Lauren through the guests. Lauren stopped several times to introduce her to small groups but managed to move on quickly. Finally, they reached the largest group, ten or twelve people clustered around a tall stately man.

The man embraced Lauren and the two touched cheeks. "Nice to see you, Mayor," Lauren said.

"I'm always glad to see ya."

Although the City Council had confirmed Victoria's hiring, she had not met any of the council members or the mayor. He turned and stretched out an elegant hand to her. She took it, expecting a firm handshake. Instead his hand felt limp as cold spaghetti. Though his cool blue eyes appraised her, he continued speaking to Lauren. "You didn't tell me Ms. Russo was so enchantin.' If her work's half as good as her looks, tourists will be flockin' here." His lips curved into a smile—or was it a leer?

"I'm pleased to meet you, Mayor Stone." She slipped her hand out of his and reached for the napkin wrapped around the glass in her other hand. His hand wasn't slimy or wet, but she needed to wipe away the unseen dirt that went along with his words. And his smile.

Being snubbed because she wasn't a southerner hadn't been so bad, after all.

"Now, Jimbo, stop it. Ms. Russo doesn't realize you're acting." A middle-aged brunette next to the mayor extended her hand. "I'm Julia Stone. Please forgive my husband. He's playing Willie Stark in next month's stage production of *All the King's Men*, and he practices every chance he gets."

Mayor Stone put an arm around his wife. "Quite right, dear," he said, adopting a British accent. He turned to Victoria. "You see, I quite enjoy pretending to be someone else. I hope my actions did not offend you."

Victoria hiccuped a laugh. "No, no, of course not. You're very good. But I didn't realize you were an actor."

"Very much an amateur, I'm afraid." His voice—the real one, perhaps?—took on a soft drawl. Southern but not as exaggerated as his character from the Robert Penn Warren novel. Instead of the cold nasal tones of the Brit, this voice brimmed with an inviting warmth. "Tell me what you think of us so far."

A lump formed in her throat. She couldn't tell him how rude and insulting the bankers had been. Or that she'd thought him to be a typical southern cad. Charlestonians had convinced themselves their city welcomed strangers and thought they extended their famous hospitality to everyone. Perhaps they did. Everyone but her.

"Yes, tell us your impressions of the city," Lauren said, emphasizing the last word. Not the people, but the city. Good thing she had Lauren's support.

"Charleston is lovely, especially this time of year." Her enthusiasm for the warm climate flowed into her voice. "Every day I see more trees and flowers in bloom. The weather is fabulous, and of course all the old homes …" She halted, aware of the smiling faces around her. Perhaps she had overdone it. "Of course, I wouldn't have accepted the job if I hadn't fallen in love with the city on my first visit."

Mayor Stone nodded. "Those of us who've lived here all our lives sometimes forget what a charming place it is. It's good to have someone from outside refresh our memories. We look forward to hearing more from you, Ms. Russo."

His smile wiped away her doubt about his sincerity. His comments reminded her why she had been chosen for the job. She just had to believe in her own abilities.

Chapter Six

The morning after the reception, laughter filtered up the stairs from the Visitor's Center concourse, breaking Victoria's concentration as she tried to make sense of the budget.

What on earth could be that funny at the information counter? She'd been here barely two weeks, but she had little doubt that the loudest laugh was Amelia's.

She pushed down her irritation and returned her focus to the laptop screen. She didn't understand why her new computer hadn't arrived. The company had promised it within a week. She'd have to ask Jennetta to check on it.

At least she had a real desk, thanks to the help of Saluki and two maintenance workers. Sure enough, the old furniture had been put in a basement storage room, and Amelia had not bothered to tell her. She could never have worked on that card table until the new furniture arrived a month from now.

This desk, faded and out-of-style, bore the scars of previous directors or managers, but it was solid wood. It had no keyboard tray, so she had to set the laptop on the pull-out writing shelf. A little high for her, but better than the shaky folding table. She had adjusted the chair so she could type, even though her feet didn't quite touch the floor.

She'd live with it a few more weeks. She had no choice. She certainly didn't intend for anyone to hear her complaining.

More laughter. As much as she hated to, maybe she should shut her door.

Better yet, she should take a break and see what was going on. She could only deal with budgets for so long anyway. She pushed her chair back from the desk and slipped to her feet.

Adjusting her tailored red jacket and skirt, she stepped out onto the balcony. She spotted Amelia behind one of the information stations, leaning across the counter toward a male customer. Three of the other female representatives had left their stations and were clustered next to Amelia. The man seemed to be enjoying the attention and had leaned over to put his head close to Amelia's. At least no other visitors were waiting for service.

When the man stood up and glanced toward the stairway, she recognized him from her first day. The cowboy carriage owner that made her heart flutter. She tried to remember his name. Roger, Ricky, Randy. That was it. Randy Lee Jackson. No, Randy Lee Jackson used to be a judge on American Idol. But she was close. Johnson. Randy Lee Johnson.

Victoria realized she had been staring at him, and he was staring back. She wanted to retreat into her office, act as though she'd just been making a routine observance of the floor. But that might seem rude. She didn't want to insult one of the city's business owners, especially one who catered to tourists.

As she made her way down the stairs, the other workers returned to their assigned positions and attempted to look busy even though they had no customers. Good. At least they pretended to care what she thought.

Mr. Johnson strode away from Amelia at the counter and met Victoria at the bottom of the stairs.

Why couldn't she stop the flutter in her stomach? His good looks and easy smile didn't help, but she had come to Charleston for a change. Change that did not include a romantic relationship.

"There's the pretty lady I was lookin' for." He held a hand out for hers as she took the last step.

As she touched her palm to his, heat ran up her arm. "Mr. Johnson. Nice to see you again." The words were meant as a formality but they sounded friendlier than she intended.

"Glad you think so, but it's Randy Lee, remember? It's

really good to see you again, Victoria."

The way he emphasized "really" prickled her skin. With him standing so close, her brain seemed foggy. They were still at the bottom of the stairway, in full view of the half-dozen people browsing the displays. She blinked. She should invite him upstairs to her office. No, not the office. "Um, did you need to discuss something? Perhaps we should—"

There went that smile again, beginning with the dimple at one corner of his mouth and spreading slowly to the other corner.

"Not today. I was just dropping off some of my new brochures. But Amelia was kind enough to take them. Said she'd put them in the racks for me."

"I see." She glanced toward the nearest literature rack and saw that Amelia had left the information counter and was arranging brochures. Policy called for all brochures to be approved before distributing them. She would need to discuss that with Amelia, but she didn't want to create a scene in front of Randy Lee. She turned back to him. "I'm happy she could take care of you."

He placed his cowboy hat on his head, positioning it low on his forehead. He nodded. "I'll be seeing you soon, Victoria."

Unsure what he meant by that, she watched him amble across the room. Before he exited, he held the large door for a middle-aged couple entering the building.

Once the door closed behind him, she approached Amelia at the literature rack. "Mr. Johnson brought some new brochures?"

"He did." She continued with her task without looking up.

"Who approved it to be displayed?"

That stopped her. Holding a small stack of the literature, Amelia faced Victoria. "I did."

"You did."

"I've been approving this kind of thing for the past year now."

"While you were acting director."

"No one's had a problem with that. Do you?"

She did, particularly with Randy Lee Johnson's brochures. Victoria's job description made her responsible for all literature distributed by the Tourism Bureau. Until she learned what was being distributed and who had good judgment, she would need to take that duty seriously. She took one of the brochures from Amelia and glanced at it.

"Go ahead and put these out. But after this, for the time being, I want to see everything before it's displayed."

Amelia pursed her lips and nodded then continued to stuff the brochures into the holder. Victoria would never grow immune to the woman's icy barrier, but she swallowed the sharp remark that came to mind and congratulated herself for controlling her tongue.

Chapter Seven

Victoria checked the sign on the window of the real estate agency to be sure she had the right address.

She hoped the tiny storefront office didn't reflect the homes for sale here. The building appeared to be squeezed between two even older buildings, five blocks from the Tourism Bureau. The faded green stripes on the awning over the plate-glass window spoke of years of exposure to the southern sun and lack of care.

She studied the flyers that covered the large window. A two-floor condo on Broad Street for eight figures. A restored four-bedroom mansion on East Bay, recently listed at nearly two million. Maybe she had come to the wrong place, and not because the homes were too small or dilapidated.

She scanned the other photos but none seemed to be in her price range. She frowned. She needed to find something, but her budget wouldn't stretch that far. Maybe she should walk away, call an agent that focused on properties farther from downtown.

But she had made an appointment and taken an extra-long lunch break. On the phone, the woman had sounded as though she could help. She took a deep breath and pulled the door open. A little bell jingled over her head.

"Hey, there," called a female voice from somewhere behind a partition. "I'll be right out."

A moment later, the voice grew closer. "Happens every time. If I want company, all I have to do—" A grandmotherly woman buttoning her tailored gray suit jacket appeared from a doorway in the middle of the wall "—is get busy back here trying to organize the storage room."

She smiled and stuck out her hand. "You must be Victoria. I was expecting you, but I lost track of the time. I'm Donna Grace Collins."

Victoria took her hand, which felt soft and smooth, but her handshake was firm. "Nice to meet you, Mrs. Collins."

The agent waved her hand. "Please, honey, call me Donna Grace. We believe in manners here in Charleston, but most of us are not big on formalities."

Victoria nodded. "So I'm learning. I guess it's a lot like New England in that sense."

Donna Grace led the way to a desk and offered a chair to her. "I think it's the modern way. I don't remember my mama calling anybody by their first name except her closest friends." She settled into a chair and began to gather up the jumbled sheets of paper on the desktop. She placed them on top of a stack of thick catalog-type books towering on the corner of the desk.

"Now then, you said on the phone you'd be paying cash?"

Victoria cleared her throat. She hoped she wouldn't have to explain about the two divorce settlements. "That's right."

"Great. Let's see what we can find that might suit you." Donna Grace tapped keys on her computer keyboard and turned the monitor so Victoria could see it. "Here are the properties in the price range you said you could afford."

The screen revealed a long list of addresses, and Victoria's hopes soared.

Donna Grace pointed to the first three. "Now, these are a little higher than your limit, but they're sweet deals for the money. And in good locations."

Victoria looked at the prices and shook her head. "I really can't go that high."

The agent smiled. "I understand. I'd say you could make an offer, but they haven't been on the market long, and knowing the way properties go, I doubt a lowball would be considered at this point."

Donna Grace adjusted her glasses and studied the screen. "Let's see what else we've got." She scrolled and clicked. "Hmmm. North Charleston's out, I guess. You said you wanted to be in town, right?"

"Yes. It's not a requirement for my job, but I think if I'm promoting Charleston as a place to visit, I should live in the city."

Donna Grace nodded. "That makes sense. The business owners will appreciate that, too, I think. Of course, not all of them live in the city." She winked. "But that doesn't stop them from judging you if you don't, I suppose." She continued to scroll, squinting at the screen, shaking her head occasionally.

Victoria crossed her legs but her foot wouldn't stay still. She uncrossed them and planted her feet on the floor. Her right foot bounced up and down. She forced it to be still. "Maybe I should just look for a better place to rent?"

"Don't you plan to stay?"

"Yes, of course, I'll stay. Where would I go?"

"I don't know. But if you plan to stay in Charleston for more than, say, a year, buying a house is a good investment. And with the current interest rates and home prices, this is a good time to buy."

"Not if I can't afford it."

Donna Grace looked at her. "Now, honey, don't you worry. I'll find you something you can afford, and in a decent neighborhood, too. It may not be in the upscale areas, that's all." She returned her attention to the computer screen. "Did you say on the phone you'd be willing to look at a fixer-upper?"

Victoria's heart beat faster. She had discovered a love affair with rehabbing old houses during her three years with Antonio. One good thing that came out of that marriage. "I would. Have you got something?"

"I don't know. I haven't been inside this one. It says it's a 'handyman special.' You know what that means in real estate, don't you?"

Victoria leaned back in the chair and blew a puff of air. "It's probably got a leaky roof, missing windows, and broken plumbing."

Donna Grace laughed, a hearty chuckle. "Down here, we figure it's one step up from a tar-paper shack. But here, look at the picture."

The two-inch photo didn't reveal much. A two-story house in need of painting. The double porch on the side reminded her of the triple-deckers in Waterbury. Victoria looked at the price, then looked again.

She could easily afford this one, but how much work did it need? "Looks like I'd have to get lots of help to fix it up."

"Well, honey, there's plenty of good help available. Do you want to take a look? The house is vacant, so we can go over there right now if you have time."

"Why not?"

Donna Grace punched some keys on the computer and the printer behind her spat out several sheets of paper. She handed the listing information to Victoria and fifteen minutes later, they pulled to a stop on Smith Street in front of the house.

Dull gray paint, chipped and peeling, scarred the outside, and several balusters were missing from the porch railings. But the four corners of the house stood as straight as the cadets at The Citadel, the military school across town.

Victoria fell in love. "It's got good bones."

She could almost see earlier owners sitting on the upper level overseeing their estate. Her heart raced ahead, imagining herself living here. With some work, this could be a real showplace. Maybe even be featured in the annual Preservation Society house tour next year. Surely that would gain her the respect of native Charlestonians.

"Look at this yard." Donna Grace got out of the car. "The lot is twice as big as anything else in this part of the city. I'm surprised someone hasn't tried to tear the house down and put up three or four new ones. Of course, the city wouldn't let that happen unless it was literally falling down." She hurried around the car and took Victoria's arm. "Come on. Let's see how bad it is inside."

The interior air bore the distinctive staleness of a house that had been closed up for several years—not unpleasant, but lonely, with memories of family meals and summer parties, fried chicken, and flowers from the garden. How many couples had been married and raised children here? Or had a spinster lived a solitary life, surrounded by beauty but tasting only isolation?

The interior exceeded Victoria's expectations—both in character and in disrepair. Decades of voices echoed through the empty rooms. Cracked and chipped plaster made the walls look like an old woman's face. But floor-to-ceiling windows provided light and access to the side porches. And the woodwork, although scratched and dulled by ancient varnish and dirt, had not been painted. Unusual in a house that had survived changing design trends for more than a century and a half.

She found a spot in the parlor where the worn wall-to-wall carpet had pulled away from the tack strips. She peeked underneath. Wood. Based on the historic house tours she'd taken, it could be heart of pine. With luck, the carpet had protected it and she would be able to restore it to a gleaming polish.

The stairs creaked as the two women ascended on the threadbare oriental-style runner. "How long has it been empty?"

"About three years." Donna Grace pushed on the newel post at the top of the staircase. It didn't give. "Got tied up in an estate dispute and was just released from probate two weeks ago. Other agents say the people who've looked at it have decided it needs too much work."

Her tone told Victoria she doubted her ability to take on the project. But Victoria was hopeful. "It will take a lot but nothing too difficult, from what I can see. I would have to borrow money for the repairs, so I'll need to get some estimates before I make an offer. Can you recommend a carpenter and a plumber?"

"Of course. When we get back to the office, I'll make some calls."

An hour later, Donna Grace hung up the phone on her desk. "All set. The carpenter will be there at lunchtime on Wednesday. I'll meet the plumber on Thursday. You don't need to be there—unless you just want to."

Victoria shook her head. "I am pretty busy this week. But … meeting with contractors doesn't seem like it would be part of your job description. I don't want to take advantage of—"

"Nonsense. You need the bids, and I can't sell the house until you get them. Besides …" She pushed her glasses up on her nose. "I hope we're going to be friends. And I go to extra lengths for my friends. Now that's taken care of, would you like to get some coffee with me? Or—have you had lunch?"

Victoria's stomach grumbled just then, and she laughed. "Obviously, I'm starving. Lunch would be great."

"It's a beautiful day. Are you up for a walk? It'll take about twenty minutes to get there, but I like to eat at the Battery."

Victoria knew about the landmark promenade by that name at the end of the peninsula. Since she enjoyed walking, she agreed, assuming it would give her a chance to try another local restaurant. She soon found out that Donna Grace intended to eat outside instead.

After buying bag lunches from a street vendor, they

headed to White Point Garden. The majestic trees filling the park had begun to get their new growth of leaves. Victoria remembered a tour guide saying they were live oaks and stayed green all year, such a difference from the oak trees she knew in Connecticut.

At the east side of the park, the two women found an empty bench that faced the harbor beyond the promenade and seawall. A young couple strolled along the walk, arm-in-arm like she and Brian had on their college campus.

Donna Grace opened the bag and took out her sandwich. "My husband and I used to love coming here and watching the ships come and go."

"Used to?"

"He passed two years ago."

"Oh, I'm sorry. I didn't know."

"Of course you didn't, honey. How could you know?"

"Were you—" She started to say "happy," but how many people were really happy in marriage? She cleared her throat. "Were you married a long time?"

Donna Grace smiled. "Almost thirty years. He died two months before our anniversary. I miss him terribly."

Victoria chewed a bite of her sandwich. "So you had a good marriage?"

Donna Grace took a drink from her bottled water then shook her head. "No, I wouldn't say we had a good marriage. I would call it a great marriage."

A breeze off the water made Victoria shiver. So some people did find happiness being married. Her parents had, in fact, until her father's Parkinson's disease cut short their life together. But she had been absent the day "happily ever after" certificates were handed out.

"How about you, Victoria? You're not married?"

"No, not now. I was …" She didn't want to tell this woman about her three failed marriages. She'd rather just forget them herself, if that were possible.

Donna Grace patted her arm. "You don't have to explain. It's not easy to make a marriage work. Lord knows, Al and I had our rough patches. But we worked through them together, with God's help."

God hadn't been of much help when Brian walked out on her. After that, Victoria hadn't had time for a god who didn't make time for her.

Chapter Eight

Victoria preferred to spend Thursday afternoon in her office and talk to no one, but she might not have a choice.

When she pushed through the doors of the Visitors' Center after lunch, the line of people writhed back and forth between the tapes and metal posts. Worst of all, not a single customer service representative stood behind the long counter.

That unsettled her stomach more than anything had in her first three weeks.

"Can we get some service here?" A short, balding man in a plaid shirt called out from the back of the line. Other voices echoed around the room, creating a rumble of unrest.

Spring breaks had started, and Charleston remained an appealing location for South Carolina families who wanted to mix some history with their school vacation. Since she liked to experience what the customer service reps did, she had been filling in at the information counter all week during the busiest times—in addition to learning her way around and working on the new ad campaign.

But now where had the reps disappeared to? Five employees—all Charleston-area natives—had reported to work this morning, and their lunch breaks should be over. And why hadn't Amelia intervened?

Victoria shifted her purse strap on her shoulder and strode toward the far corner of the concourse. Her spiky heels rapped a warning cadence. She halted in the doorway of the employee break room.

The five women surrounded Amelia, who appeared to be holding court near the coffeepot. Her back to the door, the assistant director waved both hands in the air. "You guys are important. You guys make people want to come to Cha'ston."

Victoria cringed at the exaggerated imitation of her own New England accent and Italian hand gestures. She appreciated the fact that neither Marylou nor the newest employee, Kylie, joined in the laughter. But still, they weren't at their posts.

Kylie saw Victoria. She tipped her head toward the door, probably trying to warn Amelia. But Amelia continued her act without noticing.

Victoria knew Amelia, and some of the staff who had wanted Amelia to be named director, considered Victoria a gatecrasher. But mimicking her in the middle of the workday? She forced saliva into her dry mouth and stepped into the room. Her tongue shifted into hyperdrive.

"Have you guys not noticed there are people waiting out there?" She'd used "you guys" again, but some habits weren't easily changed. "Your jobs are to make their visit to Charleston great, and if you want to keep those jobs, you'll get back to work. And this better not ever happen again."

She stopped for breath, and the five reps hustled past her to their stations. They began to utter apologies to the customers. No doubt the waiting tourists had heard her big mouth as she ranted, but at least they would know one person in this building cared about them.

Amelia pushed away from the counter and brushed past Victoria.

"Tell me, Amelia, did you win the lottery or something?"

Amelia stopped and put one hand on the doorjamb. "Whattaya mean?"

"I mean," Victoria strained the words between gritted teeth, "that you act like you don't need this job anymore. Today's behavior is unacceptable. Leaving the service desk unattended and, even worse, making fun of me behind my back."

"I don't know what you're talking about. You must be

paranoid or something."

Blood rushed to Victoria's head so fast she thought she would faint. Through the open doorway, she could see other employees—even some of the visitors—glancing in her direction.

Disciplining an employee always left her with the taste of baking soda, and she hadn't intended to let it happen in front of others. While she tried to compose herself, she straightened the jacket of her topaz blue wool suit. Underneath, her white polyester blouse stuck to her skin, and moisture trickled down her back. But removing the jacket would signal a relaxed attitude, the opposite of the message she wanted to send.

Victoria stepped closer. "I will not tolerate this sort of behavior. Do you understand what I'm saying?"

"Yeah, I got it. But I wonder if you do. I'd better go help the customers." Amelia breezed out the door, casting off the pungent aroma of outlet-store cologne.

After taking several deep breaths, Victoria strode out to help handle the long line of customers. Her hopes for a quiet afternoon working in her office had dissipated like a sandcastle in a hurricane wind.

Coffee. Victoria needed coffee. Black, strong, hot enough to wake her up.

Still wearing her extra-long Boston Red Sox sleep shirt, she shuffled through her living room. Sunlight eked its way into the apartment and she squinted to keep her eyes from watering.

The windowless kitchen was still dark so she lifted her eyelids a little more, found the coffeepot and stuck it under the faucet. She threw a packet into the basket, poured the water through the narrow opening, and flipped the switch. Leaning back against the counter, she closed her eyes and listened to the burping and bubbling, waited for the soothing aroma to reach her nostrils.

Her morning ritual comforted her. The one thing in her life that hadn't changed as she had moved from house to house to apartment, from one man to another to alone, from a colonial-era industrial New England city to a colonial-era southern port city ruled by descendants of plantation owners.

Because both cities focused on history for their tourism promotions, she had thought the transition would be simple. Her experience as assistant director in Waterbury had prepared her to run a tourism organization, hadn't it?

Once again, she was learning how wrong she could be. She poured the steaming liquid into a mug and sipped, letting the brew slide down her throat, singe her insides, and burn away the frustration.

That little scene with Amelia yesterday—in front of other employees and tourists—should have been handled in her office, in private. She knew better than to correct an employee in public. She would never win their respect by humiliating them. Even if that's what Amelia was trying to do to her.

Humiliation caused resentment and could make a person want to retaliate. Or, in some cases, to run away. Which is what had brought her to this pathetic apartment in South Carolina.

She didn't want Amelia to retaliate or to leave. The woman had valuable experience and knowledge, if Victoria could just earn her cooperation. She had to find a way.

Chapter Nine

Saluki did not know why a sophisticated lady like Victoria would invite her, but she wasn't about to pass up a free pizza.

It did feel odd to go to Pizza Shack with an adult instead of her friends. The hip-hop music playing made her feet want to move. She looked around as they entered the chrome-and-vinyl restaurant. Customers sat at a couple of the red plastic tables but she saw no one she knew. Not a surprise for Saturday lunchtime.

"What toppings do you like?" Victoria picked up a menu from the service counter and looked at her. "I like them all."

Saluki grinned. "Me too. Except anchovies." She wrinkled her nose. "Never had the guts to try them, but I hear they're really bad."

"Okay, then. Let's get the works—except anchovies." Victoria placed the order. They filled their cups at the drink machine and brought them back to a table by the window facing a parking lot.

"Thanks, Ms. Russo. This is real nice of you."

Victoria shrugged. "I want to get to know you. Tell me about your family."

"Not much to tell. I've got two younger brothers. Mama works a lot, so I've always looked after them. But now they're old enough that I could take the internship job after school."

"Your dad's not in the picture?"

"Not since I was seven."

"I'm sorry. Guess I was fortunate to have my father around as long as I did."

Saluki toyed with her straw, stirring the ice in her cup. "Is he still alive?"

"No. He died five months ago. His last few years were tough, but before he got sick we were pretty close."

"Sometimes I wish I could just talk to my dad…" Her stomach knotted, and she shook her head. "On second thought, I don't know what I would say to him."

Their order number was called and Victoria went to the counter to pick it up. From a shelf on one side of the room, Saluki got plates and napkins, as well as shakers of cheese and hot pepper.

The aroma of meat, olives, and cheese tickled her nose as she slid a slice onto her plate. She lifted it to her mouth and took a tiny bite, being careful not to burn her tongue by biting into the hot pepperoni.

Victoria asked her about school, and she explained how Mr. D. had helped her get the internship.

"I really like learning about people and cultures," she said, talking around a bite of sausage. "I plan to major in social studies in college."

"So you do plan to go to college? That's good."

"Oh, yes, ma'am. My mom didn't go to college, and I don't want to end up like her. She cleans houses during the day and offices at night. She has to work all the time just to get by." She surprised herself by talking so much to this woman she hardly knew. "I want to be a career woman like you."

Victoria winced. "Trust me. You don't want to be like me." She looked at her watch. "I've got to get going. I'm trying to buy a house, and I'm supposed to meet my real estate agent there to take some measurements." She picked up her purse then hesitated. "There's no one living there right now. Would you like to come see it? It needs a lot of work."

"Is it an old house?"

Victoria nodded. "It's not pre-Revolutionary but it is in the Radcliffborough district. It was built almost two hundred years ago."

Saluki tossed her napkin on the table and jumped up. "Sounds cool. Let's go."

A few minutes later, they pulled up in front of a huge house with a two-story porch, just like the mansions down by the river, except really run-down. A gray-haired white lady waited beside a silver car in the driveway.

"Donna Grace, this is Saluki. She works after school at the Tourism Bureau." Saluki liked that Victoria didn't refer to her as an intern like some people did, as though she was somehow less important than other employees.

The woman took her hand and the warmth of her smile radiated through her soft hand. "Glad to meet you, Saluki." She jingled a key with a red plastic tag. "Let's go in."

They stepped through the front door into a large entry hall. Victoria pointed out the dining room to one side. Saluki loved the rainbow of colors in the stained glass above the large bay window overlooking the side yard. A whole room just for eating? Of all her friends, only Dustin's family had one, but they had lots of things her family could only dream about.

While Victoria and Donna Grace measured the windows, she wandered into the other empty rooms, imagining what it might have been like two hundred years ago when the house was new. A girl like her would have been a house slave, working in the kitchen or as a maid to the lady of the house. She rubbed her arms to chase away the chill.

Odd pieces of the previous owners' lives remained in random places. A cracked plate in the kitchen sink. Pieces of contact paper clinging to the cabinet shelves. She opened a closet door and saw several empty wooden shelves. As she began to close the door, something on the top shelf caught her eye.

Was that a basket? She stood on tiptoes and looked closer. In the dim light, she couldn't tell for sure what kind of basket. She stretched her arm until her fingers touched it but she couldn't grasp hold. She jumped and tried again, grabbing the top rim and pulling it closer.

A sweetgrass basket. No way. Why would someone leave it behind? Good ones cost hundreds of dollars, even if they were made last week. The older ones could be even more valuable.

Holding her breath, she lifted the basket down and peered in it, not sure what it might contain. Empty. She exhaled, grateful not to find any critters inside. She turned it around in her hands, finding several rough spots and broken reeds. But nothing that couldn't be fixed. Aunt Ida could tell her how. She had made baskets like this until arthritis crippled her hands. Saluki had wanted to have one made by her great-aunt, but Aunt Ida always needed the money she got by selling them.

She listened to see where Victoria and the agent were. Upstairs. She could hide the basket outside and come back for it later. If she told Victoria, she might want to keep it herself. She crept to the back door and opened it quietly, scanning the backyard for a good hiding place.

Footsteps sounded on the stairs. Victoria and the saleslady were coming down. She'd have to hurry.

She stepped onto the back stoop but stopped.

Her mama had taught her better than this. Besides, Victoria had been nice to her. She didn't want to ruin that. She may have found the basket, but it wasn't hers to take. She had to show it to Victoria.

She scurried back inside and closed and locked the door without making a sound. Grasping the basket close to her chest, she crossed the kitchen and almost got hit by the swinging door when Victoria pushed through it. She jumped back.

"Oh, Saluki. Did I hit you?"

"No, ma'am. I got out of the way in time."

"I'm so sorry. That door will take some getting used to."

Donna Grace followed Victoria into the room and paused,

peering at the basket in Saluki's arms. "What have you got there?"

Saluki held it out with both hands and Donna Grace took it. "It's an old sweetgrass basket I found in the closet." She turned to Victoria. "You know, the traditional African baskets they make around here."

"I've seen them in the market. They're beautiful." Victoria took it reverently as Donna Grace passed it to her. Turning it upside down, she examined the holes. "Too bad it's not in better condition. Might be worth some money to help pay for all the work this house needs."

"I could fix it." Saluki stopped and swallowed. "I mean, I think I could. If you want me to try. My great-aunt used to make them."

Victoria smiled and handed it back to her. "That would be great if you could repair it. But I guess we should wait to see if I get the house."

Saluki took the basket to the closet where she had found it. Standing on tiptoes again, she pushed it as far back on the top shelf as she could reach. A nice lady like Victoria, not some stranger, deserved this treasure.

Chapter Ten

By midday Monday, Victoria started to wonder why the city had been so concerned about the lack of tourists. Activity at the Visitors Center had not abated, and not all the people were there on spring break.

She had been filling in at the information counter since one of the customer service representatives had called in sick. Just before lunchtime, a gray-haired man and woman held hands as the man led the way to where Victoria waited.

Elderly couples holding hands always stirred her heart. Respect for their years together battled with the awareness that she might never enjoy such sweet romance.

Once they stood in front of her, she pushed aside her envy. "I'm so sorry for the wait. We appreciate your patience. How may I help you?"

The man gave her a friendly smile that made her like him in spite of his crooked yellowed teeth. "I'm sure it's not easy to keep up when there's so many people." He released the woman's hand and leaned on the granite counter as if sharing a confidence. "Can you recommend a good restaurant? We want to celebrate."

A lump in her throat blocked Victoria's response. She swallowed and forced the requisite smile on her face into her voice. "It's always nice to see couples who have been married a long time and are still in love. Is it your anniversary? How many years?"

The man put his arm around the woman and winked. "Oh, we're on our honeymoon."

Victoria caught her breath. They had to be in their seventies. At least. She fumbled for a map from underneath the counter and unfolded it, keeping her eyes on the pair. She looked from one to the other, unable to think of a response.

The man chuckled. "Young lady, don't you know that love is ageless? Since you're wondering, I'm seventy-five, and my bride here is seventy-two. I lost my first wife three years ago, and Jeannie's husband died five years ago. When we met last fall, it was love at first sight. So we plan to enjoy every minute that we've got together. Why shouldn't we?"

Some people lucked out with multiple good marriages, but Victoria couldn't even have one. Her voice cracked. "Of course. What kind of food do you like? Seafood? Steak? Lowcountry?"

The bride spoke, the raspy voice of asthma. Or cancer. "Eddie likes seafood. I like chicken." She grinned, deepening the wrinkles around her mouth. "So seafood would be good."

Eddie threw her a tender glance. "Just so it's romantic."

It had been years since Victoria had received that kind of tenderness. If ever. She pointed to Queen Street on the map. "There are a couple of wonderful restaurants here." She moved her finger to another spot. "And here. You can get both seafood and chicken at either one. But you'll need to call ahead for reservations."

She showed the man the restaurant list with phone numbers on the back of the map.

He nodded. "These two were both mentioned by our carriage tour guide. But which one would you recommend?"

She hesitated. She could anger other business owners if she recommended one restaurant over all the others. But the way the man glowed when he looked at his wife, the tender way he touched her, made Victoria want to be part of their lives.

She lowered her voice and leaned over the counter. "I think a table by the fireplace at 82 Queen would be very romantic. That's where I would go."

The man slapped his palm on the counter. "That's where we'll eat, then."

They thanked her and headed toward the exit, their heads together studying the map as they walked.

Victoria watched them move away, forced the hollow spot in her heart to close up, and turned to help the next person in line. When she saw Randy Lee Johnson heading for her station, her pulse began to gallop.

He removed his cowboy hat and grinned at her. "Hello, sugar. I do believe I've come to the right place. Looks like love is in the air." He nodded toward the couple Victoria had just helped. "So I guess I'm here at just the right time."

What did he mean by that? Love was the last thing he would find around her.

"Why, Randy Lee, I wouldn't expect you to need any information about where to go in Charleston. What are you doing here?" She gave him a teasing smile to take the sting out of the question that sounded harsher than she intended.

He planted his elbow on the counter and leaned over, moving his bushy eyebrows up and down. "I need some very important information. Do you know a pretty lady who might have dinner with me this ev'ning?"

Her face grew warm and her eyes flitted to the customer rep on her left. Had anyone overheard the question? Thankfully, no one seemed to be paying attention, but she couldn't be certain. It wouldn't do for her employees to think she condoned flirting with the customers. "Shhh. Randy Lee, I'm working right now."

He straightened, forcing her to crook her neck to follow his motion as he switched to a serious mood. "I understand, miss." He lowered his voice to a stage whisper. "May I have the honor of your presence for the evening meal tonight?"

She stifled a giggle. It would be fun to go out with him. One dinner didn't have to lead to a relationship. "Yes, okay. I accept. Now please, I need to get back to the real customers."

He plopped his hat back on his head. "I'll pick you up here at six." He made a two-finger salute off the brim of his hat, rotated on his heels, and strode toward the exit as she motioned to the next customer in line.

A few minutes before six, Victoria freshened up in the ladies' room, checked her hair and makeup, and touched up her lipstick. She hoped the green tailored wool suit she had chosen for work that morning would be suitable wherever they went to eat. Randy Lee's invitation had been vague and hurried, so she wasn't sure what to expect.

As she waited for the last few customers to leave, she considered where she should wait. She ushered a middle-aged couple out through the large glass doors and saw Randy Lee ascending the brick steps. She felt his admiring gaze and returned his smile. He looked the part of the southern gentleman plantation owner but for his cowboy boots and western-style hat.

"There's my gorgeous date." He took his hat off and bowed low, sweeping the hat in a wide arc. "If you're ready to go, your carriage awaits."

"I'll be right with you." She stepped back inside to grab her purse. Two of the customer service reps were still at the counter. "Marylou, I'm going out the main door. Would you lock up behind me?"

She pushed through the door to the portico where Randy Lee waited. She heard the lock slide into place behind her. Randy Lee offered his hand, and she placed her smaller hand into his. He made her feel like a queen—or like Scarlet O'Hara. "Why, thank you, kind sir."

He escorted her down the steps and, when they reached the sidewalk, she caught sight of a horse and carriage waiting at the corner. She glanced at Randy Lee, unable to keep the surprise from showing on her face. "Is that for us? You really meant it when you said carriage?"

He grinned. "Yes, I thought we'd go in style."

She had taken a guided tour in a horse-drawn wagon that posed as a "carriage" and held twenty-five or thirty people, but she had not ridden in one of the private closed carriages that had room for only a few.

A two-step stool sat next to the front wheel, and Randy Lee helped her climb up then settled himself beside her. The driver, dressed in a dark blue uniform that matched the logo on the carriage, retrieved the stool and climbed onto his seat in front of them. He glanced at Randy Lee, who nodded his head, and the driver flicked the reins. The horse moved ahead smoothly, his hooves clicking rhythmically on the pavement.

Randy Lee settled against the seat and threw his arm around her shoulders. "Why would you be surprised, Miss Victoria? I do own a carriage company, remember?"

She laughed, trying not to focus on his nearness. "Of course, Mr. Randy Lee. It's just that I've never been taken to dinner by horse and buggy before."

"Well, there's a first time for everything. But technically, this would be mule-and-buggy. I only use mules."

"Sorry. I guess I should know the difference."

"That's okay, sugar. I could tell you were a city girl." His low murmur caused her to shiver. "Are you cold? We've got a blanket."

He leaned forward and pulled a folded blue blanket from beneath the driver's higher seat. He shook it out and spread it over her lap, reaching around to tuck it in on the other side. Putting his arm over her shoulders again, he pulled her close to his chest. "There, is that better?"

"I'm fine." She turned her nose into his jacket, closed her eyes, and breathed the musky smell of wool and cigar smoke. He didn't smell like a horse barn. Her eyes popped open. What was she doing? She had only known him a short time, and she had no intention of falling into the same mistake she had made too many times. It didn't matter how nice Randy Lee treated her.

She stiffened her body and sat straighter, pulling the blanket closer but putting some air between her and Randy Lee. He relaxed his grip on her opposite side but didn't drop his arm from her shoulder. The warmth felt good, so she didn't force it.

"What is it, sugar? You okay?"

She nodded and smiled, tipping her face to look at him. "I'm fine. But I don't want to rush things."

"Course not. I just don't want you to be cold." His guile-free smile reassured her. He waved his free hand at the shadows descending on the city. "It's a beautiful evening, but spring's not here yet. Wouldn't want you to catch a chill your first winter in the South."

The tingle in her body had more to do with Randy Lee than with the weather, but Victoria wasn't about to admit that to him.

Soon they left the historic district as they headed north toward one of the two rivers that bordered the city. The last remnants of sunlight reflected silver off the bridge towering above the water. Even from blocks away, the sweeping span invited drivers to adventure and excitement across the river.

But was that the Cooper or the Ashley? She had to learn which of the two rivers bordered the city on which side as they flowed to the Atlantic. She racked her brain for something that would help her remember. That bridge. A major race across it would take place in a few months. What did they call it? Something River Bridge Run.

"The Cooper." The words slipped out before she realized it.

Randy Lee nodded. "Yes, it's beautiful this time of day, isn't it? Too bad we've missed the sunset over the bridge from the restaurant. That can be spectacular."

Before they reached the turnoff to the bridge, the driver pulled up in front of Fleet Landing, an establishment Victoria had not yet visited. Going out with Randy Lee had definite advantages, since she wouldn't feel as awkward as when she ate at a restaurant alone.

"What a great spot," she said as they followed the hostess to a table by the window. Maybe she should have recommended this place to that newlywed couple this morning. "What's the occasion?"

He moved to pull out her chair, and when she was seated, he scooted her closer to the table. Leaning over, he whispered in her ear, "You are."

Predictable flattery, but it made her smile. "No, seriously, what's this all about?"

He took his seat opposite her. "Why, darlin', I'm surprised you don't know. I thought you ladies kept track of such things."

"What things?"

"It's our anniversary."

She shook her head. "Anniversary of what?"

He reached across the table and took her hand. "It's been three weeks since I met the most beautiful woman in Charleston."

Her face warmed, even though her brain told her not to take him seriously. Honestly. Did he use that line with all the women he met?

"It's not like a man to remember that kind of thing."

He lifted her hand and pressed his lips to it. "How could I forget the best day of my life?"

The waiter appeared with the wine, and she pulled her hand away. She opened her menu, burying her hot face in it.

She ordered a shrimp dinner, but when he ordered only She Crab soup, she raised an eyebrow. Handing the menus to the waiter, he shrugged. "I'm not especially hungry. I just want to feast my eyes on you tonight, darlin'."

At the soft look he gave her, she allowed her heart to do another somersault, despite the caution light flashing in her brain.

Chapter Eleven

At the sound of a horn outside, Saluki's heart flipped. Dustin waited in his dad's 1969 Dodge Charger that she thought of as a chariot.

She called up the stairs, "Tyler, Isaiah, I'm leaving."

Her brothers appeared at the top of the stairs, grinning. "Bye, sis," thirteen-year-old Tyler said. "Have fun."

"Yeah, have fun," Isaiah, eleven, echoed in a sing-song voice.

They'd been staying alone after school for a couple of years now, but this was the first time Saluki had gone out at night when Mama had to work. She hoped it wouldn't prove to be a mistake. "You've got mine and Mama's phone numbers if there's an emergency. Tyler, you're in charge. You make sure Isaiah goes to bed on time."

"Yeah, yeah. I got it." Her brother's impatient voice told her he wanted to get back to his video game. She hoped he wouldn't lose all track of time and stay up too late.

The car horn blasted again, and Dustin revved the engine. She opened the door and waved to let him know she was coming. Then she looked back at Tyler and Isaiah. Both boys had turned toward the bedroom they shared. "Isaiah, mind your brother."

"Okay. Bye." He punched Tyler on the arm and ran for the bedroom.

"And no fighting!" She blew out through puckered lips. But she wouldn't let them ruin her Friday night. She needed to go before Dustin got upset. She grabbed her purse and locked the door behind her.

Dustin waited in the car with all the windows down,

taking advantage of the unexpected warm weather. "Hurry up, babe. The others are expecting us."

She opened her door and slid into the bucket seat. "I know. I'm sorry, sweetie. Had to make sure my brothers would be okay."

He didn't wait for her to put on her seatbelt but pulled away from the curb, squealing the tires as he sped down the street. "Sure. I just hate being the last to arrive."

She breathed a sigh of relief, catching a whiff of the azaleas they were passing. He wasn't angry with her. He just didn't want to be late. The party tonight would be fun.

When they arrived at TeeJay's house, she saw only one car in the driveway. "Where is everybody? I thought TeeJay invited lots of kids."

Dustin turned to her and winked. "Like I said, looks like we're the last ones here."

He jumped out and came around to open her door. He held out his hand, and she let him help her out. Sometimes he could be such a gentleman. But he hadn't answered her question.

As she stood, he grasped her around the waist and pulled her close. "It's just the four of us tonight, babe. And TeeJay's parents are out of town."

Her heart thudded, and her body warmed at his touch. But her stomach clenched. Mama wouldn't approve of this situation. She didn't trust this "rich white boy," as she called Dustin, and didn't want her daughter ending up in the same situation that she had—pregnant and forced to marry at seventeen.

But Mama didn't understand. Saluki had no intention of following in her mother's footsteps. She would go to college and have a career. And Dustin was special. She wouldn't let him go like her mother had her father. They would go to the same college, graduate, and get good jobs, then get married.

She relaxed against him and kissed him, tasting mint on

his breath. Everything would be fine. Dustin wouldn't do anything wrong, and Mama didn't have to know that TeeJay's parents weren't at home.

The four of them listened to a new musician TeeJay had discovered on iTunes, ate chips and dip, drank Cokes, and laughed. About ten o'clock, TeeJay asked Majesty if she wanted to see his room.

Saluki couldn't let Majesty mess up her life. She jumped to her feet. "Maybe we should go home now."

Her friend looked at her like, "What's wrong with you?"

Saluki watched helplessly as her friend snuggled up to TeeJay. The pair moved down the hallway and a door banged shut. Her mouth tasted like fuzz. She didn't want to stay, but she couldn't ask Dustin to take her home and leave their friends here alone.

He tugged at her hand. "Come here, babe. Why should they have all the fun?" He pulled her onto the sofa next to him and started planting kisses all over her face.

It felt good to be wanted. Majesty had always been the one that boys noticed until Dustin had transferred to their high school.

She relaxed against him and returned his sweet kiss. She enjoyed his hands roaming over her body. But when he tried to unbutton her blouse, she brushed his hand away. "You're going too fast. I'm not ready for this, Dustin. I don't think we're ready for this."

Giggles trickled from behind the closed door down the hall. Majesty had made her choice.

Saluki looked around for her purse. "Maybe we should go home."

"Come on, baby. I just want to be with you." His voice carried an edge to it. An edge she didn't like.

She pushed him away and stood up, but he grabbed her arm and held tight.

"Oww. You're hurting me, Dustin. Let go."

He released his grip and rubbed her arm. "I won't hurt you, babe. I promise."

His pleading voice softened her resolve. She didn't want to lose him. They had something special. They could go places together. "Okay, I'll stay. But you have to stop when I say so."

He stood and wrapped his arms around her shoulders. "I will, baby." He kissed her neck, her ears, her cheek, tickling her skin with his rough whiskers. "Come on. Sit back down."

She allowed him to push her back onto the sofa. She felt so comfortable with him, like she had known him all her life. And she wanted to spend forever with him. He kissed her again, a gentle joining of their lips. She could do this without allowing things to get out of control.

He unbuttoned his own shirt and gently guided her hand until it rested on his hairy chest. She liked touching his skin, and she leaned her head against his shoulder. It was kind of like they were sitting on the beach after going swimming. She could stay here like this all night.

She'd never expected to date someone like Dustin. Someone who wasn't even African-American. Someone from a wealthy family. But it felt so right. She loved him, and he loved her.

After awhile, he began to kiss her again, whispering words of love and desire. He pulled her onto his lap and nibbled on her ear, then leaned over sideways, pulling her to a reclining position beside him. Warning bells went off in her head, and she struggled against him. He held her tight. "It's all right, baby."

She pushed against him but couldn't get up. "No, it's not, Dustin. I said stop."

"Oh, babe. Please."

"You promised to stop."

"I will. I won't, you know, do anything we'll regret. Just

stay here beside me. Please."

She managed to get a hand free and to give him a weak slap on his cheek. He reacted with force, hitting her face so hard she fell off the couch and hit her arm and her back on the edge of the coffee table. She yelled and began to sob.

Dustin jumped up and reached for her. "Jeesh, baby. I'm sorry. I didn't mean to hurt you. Are you okay?" He knelt beside her on the floor, pushing the table out of the way.

She pushed him away. "Why did you do that?" She hiccupped, her sobs easing to a whimper.

He brushed her cheek. "You caught me by surprise. I never meant to hurt you. What can I do for you?"

She pointed to the spot on her back where she had hit the table. It felt as though the sharp edge of the table had scraped her skin off. "Maybe some ice for my back, okay?" When he returned with some ice cubes wrapped in a dishtowel, she pulled the back of her blouse up. "Is it bleeding?"

He touched her skin. His fingers were gentle. "No, but you've got a bad scrape there. The ice should help." The raw skin burned. When he placed the ice pack against the spot, she flinched at the cold.

"You want some antiseptic? I could look for some in the bathroom."

"No, it'll wait until I get home." He seemed so comforting, so concerned. This was the Dustin she knew, the one she had fallen in love with. But the evening had soured. "In fact, why don't you put the ice back and take me home now?"

"Whatever you say." When he returned from the kitchen, he went to the hall entrance and called out. "Hey, TeeJay. Thanks, man. We're leaving now. Catch you tomorrow."

Saluki had retrieved her purse and waited by the door.

"You okay, babe?"

She nodded, fighting the urge to cry.

He cupped her face in his hand. "I really am sorry. It

won't happen again, I promise. I love you, babe."

He kissed her, his lips barely touching hers, and the warmth spread to her toes.

It had been an accident. Dustin wouldn't hurt her. She looped her arms around his neck and returned the kiss.

She believed in him, in their future together.

Chapter Twelve

Victoria's insides seemed to be tying themselves in twenty knots Monday afternoon as she set up presentation boards containing the new tourism campaign in the conference room.

She had worked with a local design firm to translate her ideas into billboards and print ads. Today would be her first presentation to an audience—her own staff.

She had placed notepads, pens, and bottles of water at each place around the table. Maybe this group of managers and supervisors would have some helpful comments. If they wished to remain anonymous, they could submit their suggestions in writing.

She lined the boards up on easels positioned around the room. She wanted the employees to see the designs as they came in.

No. She should present one idea at a time. She hurried to turn each board so the design faced the wall.

Laughter and chatter reached her from the hallway. The conference room door opened and the laughter stopped. Amelia entered with Phyllis, one of the customer service supervisors, bringing only silence with them. They had wiped their faces clean of any mirth.

The others followed. Most gravitated to the far end of the conference table, as if putting space between themselves and her.

No matter. That made it easier for her to practice the presentation she would make to the Old Town Business Owners Association next week. As she waited for everyone to get settled, her mouth felt like paste. She tried to soothe it with a drink from her bottle of water. Then she took a formal stance behind her chair at the head of the table.

"As you know, the Board of Directors hired me to raise Charleston's prominence as a destination," she began. "The city has long enjoyed a good reputation, but there's been a downturn in recent years due to the economy. I'm excited that you will be the first to see our new tourism campaign."

She turned the first board around, showing an aerial shot of the city and the words, "Come and See."

"We want people who have been to Charleston in the past to come back, and we want those who have never visited to come for the first time. So this will be our theme."

She waited for a reaction. Their faces remained blank.

She squared her shoulders and moved to the next panel. "We'll do a series of ads and billboards with various slogans focusing on different aspects of the city. For instance," she turned the panel over to reveal an advertisement featuring Fort Sumter in the middle of Charleston Harbor, "we're best known as the place where the Civil War began, so this one uses 'Come and See Where History Was Made.'"

She detected a flicker of a smile on Tom Peyton's face. Progress.

"We'll run some ads targeting religious tour groups, focusing on the numerous churches and the role they played in the city's growth." She turned another board around. It showed several historic church steeples with the words "Come and See the Holy City."

A few heads nodded. She stepped to the next panel.

"And this one is my favorite." She revealed a close-up of an African-American woman weaving a sweetgrass basket. She let the words on the poster speak for themselves—"Come and See an Old Art Rewoven."

She continued to move around the room, turning the poster boards over and explaining what audience each one was designed to reach. When she had finished, she took her seat.

"Well? What do you think? I'd like to know your reactions and I welcome your ideas."

Unlike the others, Tom did not look at Amelia for approval before speaking. "I think it could work." As business manager, he brought a straightforward approach to their meetings. "I like the way different audiences are targeted with slightly different messages. That could be very cost-efficient."

"Thank you, Tom." Victoria was relieved to have some affirmation for all the time and effort she had put into the campaign. Now for the hard part. The others would take their cues from Amelia, so she looked at her assistant director.

"How about the rest of you? Do you have any suggestions?"

Amelia shifted in her chair, leaned to one side and tilted her head. "Sure. It has lots of possibilities," she said in an I-don't-really-mean-this tone. "We could do a play on words and use, 'Come and See the Sea.' Since we're right at the ocean and all."

Phyllis snickered then stopped abruptly when Victoria shifted her glance to her. "Yes, ma'am. Since the first name of the city was Charles Towne, we could say, "Come and See C-Towne.' That's kind of catchy, don't you think?"

Victoria closed her notebook and stood. No sense wasting any more time. "Thank you for your attention. And for your comments. Think about it. Mull it over. If you have any other suggestions, you can write them down and give them to Jennetta, or you're welcome to …" She paused for effect. "… come and see me."

Realizing they had been dismissed, the staff gathered their things and filed out without speaking.

Tom gave her a reassuring smile, but the others avoided meeting her eyes.

After they had all left, she began to stack the presentation boards. She should have known that the staff wouldn't provide any useful comments, at least not with Amelia present.

Saluki stuck her head through the doorway. "Hey, Ms. Russo. Need some help?"

She turned, glad for the distraction. "Sure, Saluki. Can you bring these to my office, please? I'll get the rest."

Saluki kept her head averted. As she picked up the boards, the sleeve of her shirt pulled up, revealing a large, dark mark on her light brown skin.

Alarmed, Victoria touched her arm. "Is that a bruise?"

Saluki turned away, jostling the boards in her arms. "It's nothing. I—I ran into a door. At home." She hustled out of the room.

Not the action of someone with nothing to hide. Victoria quickly collected the remaining boards and strode down the hall to her office where she found Saluki setting her stack of boards on the floor in the corner. "Okay to put these here, Ms. Russo?"

"Yes, that's fine. Thanks." She crossed to her. "Here, take these, too, please."

Saluki had to face her to take the stack from her arms. As she had suspected, another bruise colored her left cheek. While the girl placed the boards neatly on the pile, Victoria closed the office door, as well as the one leading to Jennetta's office. Then she took Saluki's hand and led her to one of the two guest chairs.

"Sit." She took the other chair. "Tell me what happened. You didn't run into a door, did you?"

Saluki appeared ready to cry. She shook her head.

"Who did this to you? Your mother?"

"No!" Saluki burst out of her chair. "Don't go jumping to conclusions. Mama's not like that."

"Okay, okay. Sit down." She motioned with her hands. "Then tell me who is to blame."

Saluki sat down and fidgeted with the beaded bracelet she

always wore. "Really, it doesn't even hurt. It's nothing to worry about. Anyway, it was an accident."

"If someone hit you, there's no excuse. Won't you tell me what happened?"

"Dustin and I were foolin' around. That's all. He got a little mad, and I fell. He didn't mean to hurt me."

"Dustin, your boyfriend?"

Saluki nodded.

"He's got no right to hurt you, Saluki. It doesn't matter how it happened." Her own face ached with memories. Getting away from Antonio had taken every ounce of strength she had. She couldn't let Saluki endure that sort of treatment. "You need to stop seeing him."

Saluki jerked her head up and glared at her. "Break up with him? No way."

"You must. He's hurt you once—" She flinched. "Is this the first time?"

Saluki shook her head, just barely noticeable.

Victoria rose and paced across the room. "He'll do it again, Saluki. And it will only get worse."

"No. He told me today how sorry he was, that he shouldn't have been pushing so hard. He loves me, and we're going to go to college together. He's gonna be somebody. We'll go places together."

Victoria returned to her chair and sat, leaning her elbows on her knees so she could get closer to the girl. "I thought you wanted a career, to make something of yourself."

"I do. And I will. But Dustin and I—we're good together."

"Not if he treats you like this. You deserve better."

"You don't understand." She stood and strode to the door then turned back. "If you're such a great judge of guys, how come you're spending time with Randy Lee Johnson? Everybody knows he's just cozying up to you so he can get what he wants."

She jerked open the door and stomped through it.

Victoria stared at the open doorway. What did a sixteen-year-old know about relationships, anyway? She and Randy Lee were just friends.

Chapter Thirteen

Victoria had expected the carpenter to be a middle-aged redneck, but the tall, muscular man wearing jeans and a denim shirt appeared to be about her age. The brim of his faded orange Clemson Tigers ball cap pointed straight to the sky as he squinted at the overhang of the porch roof.

When she arrived at the house a few minutes after noon on Wednesday, Donna Grace turned and waved her over. "Hey. We just got started."

She picked her way through the dry, brown grass that had yet to show any signs of spring.

"This is the carpenter I told you about. Matt Buchanan, this is my friend, Victoria Russo."

He turned from studying the house and instead studied her as he shook her hand. "You've got rot."

She blinked. "What?"

He withdrew his hand and removed his cap, revealing curly brown hair. His full lips turned up into a smile that wrinkled his tanned face. "I'm sorry. I get caught up in my work sometimes. It's nice to meet you." He pointed to the overhang he had been studying. "What I meant was, you've got some serious rot. Up there."

"Oh. Well, that's to be expected. That roof hasn't been replaced in probably thirty years. I expect to have to replace some, if not all, of the sheathing. The soffit and fascia, too."

His hazel eyes flickered with surprise. Clearly, he hadn't expected her to know houses. "I was afraid you were planning to buy her without knowing what you were getting into."

He referred to the house as "her." She smiled in spite of her irritation with him. "No, Mr. Buchanan. I am not a real estate virgin."

His eyes widened. "That's good. You sure have a lot of work with this one."

"I'm aware of that. Is it too big a job for you?"

He studied his clipboard and shook his head. "Not for me. I've fixed up worse." He started up the steps to the front door, turned, and looked at her. "You want to tell me what you have in mind, or should I guess?"

She glanced at Donna Grace, who appeared to be fighting the urge to laugh. "Really? Is he always this rude?"

Donna Grace patted her arm. "It'll be fine. He's the best, and you'll get used to his ways."

"I doubt it." She stomped up the wooden steps, wishing she had changed from her heels to clogs so she could emphasize her irritation with more noise.

Matt squatted in the middle of the doorway studying the threshold.

She couldn't get around him, so she would have to let him lead the way. "Let's talk about the kitchen. It's through the door at the end of the hall."

He didn't budge. What was he looking at? She bent over to peer at the same spot, when he suddenly lurched out of his squat, bumping her head with his back as he rose.

"Owww!" She jumped back, rubbing her nose.

He turned. "I'm sorry, Ms. Russo. I didn't realize you were standing over me. Are you all right?"

Donna Grace hovered at her side. "Should I look for some ice?"

"No. Please, I'll be fine. Let's just get on with this." This time, Matt waited for her to enter first, followed by Donna Grace. She led the way down the hall and through the swinging door into the kitchen. "I'd like to get this done first, because it'll probably take the longest."

"You mean after the roof, of course." He jotted something

on the list on his clipboard then raised his head to peer at her. His dark eyebrows formed an upside-down vee.

"Of course. My grandpa used to say, 'No shoes, no horse.' The same applies here. No roof, no house. But maybe we could start on the roof and the kitchen at the same time."

He rubbed the scrubby whiskers on his chin. "I've only got one crew. When we have a rainy day, they could start the demolition in here, I guess. And we could order the cabinets right away." He strode to the row of cupboards on the outside wall and ran his hand over one of the doors. "Unless of course you plan to keep these old cabinets?"

He had to be joking. Didn't he? They did have character, but they were ancient. "You think we should try to refurbish them?"

"That's up to you. It'll take some work, but it could still save you money in the long run. And they add to the historical authenticity of the house."

She studied the dirty white cabinets, the chipped and peeling paint revealing pine wood underneath. She knew what Antonio would do—save money by painting them all white and call it good. She squeezed her eyes nearly closed, trying to visualize the kitchen with the cabinets stripped and finished in a natural color. "Donna Grace, what do you think?"

Donna Grace rested her hand on the peeling linoleum countertop. "I would definitely replace the countertops with granite or solid surface. As for the cabinets …" She opened the door of an upper cabinet. "I'm not sure. Matt, what would you do if it was your house?"

Victoria cringed. Why ask him? He probably stood to make more money by refinishing these old things than by putting in brand new ready-made boxes. Besides, what made him an expert on kitchens?

Matt put down his clipboard. Grasping the front of the sink with both hands, he pulled hard on the cabinet, as if trying to loosen it from the wall. Nothing budged. He opened the lower doors and peered underneath the sink, then looked inside several other cabinets. Finally he straightened.

"These are sturdy but the bottom of the lower boxes is warped in a couple places. If it were me, I would keep this sink cabinet and these two upper ones. I'd put a new false bottom in the base cabinets, and install adjustable or roll-out shelves, so inside it would seem like new."

He pointed to the section at the left of the sink. "The bottom of this one is the worst, so maybe cut it out and put the dishwasher here." He strode to the opposite wall, which was empty. "On this wall, you could put your refrigerator and new cabinets built to match the old ones. That would give you additional counter space and a more efficient work triangle."

So he did know something about kitchens. Victoria crossed her arms and tried to imagine what he described. She liked the thought of giving these cabinets new life.

"I think you could sand these old ones down and either paint or stain them, depending on which you prefer. They can be finished to match the new ones. You could even have new doors made." Matt seemed lost in thought for a moment. He nodded and looked at her, then shrugged. "But those are just my thoughts. We can do whatever you want."

She tilted her head to one side. "I have to admit, that sounds like a good plan. But won't it be awfully expensive to refinish these?"

He shook his head. "No more than good quality new ones would cost. And if money is an issue, you could do some of the work yourself. Stripping paint, sanding, even some of the staining. But it takes elbow grease and …" He scanned her tailored suit. "It's messy work."

He thought she was afraid to get dirty. "Then I'll have to make sure I wear something washable."

He grinned and seemed about to say something, but her

cell phone rang. She glanced at the display. Local area code but she didn't recognize the number. Had to be work-related.

"Excuse me. I need to take this." She turned and pushed through the door to the hallway as she answered.

"Hello, pretty lady." Her heart jumped at Randy Lee's voice, and she silently warned it to settle down. She had no intention of starting a serious relationship so soon. She had come to Charleston to build a new life, different from her past. "I'm hoping I can talk you into having dinner with me Friday."

The invitation was appealing. Her tiny apartment offered no comfort during the long, lonely evenings, and Friday nights were the worst. That had been "date night" when she and Michael were still married. Besides, she'd been working hard, and she deserved a little fun. It was just dinner, nothing more.

"Sure. Dinner would be great."

After they worked out the details, Victoria returned to the kitchen but found it empty. She heard voices in the adjoining utility room and headed toward the open doorway.

Before she reached it, Donna Grace came out, followed by Matt, writing on his clipboard as he walked. He glanced at her then continued writing. "Not too much to do in there. You ought to have an electrician look at that panel, though."

Again, he thought her ignorant about houses. She straightened her spine and tilted her chin up. "Of course I will."

He stopped writing but didn't look at her. Instead, he scanned the ceiling and walls then headed for the hall door. "Let's see the rest of the house."

By the time Matt finished his examination, Victoria expected the cost estimate to be as much as a heart transplant. He had taken extensive notes, measured rooms, and probed window sashes with his multi-tool knife. She watched him, mentally biting her fingernails and wondering what she was getting into.

As they stepped out onto the front porch, he stopped and

grinned. "It's a great house, Ms. Russo. She needs lots of work, but you'll have a real jewel when she's all done." He tapped his pencil on the clipboard. "I'll work up these costs and get the estimate to Donna Grace." With the pencil still in his hand, he touched the brim of his ball cap in a quick salute then took the steps two at a time and strode to his pickup.

Victoria turned to Donna Grace. "Seems like he knows his stuff. But ..."

Donna Grace touched her arm. "Trust me, Victoria. You'll get used to his ways, and you couldn't find a better man for this house. He loves doing renovations."

Chapter Fourteen

Maybe Friday evening could salvage what had been an exhausting week.

The thought of dinner and a cruise with a handsome man certainly cheered up Victoria. She allowed Randy Lee to lead her up the ramp of the excursion boat docked in the marina at Patriot's Point. He steadied her as she stepped onto the shifting deck, and she smiled her thanks.

They paused at the railing to look out at Charleston Harbor. Lights from the aquarium on the opposite bank winked at them as if conspiring to brighten the approaching dusk. From the east side of the Cooper River, the problems she'd had in the city seemed to blow away on the salty breeze. Even the fishy smell didn't bother her.

"Charleston's a good place to call home." Randy Lee put his arm around her waist and pulled her close. "You are going to make it your home, aren't you, sugar?"

His touch, which she couldn't force herself to resist, raised both desire and alarm. "Home" sounded good, especially the way he murmured it in her ear. But what chains did Randy Lee attach to the word?

She had begun to doubt that this southern city could ever feel like home. Not if it was filled with church-goers like Amelia who looked for ways to make her fail. "After this week, and a day like today, I'm not so sure."

"Well, now." He turned to her, but the ship's horn sounded and the boat began to move. He bent and kissed her forehead, his lips tender and warm. "Guess we'd better get to our table. They'll be ready to take our orders."

The dining room featured wall-to-wall glass on three

sides, providing spectacular views as they cruised the harbor. The waiter maneuvered between diners to show them to a table for two in the front center of the room. "Here you are, Mr. Johnson. Please let me know if you need anything."

Victoria took the chair Randy Lee held out for her, feeling as though they were suspended over the water. "Any chance we might see dolphins?"

"I ordered them just for you, darlin'. They'd better show up."

She picked up the menu and studied it. She-crab soup, salad, and a choice of five entrees. No prices. That meant expensive. She tilted her head and studied Randy Lee. As the owner of a carriage company, he clearly had money, but she shouldn't allow him to spend so much on her. Not when she had no intentions of getting serious. Her mother would not approve. "I didn't realize what you had in mind when you invited me to dinner. This must be quite costly."

"Not to worry, sugar. The owner and I exchange favors from time to time. I comp tours for his special guests, and he does the same for me." He leaned back in his chair and smiled. "I haven't had anyone to enjoy them with, so I usually give them away. Until now."

So he hadn't splurged. Typical man, trying to impress her. She should just enjoy the evening without overthinking it.

The waiter appeared with their wine and took their orders. Then Randy Lee put both hands on the table, palms up, waiting until she placed her smaller hands in his. "That's my girl." He gave her a lazy wink. "Now tell me about your day."

"As Alexander would say, it was a terrible, horrible, no good, very bad day."

He raised one eyebrow. "Alexander? Your ex?"

She laughed. "Good heavens, no. It's from a children's book that was made into a movie. Didn't you tell me you have some nephews?"

"Yeah, I do. Two. But they're more into sports than books."

"Too bad. They really should do both. Maybe you could read them some sports books."

"Right." The tone of his voice made his sarcasm clear. "So tell me about this horrible, very bad, terrible day."

"It's 'terrible, horrible—'" She pulled a hand free and waved it in the air. "Never mind. I presented the new campaign to the Old Town Business Owners. Let's just say it didn't go as well as I had hoped."

"They didn't like it?"

When the waiter brought their food, Randy Lee took the opportunity to finish his glass of wine and pour more. He motioned with the bottle to Victoria's glass even though she hadn't touched it, but she waved him off. As soon as the waiter left, she said, "I'm famished. I couldn't eat all day."

They ate in silence for a few minutes, glancing out the windows as they chewed. Fort Sumter, the humpback remnant of the Civil War's first battle, rose ahead of them. Visiting the site on her initial trip to Charleston, Victoria had found it depressing. Crumbling walls and dank compartments told visitors of the siege that led to devastation across the South and division with the North. Based on her experience so far, even after a hundred and fifty years the country had not fully healed.

As they rounded the island, the view revealed nothing but turquoise ocean stretching to the darkening horizon. Randy Lee leaned back in his chair. "Would you just look at that? It always makes me wonder who's on the other side looking our way."

She put her fork down and dabbed her mouth with her napkin. "I hadn't thought of it like that."

He turned back to face her. "Now, you were sayin' about your meeting?"

"I think a few people approved of the campaign. But some

of the others—the ones who don't like that I'm from New England—they asked some hard questions, and I felt like they were attacking me, not my ideas."

"I'm sure you handled it with flair."

She pushed a lock of loose hair behind her ear then picked up her wine glass but didn't take a drink. "No, I didn't. I said I'd have to get back to them with the information. And then—" She set the glass down hard, splashing the red liquid onto the white tablecloth. "Amelia came with me to help carry the boards and materials, and *she* answered the question."

"So, you think she made you look bad."

"Yes, but that's not all." She slammed her fist on the table, sloshing the wine out of her glass again. "She sounded like she knew what she was talking about. But her answer was wrong."

"Why didn't you say something, darlin'?" He reached over and moved her wine glass further from her fist.

"Because I should have had that information, but I didn't. And I wasn't sure that she was wrong. Not until I got back to the office and looked it up. The numbers she gave were way off. And now I'll have to send out the corrected information."

"Which means—?"

"That I'll look doubly bad. First, because I didn't know today, and second, because I have to correct Amelia. It'll look like we don't have our act together."

He grabbed her hand, stopping her before she could hit the table again. "I'm sure she didn't mean to make you look bad. When you send out the right information, they'll understand."

"No, they won't. They all like her. She's a local." She emphasized the word as if it were a curse word.

"I suppose it doesn't hurt any that Smith Alexander is her uncle. But I wouldn't let her bother you." Randy Lee tossed his napkin on the table. "Let's go out on the deck to look for those dolphins."

"What did you say?" Victoria hoped she had heard wrong.

All she needed was to have a board member's relative as her assistant director.

He pushed his chair back and stood. "I said let's go look for—"

"No." Victoria stood and looked up at him, acid burning her throat. "What did you say about Amelia and Smith Alexander?"

Randy Lee shrugged. "Oh, about him being her uncle?" His lazy eyelid fluttered open wide. "You mean you didn't know that?"

Now she understood Amelia's attitude. And realized she would be powerless to take any action against her. She shook her head slowly, her shoulders sagging in defeat. "No, I didn't know. But it explains a lot."

He caressed her chin with his large hand. "Don't worry, sugar. No harm done, right? Come with me. You need to get your mind off the whole thing."

She gave him a thin smile. Right now, she wanted to forget it all. "Sure, let's go."

The boat had completed its circuit of Fort Sumter while they ate, and now they headed back up the river. They went to the rear—he called it the aft—and leaned on the metal railing. Spotlights shone across the waves created by the boat's wake.

Randy Lee pointed. "There. They're following us, just like I figured."

Sure enough, she saw a dolphin jump. Then another. And another. They moved so quickly, dark spots breaking the water's surface, arcing into the air beyond the beam of light, and disappearing back into the churning water. She tried to count them, but she couldn't be sure if she was seeing the same one or different ones. She could tell there were at least four, though, because one would appear just as another dove under the surface.

She shook her head, enjoying the wind in her hair and

ignoring the chill of the evening. She tasted the salty spray from the waves, and for the first time all week, she giggled.

"I don't know how to thank you for getting these other estimates." Victoria sat in Donna Grace's office the following week, papers laid out across the desk. "And for introducing me to Matt. His quote is more reasonable than I expected. He acts a little odd, but he seems quite capable."

"He's first-rate, honey." Donna Grace looked up from her computer screen. "I thought you'd like him. Now, what's your offer?"

She gave her the figure, several thousand below the list price. Donna Grace nodded and tapped the keyboard. Then she called the listing agent for the house on Smith Street. While the other agent contacted the Florida owners with news of Victoria's offer, Donna Grace asked Victoria about her work.

"It's been a struggle," she confessed. Perhaps she could confide in Donna Grace. "Sometimes I feel like I'm walking on broken glass, and no one's willing to sweep it up."

"Maybe you need to clean it up yourself."

She jerked back, thinking Donna Grace had picked up a shard of the broken glass and raked her face with it. But before she could ask the agent to explain, the telephone rang.

Looking at the caller ID, Donna Grace nodded. "It's him." Less than ten minutes, and the listing agent was calling back.

Victoria listened to this side of the conversation. She jiggled her foot, ran her hands over her green skirt, brushed her hair out of her face, then examined her polished fingernails. The finish had held up well, but her cuticles were beginning to show. She'd have to go back to the nail salon in a few days. Of course, if she bought the house, she'd have no time to worry about manicures.

Finally, Donna Grace smiled and hung up the phone. She leaned back in her chair. "The sellers agreed without even negotiating. The house belonged to an unmarried aunt, and they seem to consider it an albatross. I think they are relieved to rid themselves of it."

Victoria relaxed her tense body. She hadn't expected her first offer to be accepted. Then second thoughts pummeled her. Maybe she had offered too much. She should have started with a lower number. What if the house turned out to be a money pit, like the one in the old Tom Hanks movie?

"Relax, honey." Donna Grace studied her, apparently sensing her nervousness. "It's a good deal. I'm surprised someone else didn't beat you to it. Now, let's get the contract finished up." She turned back to the computer and typed something.

A few minutes later, Donna Grace pulled several sheets of paper from the printer and placed them on the desk. "Just initial here and sign down here, honey, and we'll be done." She showed Victoria where to put her signature on the purchase agreement.

Victoria took the document and read through it. She had signed many such offers with Antonio, but she'd never bothered to read them. He'd been the expert. Now she alone would be responsible.

She had thirty days to arrange financing for the repairs or the sellers could call off the deal. Would that be enough time? She had enough for the purchase price, but without a loan, she couldn't replace the roof, much less bring the house back to its original splendor.

Finally, she looked at Donna Grace and shrugged. She had to trust her agent, despite the unfinished conversation. Picking up the ballpoint pen on the desk, she read the inscription that promoted the real estate business. *Helping You Find Home.*

She took a deep breath, clicked the pen, and signed. When

she finished, Donna Grace gathered the pages. "I'll just fax these for their signatures. As soon as they send the signed documents back, I'll get a copy to you. In a few weeks, you'll be a homeowner." She smiled and excused herself to go to the fax machine.

When the machine beeped the "send complete" signal, she walked back to her desk where Victoria waited. She handed her a copy of the contract. "Since there are three sellers, we probably won't get the signed agreement until tomorrow. I'll call you as soon as I receive it."

Victoria put the papers in the blue folder she had brought then added the estimates that Donna Grace had obtained for her. "So maybe this will make me a Charlestonian."

Donna Grace rose and came around the desk. Standing next to the chair, she patted Victoria's shoulder. "Sugar, buying a house only makes you a resident. When you make it your home, you'll become a Charlestonian."

Chapter Fifteen

Jennetta barged into Victoria's office and dropped a printed brochure on her desk. "These just came in. Amelia said I should give you one."

"What is it?" She picked up the brochure. She recognized the cover as one for the Spoleto Festival in May. She had seen the layout two weeks ago but didn't realize it had gone to press. Had her suggested changes been made?

She opened to the inside spread and scanned the copy then studied the photos. None of the changes she had asked for had been made. Her pulse pounded in her ears. She glanced up at Jennetta who seemed to be waiting for something.

"Was there something else, Jennetta?"

"No, ma'am. I think Amelia wants to know what you think of the brochure. That's all."

"Does she?" Somehow, Victoria didn't think Amelia cared what she thought. But she would tell her anyway. "Then would you ask her to come in when she has a minute?"

"Sure thing." She appeared to hide a smirk as she turned and waddled back to her office, leaving a trail of heavy perfume behind her.

Whose side was she on—Amelia's or Victoria's? Or was she one of those people who just enjoyed irritating everybody? Like Victoria's ex-mother-in-law, whose goal in life seemed to be getting other people to argue.

Not that Victoria wanted to have "sides." She had come to Charleston to build up tourism, and she expected her entire staff to be on the same "side"—with her. But she didn't see that happening yet, especially with Amelia. Maybe Amelia had "connections," but Victoria was the director. She had to be clear about her expectations.

An hour passed before Amelia strolled into her office. "You wanted to see me?"

Victoria turned from her computer where she had been reviewing the budget. "Yes, I did. Come on in." Amelia was already "in," but Victoria had a need to invite her into the office, if only to let the woman know that inviting her in remained Victoria's choice.

Amelia plopped onto the guest chair and stared at her, challenge in her features and her body language.

Victoria picked up the Spoleto Festival brochure, fighting the urge to reprimand her for ignoring her changes. "So these came in today."

"Yep. They look pretty good, I think."

She tapped the brochure on her desk, laid it down and opened it. "Yes, it's 'pretty good.' But it could have been better."

Amelia frowned and leaned forward in her chair. "What's wrong with it?"

"I had made some comments, but you didn't make my changes. I'm wondering why."

"I talked to the designer, and we didn't feel that your suggestions made sense for this piece." She leaned back in her chair, arrogance written all over her face. "You don't really know the audience here."

Victoria studied her assistant director, wondering how long Amelia thought she could get away with this behavior. "Don't you think you owed me the respect of talking to me about it? If I was off base, I would appreciate your explaining that to me."

"Well, see, we were already late, and you left early the day we had to send it to the printer. So I made the call." Accusation rippled through her words as if Victoria didn't work fifty or sixty hours a week.

"Perhaps we could have at least talked the next day so I wouldn't be caught by surprise when they showed up without the changes being made."

Amelia shifted in her chair. "I guess I could have done that. Didn't think of it at the time."

Victoria gave her a thin-lipped smile. "Next time you will think of it, I'm sure. Preferably before sending a project to the printer."

Amelia didn't respond, but stared at something on Victoria's desk.

"Do you have a problem with me, Amelia?"

"What do you mean?"

Victoria sighed and tapped her fingers on the desk. "You've not made my first few weeks here exactly easy. I believe you resent me, that you feel I came in and took the job that should have been yours."

"Hmph." Amelia stood.

"Bottom line is that the board selected me. And we are here to promote Charleston. We need to work together to do the best that we can. I need and expect your cooperation."

"I'll do my job, just like I always have. And now, if you'll excuse me, I need to get back downstairs. The reps are really busy today."

Victoria waved her hand since the conversation clearly was over as far as Amelia was concerned. Once Amelia left, she put her face in her hands and closed her eyes. She hadn't gotten anywhere with that woman.

The phone rang. She picked up the receiver and cleared her throat. "Victoria Russo."

"Hey, honey." Donna Grace's cheery voice sounded less so than usual. "I'm over at the house with the termite inspector. Do you have time to run over here for a little bit?"

Victoria had a death grip on the steering wheel when, fifteen minutes later, she pulled up behind a Volkswagen parked in front of the house. Black plastic tentacles simulating a spider encased the white car, and the words *Bug Patrol* were painted across its rounded back. She shivered as she considered the impression that passersby might get.

Donna Grace waited in the driveway next to a balding man wearing blue coveralls. As Victoria got out of her car, a light breeze attacked her nose with the sour odor of fallen Bradford pear blossoms. That tree in the front yard had to go.

Donna Grace introduced the man, who said, "Miss, can I show you something?"

She nodded, her stomach doing flip-flops. This short, fireplug of a man was not going to show her a rare plant he had discovered in her backyard. They climbed the front steps and he pointed to a small hole under a window. "I'm afraid you've got termites, miss."

Her skin crawled as if the bugs had chosen her body to gnaw holes in. Termites left untreated had killed many southern houses, she had heard, eating them from the inside. She didn't know how to prepare for that possibility when she couldn't even stop the pests eating at her own insides.

"See, here." The man poked at the hole with his gloved finger. "They're inside this wall and have eaten away this stud. Can't tell how much damage without tearing off the siding. But it's probably all the way to the sill plate. And maybe the window itself."

She felt faint. The house might as well be falling down on her.

The man caught her arm before she sank to the porch floor. "You all right, miss?"

His hand held her up and she breathed again. She blinked and said, "I don't know what to do. This is really bad, isn't it?"

He gave her a fatherly smile. "It's not good, but it can be fixed."

Donna Grace joined them on the porch. "It'll be okay,

honey. Since state law requires a termite letter for a sale, I think the sellers will pay for the treatment. Unfortunately, they were adamant about the house being sold 'as-is,' so I'm afraid you'll have to pay for the repairs."

The man held out a clipboard with a form on it. "We have a carpenter who can do the repairs, if you want. Can't give you the total until he opens it up, but here's the minimum for fixing what I can see."

Handwritten numbers filled the spaces. She looked at the figure. Money she didn't have, and had not included in her loan application.

She shook her head. "Just the treatment for now. I—I'll have to figure out something else for the repairs." Her voice sounded to her like she was speaking through water, but her mouth tasted like dried cement.

Donna Grace patted her shoulder. "Matt's a good carpenter, Victoria. He'll be able to fix this damage. You go on back to work now. We'll finish up here."

As Donna Grace and the exterminator walked around to the back of the house, Victoria got into her car. She slumped down in the seat and blinked back tears. She had been stupid to think she could buy and renovate this house. She didn't know enough about houses to take on such an overwhelming project. And if things didn't improve at work soon, she'd be forced to return home to Connecticut after all.

Loneliness won out time after time, and Victoria continued to accept Randy Lee's invitations.

After dinner one evening, they strolled up North Market Street and down South Market, stopping in some of the stores primarily aimed at tourists. At one gift shop, he bought her an oyster and a chain with a tiny cage for the pearl inside. The saleswoman opened the shell to reveal a pink pearl. Randy Lee fastened the necklace around her neck. "A rare beauty for a rare beauty."

The open-air market was shuttered for the night, the vendors packed up and gone home. But activity swirled around the restaurants and bars as patrons ebbed and flowed from one to another. Randy Lee's arm glided around Victoria's waist, and something inside her cried out to join the party.

"Come on, sugar," he murmured in her ear. "Let's get a drink."

The remnants of the day plagued her from her aching feet to the tips of her thick, black hair. She put her hand on his arm. "I'd love to, but it's been a tough day. I feel a headache coming on, so I think I'd better get home."

"Want me to take you home? I could make you feel better." His smooth voice blended with the jazz music oozing from a nearby bar, soothing the tension in her body. He pulled her close and she tried for a moment to ignore the caution lights in her brain. He stroked her back, suggesting more than a massage then guided her down the sidewalk.

Tempting. Her threadbare apartment offered no solace from the isolation she felt day after day. But she had promised herself not to get involved again. Not even with this man who comforted her and made her feel beautiful and wanted.

She stopped and tilted her head into the cushion between his arm and chest. "I appreciate it, Randy Lee, but I think I'd better just go home by myself. Besides, I wouldn't be good company."

His arm tensed. "Seems like you're always saying that, pretty lady. One of these days ..."

The statement dangled in the air between them until a cottony puff of air floated up the street from the river and whisked it away.

"You go ahead and have fun, Randy Lee." She stood on

tiptoes and pressed her lips to his cheek. "I'll see you tomorrow."

He squeezed her close. "Sweet dreams, sugar." Then he released her and headed for the nearest bar, and the chill of the evening settled around her.

When Victoria reached her apartment after the drive back to North Charleston, the emptiness threatened to suffocate her. It would have been so nice to have Randy Lee here to cuddle with, to fill the vacuum.

She decided to call her mother. They had not talked all week. It seemed even longer. She grabbed the portable phone and pressed the memory button. But after a pause, the call went right to voicemail. Mom must have turned off her phone and gone to bed.

"Hi, Mom. Just thought I'd let you know I'm all right. Busy at work and getting ready to buy that house I told you about. It's a big project." Mom would worry at that. "But it'll be great when it's finished. Maybe you can come down for a visit over Christmas. I should be all done by then and the weather'll be a lot nicer than in New England."

What else should she say? She could mention Randy Lee. No, Mom would only think she had gotten involved too soon. Again. She hadn't, had she? After all, he was not here tonight.

"I guess that's all. Hope you're okay. Call me back when you can. Love you."

She clicked her phone off and headed to the bedroom. Alone.

Chapter Sixteen

Making plans to restore the house on Smith Street would provide a wonderful weekend distraction from the difficulties at work.

Victoria added a wallpaper sample to her notebook and studied the page she'd created for the parlor. The floral border would unite the blues and grays she had chosen for the paint and fabrics, creating a muted, relaxing atmosphere. Just the right tone for entertaining. If she ever had the chance.

Paint chips, fabric swatches, and wallpaper samples were strewn across the tiny kitchen table in her apartment. She sipped her breakfast of coffee, enjoying the strong aroma. Grateful that she had not allowed Randy Lee to come home with her, the free day stretched ahead of her.

The night's rest combined with the morning sunshine had brightened her mood. She had opened the windows to let in the warm spring breezes and freshen the air. Upbeat music from the radio station helped to mask the noise from the parking lot and the jet planes flying over as they took off or landed at the nearby airport.

She enjoyed the list-making almost as much as the creative decisions about colors and patterns. She reviewed the bid from the plumber and the three-page quote from Matt. Since he would be doing so much work on the house, he had added repairing the termite damage for just a thousand dollars more.

The electrician Donna Grace preferred was out of town for two more weeks, so she had estimated the cost of adding a few outlets and switches. Her experience helping Antonio gave her an idea of what electrical work should cost.

The total for the renovations was within her budget, though just barely, and the contractors had been gracious. Buying and fixing up the house should help to make her part of the Charleston community.

She glanced at the schedule she'd created, reviewing the order of what needed to be done first. According to the bank's appraisal, the repairs she planned would more than double the value of the house. If approval on her loan application came through in time, the real estate closing next week would be the final step.

No, that would be the first step, really. She would sign the loan documents, turn over her own funds, and the deed would be transferred to her name. Then the work would start in earnest.

She hoped she had convinced the lender that she could oversee the work herself, saving the usual twenty-five percent for a general contractor. But she also planned to do most of the cosmetic work herself, to keep her costs down.

She bit the end of her pen as she studied the growing list. Patching plaster, cleaning woodwork, refinishing the kitchen cabinets and wood floors, painting, and wallpapering. Was she trying to chew more than she could swallow?

The coffee churned in her otherwise empty stomach. She had owned property before—but only with Antonio. Her second husband had been the one to handle the paperwork, the financing, the permits, and the contractors. Had she forgotten anything? Overlooked an expensive item? Would there be budget-busting surprises?

Antonio had always said to plan for the unexpected, and she had tried. She had included a contingency in her budget of double the bank's required ten percent.

Her cell phone jangled and she dug it out of her purse.

"Ms. Russo?" The drawling voice sounded familiar.

"This is."

"Robert Young. Bank of Charleston."

Her heart tripped over itself. She hadn't expected a call from the bank president, especially on a Saturday. A professional courtesy, perhaps, since he served on the Chamber of Commerce executive board. He would tell her she had been turned down for the loan. She only hoped he wouldn't gloat.

"I'm calling." He cleared his throat. "I wanted to inform you personally that your loan application for rehabilitating the property at 135 Smith Street has been approved."

Approved. It took a moment for the word to sink in. The lists and swatches on her table swirled in front of her eyes. She leaned her head back and tried to visualize the renovated house.

But dollar signs and images of unfinished projects crowded her vision. The bank's financing allowed only six months to complete the work.

Would this purchase be her opportunity or her downfall?

Saluki's world had just been rocked by her favorite teacher.

"What do you say, Saluki? This is quite an opportunity." Mr. D. stroked his gray beard as he waited for her answer. A locker slammed out in the hall. Voices drifted away as most of the students rushed from the building.

She couldn't believe the reason Mr. D. had asked her to stay after school. "I could go to Charleston Academy next year, and I wouldn't have to pay a cent?"

He nodded, his serious eyes squinting at her. "That's right. You could win a scholarship based on your grades and your internship at the Tourism Bureau. You just have to complete the application and meet with the interview committee. You'd be able to finish your senior year of high school and get college credit for most of your classes at the same time."

She slouched in a wooden desk in his classroom, studying the carvings in the desktop. Initials of kids she knew and scratched memories of students long graduated. She had history here at East Cooper High. Charleston Academy had been open only two years.

"What about the other kids? They're all S-O-Bs and S-N-O-Bs, aren't they?" People who lived south of Broad Street or slightly north of Broad had a reputation for being cliquish. She'd be treated like sour milk.

Mr. D. rearranged his soda-can pyramid, adding some new cans to it. "Not all rich people are stuck up, Saluki. Yes, it's an exclusive school, but knowing you, you'll get along just fine."

She shook her head. He didn't know where she came from. "I don't dress like them. I don't talk like them. I don't even have two parents."

He leaned his elbows on his desk. "A lot of those kids come from split families, too. Or blended families. They're not that much different."

"How many black kids go there?"

"I don't know the answer to that. Does it matter?"

She shrugged. "It does if I'm the only one."

"I don't think you'll be alone. Some black families can afford to send their children to the Academy. But you will be outnumbered." He hesitated. "Sort of like Dustin is here. Or like I am. Does that stop me from teaching here?"

Oh. Sometimes she forgot. She should ask Dustin how it felt to be in the minority at school.

But she would never make friends at that school—not friends like Majesty, TeeJay—and Dustin. Besides, what would Dustin say if she changed schools?

Maybe Mr. D. just wanted to get rid of her. Sometimes she annoyed him with her questions in class. No, he never tried to shut her down, and he never ignored her. In fact, he challenged her to think for herself. He had even helped her get the internship at the Tourism Bureau.

"So you think I could do it?"

He nodded. "I know you can, Saluki. If you want to succeed badly enough, you will."

She fingered the papers he handed her. Three pages. That seemed too simple for a chance to go to the Academy. Guess it was worth giving it a shot. She folded the papers and stuck them in her backpack.

"Okay. I'll fill out the application."

Chapter Seventeen

Victoria thought she would suffocate in the crowded room. The historic office building apparently had no spacious rooms to accommodate all the lawyers and agents needed for a modern real estate closing.

The first of April. A new month, a new home. Sunlight streamed through the tall wood-framed windows, throwing a slanted checkerboard pattern across the scuffed oak conference table. A musty odor mingled with the heavy cologne of one of the three sellers and made Victoria's eyes sting.

Next to her, Donna Grace chatted and joked with the sellers' agent. She provided a comforting presence among all the strangers, but Victoria couldn't appreciate the jokes.

The attorney recommended by Donna Grace explained each document before she passed it across to Victoria. Papers were then shuffled around the table as if this was an endless card game. After Victoria signed, each of the sellers had to sign every document. Victoria's fingers cramped after what she thought was the twenty-ninth time she signed her name.

By the time she got to the disclosure statement for the rehab loan, Victoria's stomach churned. She tried to bring the numbers into focus, but they insisted on jumping and swirling and fading in and out.

She knew the dollar amount. She had added and re-added all the estimates until she saw the figures in her dreams. Her salary could handle the monthly payments with enough left over for other necessities, like food.

The familiarity of the room should have been a comfort. She and Antonio had sat in rooms like this half a dozen times as they bought and flipped fixer-up houses in Waterbury and

Naugatuck. But the projects had been Antonio's. She had only been unpaid labor. Oh, she had chosen paint colors and light fixtures, sought out bargains on doorknobs and cabinets, helped with cleaning and sanding. But the major decisions, the responsibility, had been his.

Now, her name sat alone on the line above the words "Buyer" and "Mortgagor." This time, if she failed, she failed alone. The bank would own the house, and she would lose everything—her share of profits from Antonio's projects, along with the money from her most recent divorce.

"Did you have a question, Ms. Russo?" The attorney on the other side of the table stared at her.

The late afternoon sun hit the back of her head, leaving an oval shadow on the surface of the table and creating a glow around her. Victoria squinted to see the woman's face, trying to remember why all these people were here.

Donna Grace patted her arm and whispered, "It's all right, dear. Take your time."

Victoria glanced around the room. The sellers fidgeted in impatience, and their attorney looked bored. The bank representative drummed his fingers on the tabletop.

She lifted the legal-size page and studied it—the last document requiring her signature. She had no choice; she wanted to make her home in Charleston, and this house would become a showcase. The smooth paper soothed her burning fingertips.

Sucking air between her teeth, she grasped the thick pen marked with the bank's name. And once more, she signed her legal name.

Victoria Jane Poveromo Russo.

Chapter Eighteen

Saluki relished the chance to return to Aunt Ida's place on James Island.

Her family used to spend Sunday afternoons there once a month until Mama had to start working two jobs. Saluki missed seeing the sweet old woman and wanted her help with the sweetgrass basket she'd salvaged from the old house.

Victoria brought the basket to the office the day after signing the papers for the house, so Saluki had gone to visit her aunt for the first time since Christmas.

The April breeze rustled the trees, making their shadows dance in the warm sunlight. The songs of crickets contrasted with the rhythmic sound of Aunt Ida's worn rocking on the rough wooden porch. Across the yard, grackles perched on the rusty clothesline seemed to be scolding them for working on a Sunday.

Next to Aunt Ida sat a washtub full of soaking reeds and pine needles. She handed pieces to Saluki as she needed them. Her aunt's arthritis kept her from making baskets now, but she could teach Saluki how to make the repairs. "Take this piece and stick it under this one and over that one, honey. Keep going all the way across. You don't want it to come out."

The wet fibers smelled fresh and new, unlike the dried-out odor of the old basket. Seated on a low wooden stool next to her aunt, Saluki used a spoon handle to hold a space open so she could force the new grass between the old fibers.

She still had not told Dustin she was going to apply for the scholarship. Would he be angry that she might go to a different school next year? He might even look for a new girlfriend since she wouldn't be around all the time.

Maybe he would consider going to the Academy, too. Surely his parents could afford to send him.

Aunt Ida stopped rocking her chair. "What's bothering you, child?"

"Huh?" She glanced into her aunt's knowing eyes then tucked her chin down and focused on her work. "Oh, nothing. I'm just concentrating on this basket."

"I know you better than that, Saluki, darlin'. You never quiet, no matter how hard you working. You used to chatter like a magpie when we was picking beans together in the garden." The old woman chuckled. "I think your chattering kept the skeeters away, though. I never did get a bite when you was helping me." She resumed her rocking. "Now tell me what's on your mind."

Saluki bent her head closer to her work, hoping to hide like she had when she was five and stole a cookie fresh out of Aunt Ida's oven. But her great-aunt didn't miss a thing. She might as well tell her. "I got a chance to change schools next year and go to Charleston Academy. But I'm kind of scared."

Aunt Ida reached out with her wrinkled arm. Her gnarled fingers touched Saluki's chin, turned her face to look at her. "Now you're a smart girl. Sounds like this is a good thing, so why should you be scared?"

"Cause it's the Academy. It'll be college-level courses—and all those rich kids. I won't know anybody."

"Mm-hmm. You don't want those rich kids to know how smart you are."

"No! That's not it. But—"

"Well, how many people you gon' know when you go to college?"

She shrugged. "Not many, I guess. But Dustin'll be there with me."

"Maybe. Maybe not. He could change his mind."

Her aunt's flat statement made her shiver. He wouldn't do

that. Would he? "We've got it all worked out, Auntie. But that's my problem. This new school—well, it wasn't in our plans."

"And you're afraid your boyfriend won't like you changing the plan?"

She nodded. A tear threatened to leak from one eye. "What if he—?" Her voice sounded like that five-year-old cookie thief.

"What if he what? If he don't wait for you? If he finds somebody else?"

Saluki's chin quivered, and she wiped at her wet eyes. Her aunt had voiced the concerns she didn't even want to admit to herself.

Aunt Ida stroked her head, smoothing a strand of hair behind her ear. She patted her cheek. "If he don't wait for you, child, then he don't know what he giving up."

Victoria had not expected a response to her permit application only three days after the real estate closing.

And she certainly hadn't expected this.

"Denied."

The smudged block letters stamped across the form taunted her from the kitchen table in her small apartment. No cover letter, no explanation for the denial.

She had nearly missed the envelope when she retrieved her mail after work. Just before tossing the junk mail into the recycling bin, she had spotted the white envelope with the return address of the Charleston Building Department.

Now she sat, elbows propped on the table, staring at the form she had so carefully completed. Her shoulders sagged, weary from a busy day and defeated by this single sheet of paper.

Torn between the need to cry and the urge to scream, she banged her fist on the table. What kind of idiots turned down an applicant who would restore a house that so desperately needed saving? Without the necessary permits, she would have nothing more than an empty shell.

She loved the house, and she had been sure rehabilitating it was her key to opening doors in Charleston. But she might be forced to sell it right away. She picked up her phone and called Donna Grace.

"Donna Grace, they denied my permit application. What am I going to do? I can't afford to keep a house that I can't live in. I'll need to put it right back on the market. Why would they do this—"

"Whoa, sweetie." Donna Grace broke into her ranting. "Calm down. I think you need to come over here, and we'll talk."

Twenty minutes later, she sat in a comfortable wing chair in Donna Grace's den, a cup of steaming coffee on the side table. The small paneled room created a cocoon around her, as if she were wrapped in a plush blanket. A long-haired tabby named Max rubbed against her legs, and she leaned over to stroke him. Patches of gray fur on his face and head betrayed his age. As she rubbed his back, his purr rumbled, calming her and bringing a smile to her face.

"I don't get it." She shook her head. "I filled out the forms and gave them a detailed list of the repairs. I want to preserve the historic character of the house, which will only help the neighborhood. Why would they deny my permit?"

"I don't know, dear. I do have my suspicions, though." From the matching chair, Donna Grace reached over the small table and patted her other hand. "But don't worry. I know some people. I'll find out what's going on. And Matt knows his way around city hall."

Victoria picked up the cup and inhaled the hot steam,

cradling the cup between both hands. "I wouldn't have borrowed all that money if I had known I couldn't get a permit to fix the house." She leaned her head against the back of the chair and closed her eyes. "I shouldn't be doing this. It's too big a project for one person. I'll have to sell right away."

"Nonsense. You've got your plans all laid out. All you need to do is take it one step at a time. And the first step—"

"No, I don't even belong here." She emptied her cup and set it down. "I should just make everybody happy and go back to Connecticut."

"Not everybody." Donna Grace pressed her lips together in a thin smile. "Running from your problems wouldn't make you happy."

Victoria had enjoyed Donna Grace's company for coffee and lunch the last few weeks. She'd helped her get the bids quickly, and her name had opened doors at the bank. They had similar tastes and Victoria valued her opinion on decorating ideas. It felt like having her mother nearby. "Running from your problems just causes them to chase you. That's what my mother always says."

"A wise woman. I think I'd like her." Donna Grace rose. "I think what you need is a good game of Scrabble. I find it takes my mind off my worries."

"Scrabble? I've only played that a few times. I wouldn't be very good."

Donna Grace moved to a small game table at the other side of the room. "Come on. Give it a try."

She opened the box and set out the board. Victoria stood and crossed the room. The letter tiles lay jumbled in the box. How could a mess like that make her feel better?

"Sit. We'll just have a little practice game." Donna Grace sat in one chair and Victoria obediently took a seat opposite her. As they each chose their seven tiles from the box, Donna Grace hummed an unfamiliar tune.

Victoria arranged her tiles on the wooden holder. She had selected five vowels, an H, and an S. "I'm not sure what I'm doing. You go first."

Donna Grace placed an "O" tile on the center square then carefully positioned other letters to the right of it. "Order," she said. "Ten points." She leaned back and smiled. "I think finding a good word among the jumbled letters is very soothing."

Victoria played the word "house" for eight points. After a few more turns, Donna Grace went to the kitchen and returned with ham sandwiches and more coffee. They ate between turns, sharing about their childhoods and families.

Even though Donna Grace lived simply, with only Max for company, she seemed content with her life. Victoria envied her calm spirit and peaceful attitude. Maybe if she were able to finish the house, she would find similar satisfaction.

"Q-U-A-S-E." She placed the first tile over a "double letter" square. "Forty-eight points."

"Seriously?" Donna Grace leaned over the table to stare at her, a glint in her eye. "You think that's a word? Do we need to get out the dictionary?"

Victoria laughed. "I don't know. You've played some words that I've never heard of."

"Honey, I've been playing this game a long time. You can learn some good words, but I don't think that's one of them."

By the time they ran out of tiles an hour and a half later, Donna Grace had three hundred points to Victoria's embarrassing score of barely two hundred.

Victoria shrugged. "I warned you I wouldn't be much of a challenge."

"Doesn't matter. It's the process that I like. Making sense out of what looks like chaos. You'll get better with practice. Want to play again?"

She stretched. "No. I'd better get home and get to bed. At

least try to sleep."

"Of course, dear. I'll talk to Matt first thing in the morning and see what we can find out about your permit." She walked Victoria to the door. "It will work out, you'll see."

Chapter Nineteen

The front doorbell in the empty old house gave a half-hearted attempt at a chime. Victoria had to get that fixed or replaced. One item she had not included in her budget.

She dropped the worn blue sponge into the bucket of dirty water, tugged off the rubber gloves she'd worn to protect her hands, and reached for the edge of the kitchen counter to pull herself off her knees, grateful for a break from scrubbing the insides of the cabinets. In spite of uncertainty about the building permit, she had decided to spend Saturday tackling the grime that permeated the house.

She padded through the hallway and approached the door cautiously. The neighborhood seemed safe enough, but she hadn't expected anyone. Mother had taught her to be careful of opening the door to strangers, especially when she was alone.

Through the dingy glass in the door, she recognized Randy Lee. She released the breath she'd been holding and unlocked the door. He stood on the porch holding a pizza box and something in a plastic bag.

"Come on in." She swung the door wide open. She had forgotten to eat and now her stomach rumbled at the aroma of pepperoni. "You're just in time. I am so ready for some help."

"At your service, sweet lady. I heard there was some heavy lifting going on here." He elbowed the door shut behind him and bent to kiss her cheek.

She laughed, the first time in days. It felt good. "More like heavy sweating."

"That's where you're wrong, sugar. Don't you know a southern lady does not sweat? She perspires."

"Is that right? Does that mean you think I'm a southern

lady?"

"You live in the South, and you're a lady." He set his offering on the bottom step of the staircase, removed his cowboy hat, and swept his arm wide as he bowed deep, like Rhett Butler. "Works for me."

Pleasure rose from her toes to her stomach and back down. She grabbed the pizza box and headed for the kitchen. "Come on. Let's eat this gourmet meal you've prepared."

From the grocery bag she had left sitting on the floor, she pulled two paper plates and dropped them on the yellow linoleum countertop. Plastic cups followed. She took a jug of lemonade from the ancient refrigerator and poured some in a cup.

When she held it out to Randy Lee, he shook his head and held up the mysterious bag. "Brought my own." He removed a six-pack of beer and tossed the bag toward the back door. "Want one?"

"No, thanks. I'll drink this." She drank the lemonade eagerly, letting the sweet-sour liquid rinse away the exhaustion of the morning.

She had not bought chairs yet, so Randy Lee hefted himself onto the countertop. He offered to help her up beside him, but she declined, choosing instead to lean against the cabinet.

After devouring one slice of pizza, she told him how she had spent all morning scouring dirt. "Seems like cleaning will take forever, much less the remodeling. I don't know how I'm going to get it all done in the time the bank expects. And now the city is hassling me over the permits."

"What sort of hassle?" He reached for another piece of pizza.

"They sent me a denial notice with no explanation. But Donna Grace found out why."

He raised his eyebrows in a silent question as he bit off the end of the pizza slice.

Victoria moved the last piece to her plate. "They're claiming the house is in a conservation district, and I can't do anything to the outside without Historic Commission Approval, even though nothing about that turned up in the title search."

"So you think the commission won't approve of your changes?"

"No, it's not that. My changes aren't major—just fixing the porch and painting the place a different color. From what I understand, the colors aren't an issue in this district. But the Building Department rejected it because I didn't go through the commission first. And they won't even meet to review my application for three more weeks. I can't afford to lose that kind of time."

He picked up his beer can and waved it in a circular motion. "This sounds like a time to follow my favorite piece of advice. Do what you need to do and ask forgiveness later."

She laughed. "That works for you, does it?"

He nodded. "Every time." His face remained serious.

Antonio had taken that approach on several projects and had paid large fines as a result. He claimed it was a cost of doing business and that it had saved time. And to him, of course, time was money. But she had no desire to emulate any of her ex-husbands.

She picked up the empty pizza box and bent it in half. "I'm trying to be accepted by the civic leaders of this city. I don't think ignoring their rules is the way to do that."

Victoria learned Monday that Matt knew how to work within the system to get what he needed. He called her just before lunchtime.

"I can get a preliminary permit." His husky voice seemed

to be hiding something.

"That's wonderful, Matt! How would you do it?"

"I'll need you to sign some papers. Can you meet me at the house in thirty? I'll explain then."

Charleston continued to amaze her with its brilliant colors of spring around every corner. Back in Connecticut, there would only be daffodils and possibly cherry blossoms by now. She drove with the window down to enjoy the fresh-air fragrance, scented by flowering bushes she would never learn to identify. When she arrived at the house, she found Matt sitting on the porch steps eating a sandwich. Her stomach growled in complaint. She wished she had thought to stop for some fast food on the way.

Matt looked up at her. "Hey." He waved the sandwich at her. "Thought I'd be done with this before you got here. Sorry."

"That's okay. Go ahead and finish." She stood in front of him, not wanting to risk getting dirt on her pants suit by sitting on the wooden porch.

He stuffed the remainder of the sandwich in a black metal lunchbox beside him and jumped up, brushing off his hands. "Do you want to talk inside?"

She nodded and headed up the steps, key in hand. He picked up some papers from under the lunchbox and followed her, the screen door slamming behind him. In the hallway, she turned to him. "So how did you convince them to issue the permit without commission approval?"

"Well, they haven't yet, but they will if you complete this." He held out the papers.

"What is it?" She didn't take it.

"It's a hardship application requesting they waive the requirement for commission approval. It's only for the roof and repairing the rot on the exterior."

She took the papers and looked over the form. "Hardship?

Won't it upset the commission members if we bypass them? I can't afford to make any enemies."

He slapped his hand against his thigh, tapping out a beat on his denim dungarees. "Nope. This is not unusual when a house has fallen into complete disrepair. You'll still have to go before the commission to get approval for the paint colors and replacing the shutters and porch railing."

She tilted her head to look at him. "The porch railing? Why would that be an issue? I just want to put back what used to be there."

He chuckled. "It won't be an issue. You've got photos of the original house to show them, and I'll give you a drawing to show that what I'm going to make will be a faithful reproduction." He looked around the hallway and lowered himself onto the fourth step. "Besides, I've met with them on several projects. They're reasonable people. Mostly."

She started for the kitchen where she could use the counter to fill out the form. But when his last word pushed through the fog in her brain, she turned back toward him. "Mostly?"

His hazel eyes twinkled, belying the serious look on his face. "Well, I've only known 'em to kill and eat one person, but she wanted to paint her house orange and purple. I think you'll be fine."

Chapter Twenty

A thunderclap jerked Victoria out of a deep sleep. She had dragged herself back to her apartment at midnight, exhausted after spending Thursday evening removing old varnish from the dining room woodwork.

She rubbed the gunk out of her eyes and squinted at the clock. *4:12.*

Rain pelted the glass and wind whistled through the gaps around the metal frame of the bedroom window. April thunderstorms weren't frequent, but they were not uncommon, Matt had said. She hoped his workers had secured tarps over the unfinished roof.

Speaking of Matt, she was supposed to meet him at seven this morning to give him a check and discuss his progress. After finally obtaining the preliminary permit, his crew had started work on the roof a week ago.

"With any luck," he had told her as they stood in the front yard watching the materials being unloaded, "we'll have a good couple weeks and can get 'er covered without any problems."

She squeezed her eyes shut and pulled the blanket up to her neck. Maybe the storm wouldn't last long, and the men would still be able to work today. A flash of lightning and another crack of thunder answered her.

She lay there for several minutes, mentally reviewing her checklist of tasks and projects. Then she began to add up the expenses that were due—materials from the lumberyard, Matt's work so far, plus the deposit for the plumber. She already feared that her estimates had been too low.

The next bolt of thunder shook the window glass. What

was the use? She tossed aside the blankets and swung her feet out of bed. There'd be no going back to sleep today. She might as well get up and accomplish something before work. She could bring clothes for the office with her and change after the meeting with Matt.

Using only the night-light, she pulled a wrinkle-free skirt and jacket from the closet. Folding them loosely, she placed them in a red gym bag. She hadn't worked out in a month but the bag had come in handy for carrying old clothes she could use at the house after she left work each day. This time, her good clothes would go in the bag.

She added heels and jewelry then zipped the bag and left it by the door. After finding her jeans drawer empty, she grabbed yesterday's pair out of the overflowing laundry basket. Tonight she had to wash clothes. Lightning crackled, throwing a slash of light across the room as if to endorse the promise to herself.

At least she had one more clean t-shirt. It was her favorite Red Sox shirt, so she'd have to be careful not to ruin it by splashing varnish remover on it.

About halfway into town, she realized she had made a bad decision. The storm dumped buckets of water on her windshield, obscuring her vision for what seemed like minutes at a time. She drove just over the minimum highway speed of forty, at times slowing even more. Thank goodness few other cars were out this early.

When she pulled into the driveway of her house at five thirty, the storm had given no indication of letting up. She checked the weather on her phone. Great. Eighty percent chance of rain for the next three days. So much for Matt's crew resuming work on the roof anytime soon.

She had cleaned the baseboard on two walls of the dining room by the time Matt knocked on the front door a few minutes before seven. She rose and brushed off her jeans, pleased with her progress. She might even finish this room after work tonight.

Water dripped from Matt's rain jacket as she opened the door. He lifted his eyebrows when he saw her. "Have you been working all night or something?" He shed the jacket and dropped it on the porch before stepping inside.

"It feels like it." She ran a hand through her hair. "I must look a mess. The storm woke me a little after four, and I couldn't get back to sleep. So I figured I'd get some work done. I've got coffee made if you want some."

"Smells good. I could use a cup." He followed her to the kitchen, where she poured some of the brew into a Styrofoam cup and handed it to him. "Black, right?"

He grinned. "Yes, ma'am. Good of you to remember."

She took her checkbook out of the purse she had set on the kitchen counter and began writing. "Please don't call me ma'am, Matt. Makes me feel old enough to be your mother—which I'm not, by the way." She handed him the check.

He took it, folded it without looking at it, and stuck it in his shirt pocket. "Believe me, Ms. Russo, I know you're too young to be my mother. My older sister, maybe ..." His grin let her know he was testing her.

She put a hand on her hip, pretending to be serious. "If I'm your older sister, you can just call me Victoria."

"Yes, ma'am—uh, Victoria." He took a sip from his cup. "Good coffee."

"Glad you like it." She picked up her own cup. "Looks like you won't be able to work on the roof for the next few days."

"Afraid not. I thought I'd check the attic to see if we have any leaks. The way the winds were blowing, I'm a little worried whether the tarps are holding."

She swallowed her now lukewarm coffee. "Of course, let's do that now. Want a top off?" She held out the pot.

"Nope, mine's good for now. Thanks."

She filled her cup then picked it up and led the way upstairs.

Matt moved a ladder in the upstairs hall so he could reach the attic hatch. After pulling himself through the opening, he peered down at her. "Want to come up?"

She hesitated. She had yet to go into the attic, having put her trust in Matt and the home inspector she had hired before the closing. She imagined mice, cobwebs, and head-crunching beams. And she had to go to work in less than an hour.

"Come on. It's pretty cool up here. I've got something to show you." He stuck his hand down toward her and wriggled his fingers.

She set her coffee cup on the floor and started up the ladder. "Okay, but promise not to get me too dirty."

After he helped her crawl through the opening, she found the space to be better than she expected. A musty smell reminded her of the attic in her parents' house. Rain drummed on the roof, setting the hanging cobwebs into gentle motion.

But she had lots of room above her head. Boards positioned across the rafters allowed for easy movement throughout most of the space. "We could make another room up here!"

"You could, but the ceiling would be a bit low for some people." Matt's Clemson hat brushed the bottom of a beam. He stopped and studied the framing. "But if you want to, I think we could move these collar ties up enough to make it work."

She wrinkled her nose. "That sounds expensive. I think we'd better put that idea on hold until the rest of the work is done. What did you want to show me?"

"Right. It's over here." She followed him to the front corner, where the roof sloped to its lowest point. They had to crouch as they got close to the front wall. "Look." He pointed to a black chunk that seemed to be embedded in a beam. It was about a foot across and looked like a crushed rubber ball.

"What in the world?" She reached out and touched the smooth, cold surface. It felt like some kind of metal. "Any idea how that got *here*?"

He placed his hand next to hers on the metal. "I'm not positive, but I think it's a cannonball from the war."

She blinked and gazed at him. "You mean, *the* war?"

"Yep."

"But … how?"

"I'm guessing it landed here while the North was shelling the city. The owners must have repaired the hole in the roof and just left the fragment in place."

"Oh." She hadn't realized the house contained a memento of the Federal bombardment of Charleston. Much of the city had been destroyed, so evidence her house had withstood the year of attacks should count for something. "Shouldn't it be removed and displayed or something?"

He shook his head. "That's for you historians to decide. I reckon you'd have to get approval from the powers-that-be. Taking it out might jeopardize the integrity of that beam, but we could always build a sister joist beside it before removing the shell."

She thought about that. Displaying a piece of the Civil War from her own house would add to the authenticity of the place. But she couldn't afford to add more to Matt's list of work to be done. "Is it—safe—to just leave it here? At least for now?"

"Sure. It's been here a hundred and fifty years, and the house hasn't fallen down." He winked at her. "Yet."

She drew a deep breath. "Okay, then. We won't worry about it until the rest of the house is finished."

"I didn't say that. You still ought to tell the Historical Society and let them take a look." He moved back to the center area and stood up, rubbing his back. He craned his head and appeared to be inspecting the roof.

She followed him and stretched her own back as soon as she had enough room. "I'll call and ask them to come look at it. Find out what they think." She stepped closer and followed his gaze. "Any leaks?"

He glanced at her. "Were you worried?"

"A little."

"Well, you shouldn't have been. My guys know what they're doing." He smiled.

"But you said—"

"I did want to check. But mainly I just wanted to see if I could get you up here in the dusty attic." He held his hands out in front of him. "You always look so neat and tidy. I thought you needed an adventure."

She shook her head as he helped her climb down through the attic opening. She hardly needed more adventure than what she'd experienced since leaving Connecticut.

Chapter Twenty-One

Saluki had almost reached the door of the classroom when Mr. D's voice pulled her back.

"Saluki, can you stick around?"

Majesty looked at her and, nodding toward the hall, mouthed, "I'll wait for you."

While Mr. D. erased the chalkboard, she stood by his desk, rearranging the empty soda cans displayed there. He would ask about the application for the Academy scholarship that she'd been carrying in her backpack for two weeks. She had filled it out after talking to Aunt Ida, but when she read the part about making a speech, she had folded it and stuffed it away.

When the classroom was vacant except for the two of them, he put down the eraser and turned around. Leaning against the chalkboard, he crossed his arms. "I haven't seen your scholarship application yet, and the deadline is tomorrow. What's going on?"

She shrugged. "I'm not sure I want to go to the Academy." She wanted it so badly she could taste it, but not enough to give a speech about her reasons. She envisioned getting all dressed up and standing in front of an audience, only to have them feel sorry for her. Much like her eleventh birthday.

But he wouldn't understand. "You know, I'd have to leave my friends and all. Maybe I want to just graduate with my class here."

He gazed at her, his eyes lasering through his glasses like he could see through her head. He stepped over to his desk, shuffled some folders, pulled one out, and opened it.

"I will do whatever it takes to achieve my dreams, even if it means stepping out of my comfort zone."

Saluk shifted, her gaze on the floor as he continued to read aloud from her application for the Tourism Bureau internship. "I don't believe anyone should be limited by her family, her income, or her fears. The only thing I will not do is hurt my family by ignoring them or pretending they don't exist." He closed the folder and tapped it on the desk. "What happened to that girl? What are you afraid of, Saluki?"

How did this man understand her so well? If she didn't know better, she would think he could read her mind. She dropped her backpack on the floor and flopped into a desk on the front row. "I'm not afraid of going there. But I'm not sure what difference it'll make."

Mr. D. moved to the desk next to the one she sat in and, squeezing himself into it, faced her. "You're right in one sense. Going to the Academy won't change your life. It's your ambition and your abilities that will help you achieve your dreams."

"Okay, then. I'll stay here." She wanted to get up and leave, to demonstrate that the decision was fine with her. But it wasn't. Not really. She didn't budge, but she couldn't look at him either.

"On the other hand, one of my students said recently that no one should be limited by fear. If you don't face your fears, Saluki, you will never be all that you were created to be. Why don't you tell me the real reason you haven't filled out the application?"

"I did—" She hadn't meant to blurt that out. Now it was too late. She bent over and grabbed her backpack, unzipped the pocket, and pulled out the application—her answers neatly printed and the paper only slightly wrinkled. She smoothed it out with her hands and handed it to him. "I filled it out right away. I was so excited. But …"

He took it and looked it over, pausing to read her answers about her plans for the future and her reasons for wanting to attend the Academy. He nodded. "Good answers." He turned to the back where she had underlined the other requirements—with a double underline under the statement about making a five-minute presentation to the committee.

He looked up. "Is that it? You're worried about the committee interview?"

She nodded, running her finger over the carvings in the wooden desk. "I don't like talking to a group of people I don't know. I had to do that at church a couple years ago, and I wound up crying. I was so embarrassed."

He blew a puff of air. "Thank you for telling me. You don't seem to have a problem in class, so I would never have guessed."

She blinked back the tears that threatened. "I know all of them. They're my friends. But a bunch of grownups I've never met? Uh-uh."

He reached over and touched her shoulder. "What if I help you practice? And—I think I can arrange to be there, so you will know someone."

She looked at him. "You'd do that for me? How come?"

He smiled. "Because I believe in you. I want to see you achieve your dreams, and I know you can. But you need to confront this fear."

If only her father had believed in her that much.

"Can you come to school fifteen minutes early for a few days? We'll go over your speech until you know it cold. And I'll give you some tips on overcoming your fear while you're speaking. What do you say?"

Maybe she could do this. She didn't want to be a coward all her life and miss out on opportunities like this one. She nodded. "Thanks, Mr. D. You're the best."

He held up her application form. "Ready for me to turn

this in?"

She shrugged. "I guess so. What's the worst that can happen, right?"

Other than losing Dustin and her friends.

On top of the Saturday lunchtime roar at Papa Joe's Grill, the voices of her friends threatened to give Saluki a headache. The thick burgers and affordable prices meant that students filled the place after school and on weekends.

Majesty held a half-eaten French fry between her teeth. "You're kidding, right?"

TeeJay blew a low whistle through his teeth. The remainders of burgers and catsup littered the table of their booth.

"Papa Joe," as he liked to be called, had opened the tiny restaurant three blocks from the high school after he retired from teaching. He wanted to offer a safe hangout for kids from the neighborhood, he always said. Papa Joe played the most recent pop and hip-hop hits. Since he could turn off his hearing aids, he didn't care how loud the noise got. His only rule was posted on a sign by the cash register: "Be nice."

Dustin draped his arm around Saluki's shoulders and squeezed. "Of course she's kidding, ya'll. Saluki's not going to leave us to go to some preppy school. Right, babe?"

She shook her head, slowly. "No, I'm not kidding. Mr. D. says it's a great opportunity and I should go for it. I've already turned in the application."

Dustin pulled back his arm. "Without talking to me first?" His look pierced her calm resolve. She should have told him before this.

"Well, I might not even get the scholarship. There'll be others applying, too, so …" At the hurt in Dustin's eyes, her stomach tightened. "It doesn't change anything with us, sweetie. You ought to know that." She waved her arm at the two across the table. "We can all still be together when we're not in school or working."

Majesty snorted. "Sure. It'll be just like old times. The four of us hanging out—when you're not too busy with your new, rich friends."

TeeJay grabbed his milkshake and slurped the last of it noisily. "Girl, you gonna be hanging with some smart dudes. You'll be too good for the likes of us. We get it."

"No, it's not like that." She tried to reassure them. "Ya'll are my best friends and always will be. But going to the academy will improve my chances of getting college scholarships. And …" What would Dustin think about the college credits that would make her a sophomore when they entered college in a year?

He picked up his burger and finished it in one bite. After he swallowed, he turned to her and put his face close to hers. His onion-breath turned her stomach. "And what?"

She smoothed the wrapper from her cheeseburger and folded it in half then folded it again. She didn't look at any of them. "And I'll get college credit for most of my classes next year. That'll save me a whole year of college tuition."

Dustin crumpled his own wrapper and tossed it on the tray at the end of the table. "Good for you. So much for taking classes together. Maybe you can tutor me in freshman English, since you'll have already taken it."

"You won't need tutoring—" She saw his face and closed her mouth. This was no time to disagree with him, even over something so obvious.

"I guess all good things have to end." Majesty shrugged. "I just didn't think it would be so soon. Thought we'd share the senior experience—homecoming, prom, graduation, all that stuff."

Saluki sucked on her straw then shook her cup. The ice in the almost-empty container sounded as hollow as her answer. "It's not like I'd be leaving town, you know. I could still go to dances and ballgames at East Cooper." She reached across the table to grasp Majesty's hand. "I'm definitely gonna be there when you're crowned Homecoming Queen."

Majesty pulled her hand away and gathered her empty cup and wrapper. "I always thought we'd both be part of the Homecoming court. But don't worry about me. I'll find somebody to share the excitement with." She stood. "Come on, TeeJay. I gotta get home to help Mama plant the garden."

"Yeah. This bites. Bye, Saluki." He slid out of the booth and held a hand out to bump fists with Dustin. "Catch you later, man."

Dustin got up, too. "You need a ride home?"

He always took her home, even though she lived only five blocks from the restaurant. What happened to his manners? She shook her head. "No, that's okay. I guess I can walk."

"Cool. See you around then."

See you around? That's all he could say? She had not even been accepted at the academy yet and already she felt abandoned.

Chapter Twenty-Two

A brisk wind carried the fragrance from the azaleas by her side porch as Victoria scrolled her finger across her tablet computer. Now that Donna Grace had told her what plants were in the yard, she kept trying to memorize their names. So far, she had learned azalea and clematis, but none of the others.

The builders of her house had known what they were doing; the porch provided an ideal spot to catch the breezes coming from the bay. She enjoyed the opportunity to try out the wooden swing that Matt had re-installed for her that morning, the first clear day in the last couple of weeks.

She checked the time in the lower right corner of the tablet screen. How long did it take to inspect the wiring in a house? She could only accomplish so much work on the tablet, and she needed to get back to the office soon.

Brushing her hand across her forehead, she scanned the street. Quiet in the middle of the day. An occasional car passed but no high schoolers revving their engines or cruising the block with their windows down and radio blasting.

She liked the neighborhood, even with the boys trying to act tough. Just as the aging houses included a mixture of well-kept family homes, sprawling mansions converted to apartments or condos, and rundown-at-the-heels structures like hers, the residents were varied as well. Like the proud widow who had raised five children in the home two houses down and whose face now looked as weathered as the siding and whose body sagged more than her porch.

Or the lawyer and her banker husband further down the street who, along with their teenaged son and daughter, were renovating a Charleston single house that had been in her family for three generations.

In the converted duplex across the street, a single mom struggled to keep her three grade school children from running wild while she worked.

Victoria surprised herself by how much she had learned about her neighbors in a few weeks. She had taken several walks and stopped to introduce herself when she found someone outside. Everyone had greeted her warmly and seemed genuinely interested in her New England background. They had all made her feel welcome, much to her surprise.

But sitting here musing about her new acquaintances wouldn't get her work done. She had to find out what was taking the electrician so long. She stuffed the tablet into her rolling briefcase and stood to go into the house. The screen door opened and the electrician emerged from the dusky interior.

"Ms. Russo, I'm all done." The man reminded her of a football player in blue coveralls. He swiped his sweaty forehead with a red handkerchief. "Most of your wiring is in good condition. We'll just run the new wire to add some outlets like you asked."

She released a breath. Having to replace wiring throughout the house could have cost thousands. "That's good news."

"Yes, ma'am. But I want to show you something." He turned abruptly and headed back into the house. She followed him down the hall, through the kitchen, then into the utility room where she planned to install a washer and dryer.

He opened the metal door of the electrical panel. "Now, look here." His voice carried an undercurrent of warning.

She studied the breaker box, not seeing anything wrong. The rows of black circuit breakers lined up in formation. She had been grateful the house had been modernized instead of still using fuses. Antonio had spent more than five thousand to upgrade the electrical service at one house he'd remodeled.

Paper labels marked only three of the switches, but that could be easily fixed by testing outlets and lights, as she and Antonio had done on several occasions. She shrugged her shoulders.

"You see this brand name." The electrician pointed to a small metal plate with the manufacturer's information. "This company—look at me, now—"

Surprised by the brusque command, she turned to face him.

He pointed his finger at her chest. "This company went out of business, probably to avoid being sued after some of their boxes caught fire."

Victoria gasped. "What does that mean?"

"It means, little lady, that you could have an electrical fire. You ought to replace the whole panel."

Her knees turn to gelatin, and she looked around for a place to sit down. Nothing, of course. She leaned against the wall for support. "That—that sounds expensive."

He nodded. "It's not cheap. Couple thousand. You okay?" He reached out to grab her elbow. "Now, you don't have to decide today. But I wouldn't wait too long, you hear me?"

She breathed deeply and straightened her back. "Yes. It's a fire hazard, and I need to replace it. Do you think it will be okay for a couple of months?"

"Can't say. It's not something you can predict, you hear me?" He stepped back from her and dropped his hand. "Depends on how much of a risk-taker you are."

She snorted. "I guess I'm big at taking risks. I bought this house, didn't I?"

He wiped his hand through his greasy black hair and grinned. "Yes, ma'am, I guess you are. I'll write up an estimate and call you tomorrow."

"Thanks. I'll see what I can do after I get your estimate, I guess."

After he left, she wandered through the house, mentally listing the work to be done and adding up the expenses. What other surprises lay ahead?

"Now, sugar, it can't be as bad as it sounds." Randy Lee rubbed Victoria's upper back as they sat together on the porch swing that evening after work. She had taken a break from restoring woodwork when he showed up.

The air hung heavy with moisture from another pending storm. The neighbors had retreated inside, leaving a vacuum as the sounds of activity were missing. Only the birds continued to chatter about the rain that was on its way from the ocean.

She used to love the smell of rain. But today it reminded her of a muddy creek. The storms kept coming, preventing Matt's crew from shingling the roof. The job should have been finished two weeks ago, but Matt wouldn't continue work on it until the forecast called for a week of clear weather. At least the tarps continued to keep the attic dry.

"It is, Randy Lee. I have to have the electric panel and all the breakers replaced."

He stretched his legs out in front of him and stopped the swing. "Surely it doesn't have to be done right away. It's been okay up to now, right?"

She leaned her head back on his arm, comforted by his presence. "I guess. But I can't risk a fire. That would be disaster."

A breeze blew his hair across his forehead, giving him that charming little-boy look. "I hear what you're saying, but how do you know this guy's not just making up this stuff?"

She lifted her head and stared at him. "Why would he do that?"

"To get your business."

Sometimes people did say things just to gain an advantage. Could that be the case now?

She shook her head. "I don't think so. Donna Grace recommended him. If she says he's trustworthy, I'm sure he is."

He held out his free hand. "I'm just trying to look at it from all angles. It's business, so you need to keep the emotions out of it."

Keep the emotions out of it. Sounded like what Antonio would say when he was about to bargain for a better price. "It's not emotions. It's practicality. If there's a fire, even a small one, I might as well forget about finishing the house in the time the bank allows."

He gave the swing a push with his foot. "You probably won't have a fire, sugar. And even if you did, I'm sure the bank would extend the deadline. You've got insurance, right?"

"Of course. But I can't stand the thought of an electrical fire." She shuddered, remembering when her mother had set the kitchen on fire three years ago while cooking bacon. Her parents had been lucky to get out of the house, especially since Parkinson's had limited her father's walking ability by that time. The firefighters had managed to save the house, but the repairs had taken three months before her mother and father could move back in.

Randy Lee patted her shoulder. "See, I think that guy just wanted to scare you. Maybe you should at least get another opinion."

She could Google the manufacturer of the panel to see what had been reported about the problems, but it wouldn't hurt to get a second estimate. "Like a doctor, huh? That's not a bad idea. At least I could compare prices."

"That's my girl. I've got a friend that could look at it for you. Want me to call him?"

She leaned her head back again. "Sure, that would be nice."

A few minutes later, he clicked off the phone call and grinned at her. "He's out of town this week but he'll come by next Saturday."

She forced her stomach to relax. If another electrician thought it could wait a week and a half, she surely didn't need to panic.

Saluki spent every morning for two weeks practicing with Mr. D. She had memorized her speech and could repeat it flawlessly for him. But bumble bees buzzed in her stomach when she thought about appearing before the scholarship committee.

"Now remember," he told her Thursday morning before the committee meeting Sunday afternoon. "Make eye contact with each member of the committee once, then focus on me. Forget about them and pretend it's just you and me in the room. Just like now."

"Easier said than done."

"I know. That's why I want you to give the speech in class tomorrow. One last practice. Then you can relax for the weekend."

"In front of the class?"

He smiled. "You said you didn't mind talking in front of your friends. It'll be good practice for speaking to a group, and focusing just on me. Then the committee of three will seem like a merry-go-round."

"More like a roller coaster, you mean."

He laughed. "Okay, but it'll be the last downhill slope. You'll be fine."

But she wouldn't be fine. Even the thought of giving this

speech to her friends made perspiration break out on her forehead.

The next day, as Mr. D. explained to the class why Saluki was making a speech, she felt rather than heard the murmurs.

She stood robot-like and moved to the front of the class. When she turned to them, the room became a Tilt-A-Whirl, their faces spinning out of control, blurring together. These were her friends, and she couldn't look at them. She searched frantically for Mr. D., found him standing in the back, arms crossed, nodding at her.

She focused on him like he had told her and tried to block out the rest of the room. But she could still see them in her peripheral vision. Were they laughing, or was she imagining that? She blinked and settled her eyes on the spot on top of Mr. D.'s head where his hair was almost gone.

"My name is Saluki…" Her voice sounded like a frog's. And they knew who she was. She should have skipped that part. She cleared her throat and started again. "I want to go to Charleston Academy because of the academic opportunities it offers and the courses that are not available at East Cooper High School. My goal is to attend the College of Charleston …"

She didn't remember making it through the rest of the speech, but she must have, because Mr. D. applauded. Most of the students clapped politely, but she didn't think they were impressed with what she had to say. Or maybe it was the way she said it. She must have sounded as much like a robot as she had felt.

After class, she asked Majesty to wait for her. Her friend shrugged and left the room with TeeJay and Dustin. She approached Mr. D.'s desk. "That was awful, wasn't it?"

He leaned back in his chair. "No, not awful. You'll do fine. The committee isn't looking for a professional public speaker. They want to hear your heart. Try to relax and let them see that you mean what you're saying."

She shook her head. "Relax. Right. Maybe I should get hold of some Prozac to help me relax. That's the only way I'll make it through this."

He smiled. "I hope you're kidding about that. Now go enjoy the weekend. I'll see you Sunday afternoon."

She hurried to her locker to collect the books she needed for homework, expecting to find her friends waiting for her. But the hall was empty. Friday afternoon and everyone had cleared out. She quickly gathered her things and stuffed them in her backpack, closed her locker, and hefted the heavy bag over her shoulders. She jogged down the stairs and out the front door, expecting to catch up with Dustin and the others.

Why hadn't they waited for her? Since she had worked late on Wednesday and Thursday, she had already filled her hours for the week and could go for ice cream with them. They had talked about it at lunch.

She spotted the trio getting into the Dodge Charger. She hurried over. By the time she reached the car, Dustin had started the engine and seemed to be ready to back out of the parking spot. Majesty was in the passenger seat, and TeeJay sat in the back.

She put her hands on her hips and stared. Dustin saw her finally and put his window down. "Make sure I don't get in your way."

She leaned down and looked in his window. "What is that supposed to mean? And—why didn't ya'll wait for me? I thought we were going for ice cream together."

Majesty leaned around Dustin. "Didn't sound like you wanted to hang around with us anymore. Go have yourself a good time at the *academy*." She emphasized the last word as if Saluki were going to Europe or something.

What had she said to make them react this way? "You know I don't want to leave y'all. I just want a better education than I can get here."

Dustin looked away. "Sorry we're not good enough for you. Watch your toes." He put the car into gear and rolled it backward, forcing her to jump back. As he turned the car and peeled out of the parking lot, she stood like a mannequin, watching as her three best friends roared away.

The empty spot she'd had in her stomach since the day her father left had just doubled in size.

Chapter Twenty-Three

Victoria might run out of money and time before she finished restoring this house, but it would not be because she didn't try.

She moved the stepladder to the end cabinet and climbed to the fourth step. It had been a month since she took possession of the property. Since then, she had spent weekends and nearly every night—when she didn't have civic meetings to attend—working on the house.

She tugged at her rubber glove then reached into the large metal coffee can to retrieve the piece of steel wool. She turned her face away to keep from breathing in the tart odor as she squeezed the excess paint remover out. Then she applied the pad to the front of the upper cabinet.

At the other end of the row of cabinets, Donna Grace scrubbed off the residue of their efforts. "My Al would have liked you, Victoria. He'd say you've got spunk."

The comment warmed Victoria, like the sunlight streaming through the large window above the sink. She could finally see progress. They'd had a week with no rain, and Matt's crew had completed the roof and repaired the termite damage.

He wanted to start work on the kitchen on Monday, so she hoped to finish stripping the paint off the cabinets today. With Donna Grace's help, that just might happen.

She glanced at her friend, who had removed her safety goggles in favor of her regular glasses. Through her own goggles, Donna Grace's face blurred. "Me? Why would he say that?"

Donna Grace attacked one of the base cabinets with a

metal scraper. "Isn't it obvious, honey? You taking on this house all by your lonesome speaks for itself. And before that, you picked up and moved from New England to take a job here where you didn't know a soul."

Victoria shook her head. "I didn't really have a choice. I had to leave." She swiped the wet pad across the cabinet in short, choppy motions. As she dunked the ragged steel wool back into the liquid, she noticed that Donna Grace's eyebrows formed a question.

"Something bad happened to prompt you to move." Donna Grace met her eyes. Then she went back to her task. "If you want to talk about it, I'm here."

How much did she want to tell? The pain was still raw. She stretched her arm to reach the uppermost corner of the cabinet. "Michael and I—Michael was my last husband—we worked together in Waterbury. That's where we met. Things were great for a couple of years until I found out he was cheating on me with a co-worker."

"Oh, my." Donna Grace whistled softly. "Some men don't have the sense to put their pants on one leg at a time."

"The worst part was, apparently everybody in the office knew about it before I did. I confronted him, and he chose her over me. Story of my life."

Donna Grace rose from the floor, rubbing her bottom. "These old bones aren't used to sitting on a hard floor." She emptied her bucket of water in the kitchen sink and gazed out the window. "Of course, I don't know Michael or the other woman, but it seems to me he missed the mark when he made that choice."

"No, it only makes sense." Victoria climbed down the ladder, carrying the empty can with her. "She's tall and thin, looks like a model. She's loads of fun to be around, and she'll probably become director there. I liked her."

She pulled off her gloves and goggles and tossed them on

the edge of the sink. "We used to go out dancing with her and her husband. I had no idea what was going on right under my nose, and neither did he."

"Whew. That would be hard." Donna Grace grabbed the gallon jug of paint remover and poured a liberal amount into the coffee can Victoria had set on the counter. The rush of fumes burned Victoria's nostrils. "So you decided to get out of town."

"Pretty much. As soon as I could. The last three months were torture—going to work and seeing the two of them, feeling the pitying looks and the whispers." She turned abruptly and opened the back door, sucking in the fresh air. "But it's not like I hadn't been through it before."

"Oh?" Donna Grace capped the chemical container and stretched a piece of plastic over the coffee can. "How about a cold drink? Got some sweet tea?"

"Yeah. That sounds good." Victoria pushed away from the doorway and grabbed two plastic cups from her stash in the closet.

Donna Grace got the pitcher from the refrigerator and filled the cups then handed one to Victoria. "I can't say that I know how it feels, but I know that the problem wasn't with you. It was with him. He made the poor choices, not you."

Victoria snickered. "The problem with that statement is that Michael was my third husband. The other two didn't turn out much different." She didn't even want to think about Brian and Antonio. "Not to mention the in-betweeners that I didn't marry. All of them were bad choices. I can't seem to tell a keeper from a throw-away."

She took a sip from her cup. "Anyway, I came to Charleston to forget about Michael and get a fresh start. But tell me about Al. How did you meet him?"

Donna Grace's lips curled up at the ends and her eyes sparkled. "Now that is a good story." She held up her cup.

"Let's take a break on the front porch, and I'll tell you."

They settled in the porch swing. Somewhere down the block, a lawn mower purred. A door slammed across the street and a teenage girl ran to a car waiting at the curb. "We met at my birthday party."

"You didn't even know him? What was he, a party crasher?"

"My friends gave me a surprise party at church when I turned thirty. Al and his two children had just moved to town, and they invited him so he could get to know people. The funny thing was that he forgot my name. When he saw me at church the following Sunday, he called me Debbie Grace." She chuckled. "Since he met a lot of new people that night, I forgave him. Of course, I did tease him about it over the years."

Victoria used her toe to push the swing into motion. "Did you say you were thirty when you met? Had you been married before?"

"No, sweetie. I had dated a few men, but none of them seemed to be the man God had for me. I had a full life—a job I loved, lots of great friends, and I had my cat, of course."

"But didn't you get lonely?"

"Sometimes. But mostly, I was grateful that I had time to help out with some of the ministries at church. I had grown content to be alone my whole life. Of course, I was never really alone."

"You said Al had two children. What about his wife?"

Donna Grace nodded. "She had died of cancer about a year earlier. His family was here, so he moved back to Charleston where he would have help with the kids. They weren't even in school yet, poor things. They're great kids. Well, they're grown now and have kids of their own. I think of them as my grandchildren, even though they aren't mine biologically. I don't think that matters."

Victoria swung her feet, barely grazing the porch floor

with her toes. "So was it love at first sight? Was it a short romance?"

"Gracious, no. He needed to get over losing his wife, and I had to adjust to the idea of sharing my life with a husband and two children. We didn't marry until three years later. But God gave us thirty wonderful years together."

Victoria had dated Brian all through high school, nearly four years. Everyone, including her, thought God had brought them together. And look how that turned out.

Donna Grace sipped her drink. "Mmmm. You've learned to make real good sweet tea since you moved here."

She smiled. "Glad you like it. I only needed umpteen lessons from you. The first time a waitress asked if I wanted sweet or unsweet, I didn't know what she meant. We always called it iced tea up north, and you sweetened it the way you liked."

They swung in silence, the chains that supported the swing creaking against the hooks in the porch ceiling. Victoria listened to the grasshoppers and the children playing down the block. A pickup truck roared past, spewing fumes behind it.

"So are you pleased with Matt's work so far?"

Donna Grace's change of subject caught Victoria by surprise. "Yes. He's doing a wonderful job. I'm so grateful you told me about him." She swirled her glass and watched the melting ice cubes chase each other in a circle.

Donna Grace stopped the swing and set her glass on the porch floor. "I'm glad it's working out. Matt is a good man." She looked at Victoria, her forehead wrinkling. "He'll make a grand husband for some lucky woman."

Victoria's face warmed. What was this about? She wasn't looking for a husband. Three times had been enough. Besides, Matt deserved someone—well, someone less "experienced," with less baggage. "I'm sure he will. I'm surprised someone hasn't snapped him up already."

"Oh, there've been plenty of girls chasing him. But he told me he was waiting for God to send the right woman."

She snorted. "What makes him think that'll happen?"

"What do you mean?" Donna Grace pushed the swing with her foot, setting it into a gentle motion. "Sugar, don't you trust that God brings men and women together just as sure as he turns the world on its axis?"

"I used to think so. I thought Brian—my first husband—was God's man for me. Everybody said it was God's plan for us to marry. Our parents, people at church. Brian himself. Until he walked out on me after six months."

"I see." Donna Grace touched Victoria's arm. "That must have hurt a lot."

"It left me reeling. I feel like I've been on a roller coaster ever since."

"So that's why you quit going to church?"

"Pretty much." Victoria tried to stir up a breeze by pumping her legs to get the swing going faster.

"Tell me something, Victoria. Where do you see yourself in five years?"

"Five years? Seems to me they asked me that at my job interview."

The older woman chuckled. "I don't mean it that way. I mean in your personal life."

"Guess I haven't thought about it. I came here looking for a new start. I don't want to get married again, that's for sure. But I don't especially like living alone."

"I understand. It was really hard the first year after Al died. I had Max to keep me company, but that wasn't really the same. Once I got smart and started talking to God about it, I quit feeling so lonely."

Victoria shook her head. Talking to God didn't seem to be the answer for her. "Maybe I should get a cat."

That night in her apartment, she settled on the couch and

called home. A dog or cat might help pull her mother out of her depression. At least, she could suggest the idea.

"Victoria, I'm so glad you called. You'll never guess who I saw today."

Mother hadn't sounded so excited in months. "I can't even begin to guess. Just tell me."

"I went to the grocery store, just to pick up some bread and cheese. And there, in the dairy aisle, I ran into Brian."

A cord clenched Victoria's stomach. Mother still believed the divorce had been Victoria's fault. Maybe she'd been right. After all, his second marriage had lasted so far.

For that reason alone, they could never reconcile. But Victoria had been unable to stop her mother from persisting in that hope. After each of Victoria's breakups, Brian's name had come up again, as if he were the solution to her problems. Never mind that he and his new wife had two—no, make that three—children.

"His two boys seem so grown up now. And that little girl is just adorable." Longing laced her mother's voice, the desire for grandchildren she would never have.

Victoria finally found her voice. "Mother, please—"

"Oh, and here's the best part, dear. He's divorced now, too. He asked about you. And he told me he'd love to see you again."

No. She pulled the phone away from her head and rubbed her ear. She would not allow Brian to break her heart again.

She put the phone back to her ear. "I am not interested. I'm doing just fine down here, Mother."

"Of course you are, dear, but don't you think you could give him another chance? He's such a nice man."

He had not been nice when he left her. Nothing could change that. "We are not having this conversation. I called to suggest that you consider getting a cat. Or a dog."

Maybe a Pit Bull. Mother could name him Brian, since she

liked the man so much.

Chapter Twenty-Four

Victoria's muscles rebelled as she climbed the stairs to her office Monday morning. A whole weekend scraping and scrubbing, on her knees, or climbing up and down the ladder, had left her sore and stiff. Maybe she would take tonight off to rest.

She unlocked her office door and plopped her bag on the new desk that had arrived last week. Her office finally had taken on a professional, yet warm and inviting, look. This afternoon she would make the final presentation on the new tourism campaign to the Board of Directors. She probably should have polished it over the weekend, but she hadn't thought about it since finishing it up on Friday. She hoped she was ready.

Booting up her computer, she pulled up the PowerPoint slide show and started to review the presentation. Halfway through it, she froze. That transition made no sense. Wait. What happened to the beaches slide? She clicked through a few more then went back. Maybe it was just out of place.

No, it was gone. She continued through the slides, her mind whirling. She almost didn't realize that others were missing too. The ad highlighting Philip Simmons' gates. And the one for Fort Sumter. No one would create a tourism campaign for Charleston without mentioning Sumter.

No computer glitch would have caused those ads to disappear. Someone had tampered with her presentation. Only Victoria and Amelia had access to that file on the server. Victoria had tried to work with the woman, but this constituted outright treachery. She rose and charged through the middle office, past Jennetta's vacant desk.

Flinging the door to Amelia's office open, she ignored Jennetta and Leslie sitting in front of the desk, and looked straight at her assistant. "I need to see you." Her voice was too loud but she couldn't tone it down. "Right now. In my office."

She turned away and marched back the way she had come. She waited at the door until Amelia sauntered in, trailing orange-blossomy perfume as she passed.

Victoria slammed the door with a thud that made even her cringe. "What do you think you're doing?"

Amelia plopped into one of the guest chairs, her attitude indifferent. "I don't know what you're talking about, Victoria. Maybe you should explain why you're upset."

She stalked across the room and stood in front of her. "You know exactly what I'm talking about. You're trying to sabotage my presentation. I could fire you for that. I should fire you. You've gone behind my back one too many times. You're trying to ruin me, and I won't stand for it."

Amelia raised her eyebrows. "What makes you think I'm trying to ruin you?"

"You've disliked me since the day I came. You want my job, and you'll do whatever it takes to get it, won't you?"

Amelia stood, so close the friction made Victoria's arms tingle. "You don't know anything about Charleston. I don't see why the board thought you could do a better job of promoting Charleston than I could."

Victoria refused to step back, even though their closeness meant she had to tilt her head to see the other woman's face. "Besides the fact that I studied tourism promotion and have more experience than you? The fact is, they chose me, not you. And you don't have the right to go behind my back. Ever."

"You're spittin' into the wind. You can't prove I did anything." Amelia's eyelids closed nearly shut, all but obscuring the burning light in her eyes.

"I don't need proof," Victoria hissed. "You're the only

one with access and motive."

Amelia crossed her arms, brushing her sleeve across Victoria's face. "I don't appreciate your accusations. I think Uncle Smith would agree that you owe me an apology."

Victoria tried to catch her breath. Without solid proof, she had no grounds to fire the woman. But she had to do something, even if Smith Alexander objected. "Tomorrow, I will be writing up a warning notice for your personnel file. Right now, I have to repair my presentation."

She turned and strode to the door, jerking it open in silent notice of dismissal. Never in her career had she been so angry.

Disaster avoided, no thanks to Amelia.

Victoria had managed to replace the missing slides in her presentation in time for the afternoon meeting, and the Board of Directors had approved the campaign.

Two out of the three said they liked her ideas. As usual, Smith Alexander remained noncommittal, but he had—begrudgingly, it seemed to Victoria—voted to move forward. The man had a sadistic streak like his niece, no doubt about it.

Alone in the conference room, she packed up her laptop computer and wondered if she had energy left to get any sanding done in the house tonight. Probably not. By the time she got home, ate dinner, and changed clothes, it would be after eight. That was the problem with these late afternoon meetings. Taking a night off sounded better and better.

The conference room door opened and Lauren glided in. Surprised that she had come back, Victoria paused in wrapping up the computer's electrical cord.

"Victoria, I want to tell you that you did a fantastic job. Gary and I think your campaign is brilliant, and even Smith admitted that it has potential. Coming from him, that's a great compliment."

Potential? Smith had said that after he left the meeting? Apparently he didn't want Victoria to know he had anything positive to say. That was okay. Just the fact that he had said it to the other board members felt like a victory.

Victoria stuffed the cord into her computer case. "I'm glad you like it. Now that it's approved, we can start placing the ads."

"Yes, and that should get people to come for the Fall Festival."

Ah, the big festival. Her next test. "I hope so." She added the mouse to the laptop case and pulled the zipper closed. "If you have a minute, I'll walk out with you. Let me just put this in my office."

Lauren agreed, and she waited on the balcony while Victoria locked her office door. "How's the work on your house coming along?"

"It's fine. The contractor was finally able to finish the roof last week." Victoria's banker and Lauren saw each other at social gatherings, so she wouldn't admit her concerns about meeting the six-month deadline. Or about running out of money.

They started down the stairs. "That's got to be a relief. Now you can get the inside done without being worried about leaks. I'd offer to help you paint, but when my house was being restored, I found out that I am totally inept at painting. I got paint everywhere except on the walls."

Lauren didn't seem to be inept at anything, but Victoria couldn't quite imagine her wearing a paint-spattered t-shirt and jeans, either. "That's okay. I'll manage. My real estate agent has already offered."

"Really? I didn't know that was a service they provided."

Victoria laughed. She opened the door leading to the employee parking lot and inserted her key in the lock. "I don't think most do. But she's also become a good friend."

Lauren exited the building and watched as Victoria locked the door. "I'm glad to hear that. Restoring an old house is a lot of work, but it helps in making connections, doesn't it?"

Making connections … and a good impression. Victoria hoped bringing the old house back to life would help her to create a new life as well.

Chapter Twenty-Five

Ferreting out the stories behind the historical facts appeared to be Saluki's hidden talent, Victoria discovered. And she had a way with telling them in a few words.

Victoria had asked Saluki to come up with ideas for the new display as part of her internship. Historical tidbits could hold more interest for visitors than straight facts, she had explained. Saluki's results had captured her attention.

"You've done a great job with these." She handed the sheets of paper to Saluki across the polished cherry desk. "I've marked a few changes, but overall, I'm very pleased. I think these will really add to the exhibit."

The Friday afternoon sun had edged its way across the floor of her office, highlighting the still-empty bookshelf. A weekend of scraping and painting waited at the house, and Victoria needed to get started. But Saluki seemed to be lingering.

Saluki had not mentioned her boyfriend since the day when she had bruises. Surely she'd not let him hurt her again. Or maybe she'd received bad news about the scholarship to Charleston Academy.

"Is something bothering you, Saluki?"

"No, ma'am." Their eyes met and Victoria saw a flash of guilt—and pain. "Yes, ma'am. I was wondering ..." She shifted in her chair, fiddled with the papers on her lap.

Victoria waited, tamping down the desire to pull the question out of the girl's mouth.

"How do you hold onto a guy you're in love with?" The words seemed to rush out as if she had to expel them before they burned her lips.

The question pushed Victoria against the back of her chair. Wasn't that the question she had struggled with since Brian left? Saluki stared at her, waiting for an answer. But Victoria was the wrong person to ask.

"You can't." Her throat had dried up and the words sounded like sandpaper scraped across a wood rasp. She sipped water from the cup she kept on her desk and cleared her throat. She had avoided this subject for fifteen years, and it felt like digging up a dead body.

"I had the perfect marriage. Or so I thought. We—Brian and I—grew up together. Our parents were good friends. We all went to the same church, and he and I were inseparable."

She picked up a pen from her desk and pulled the cap off then put it back on. "We believed God had brought us together, and that we were perfect for each other. We got engaged our junior year and had a big wedding two weeks after graduation. His parents were just as thrilled as mine were." She dropped the pen on the desk and drank more water, noting how captivated Saluki seemed.

"Everything was great for about six months. We both started college that fall, and we were super busy. At first we studied together, of course, but since we had different majors and none of the same classes, he started studying with a group at the library."

She stood and paced across the office, recalling the end of the fairy tale. "Then, two weeks before Christmas, he packed his bags and told me he was leaving. He said he never should have married me, and he didn't love me."

Saluki groaned. "No way. That rots."

Victoria sank into her chair again. "I'm sorry. That's not encouraging, I know, but the truth is that it doesn't matter how much you love somebody. If they don't love you back, there's nothing much you can do."

That sounded like it came from a movie script. But it

wasn't something she had thought about before. At least, not that she'd admitted to herself.

"Yeah. But a dad's supposed to love you no matter what, right?"

Victoria blinked at the change from talking about romantic relationships to fathers. "You don't think your dad loves you?"

"Huh. The last time I saw him—no, the last time I was supposed to see him—we were going to meet at Hampton Park on my eleventh birthday. I was so excited. I got there thirty minutes early. Some of my friends were playing Frisbee but I had worn my best Sunday dress. I wanted to look nice for him. I hadn't seen him in two years. So I sat on a bench and watched them play while I waited."

Saluki clenched her fist and hit her thigh. "I kept thinking he just got delayed, maybe stuck in traffic, or car trouble, you know? My friends kept looking over at me. Majesty even came over and asked if I was okay. But I told her I was fine, that I knew my dad would come."

A tear leaked out of her eye. "I waited for two idiotic hours. Finally I gave up and walked home. The kids all stopped playing to watch me leave. How lame is that? They knew. They *knew*. My own dad stood me up."

Victoria kept silent for a moment, allowing Saluki's words the weight they deserved. "Did he ever tell you what happened, why he didn't come?"

"He called the next day and told Mama he forgot. He forgot his own daughter's birthday." She crossed her arms. "I haven't talked to him since. The biggest day of my year—my life—and all he can say is he forgot?" She shook her head. "What kind of a parent does that? He didn't even care."

Indeed. Victoria wanted to respond based on her experiences with men—all except her father. To tell her to forget about him, that he didn't deserve the effort she wasted missing him. But Saluki was too young to have to face that reality.

"I'm sorry, Saluki. He has no idea what he's missing by not spending time with you, getting to know you." And Brian had no idea what he had missed by walking out on Victoria.

Saluki brushed her hand across her eyes and blinked. "Hey, it's okay. I'm over that now. I've got Mama. And Dustin, if he stops being a jerk. That's all I need, right?" She grinned, drawing a curtain to hide the hurt. She held up the sheaf of papers. "I'll make these changes on Monday."

Victoria stayed at her desk long after Saluki had left the office. She couldn't understand a man who didn't love his own child. Hadn't God built that fatherly love into every man? But then, God didn't exactly act the way she expected. Maybe Saluki's father, like God, didn't love someone who stopped loving him.

But Saluki had not stopped loving her father, in spite of the way he treated her.

Not only were the stories behind the facts more interesting; they could also be more painful.

The envelope seared Saluki's hand every time she reached in her back pocket Thursday afternoon. She longed to rip it open and read the letter, but some part of her didn't want to know what it contained.

Today, working alone in the basement storage room suited her. She could take her mind off the question by playing her favorite radio station on the old boom box in the corner. The louder the better and no one would come down here to make her turn down the volume.

Besides, she didn't want to answer any questions about Charleston Academy. Even if the letter said she had won a scholarship, she hadn't decided if she would accept it.

With her left hand, she held a tack against the wood frame of the display backdrop she had built yesterday. As soon as she finished stretching fabric over the frame, she could arrange the photos to see how the completed exhibit would look.

Her internship provided a variety of tasks, but this was the first project she could say was her own. She'd suggested the idea of an exhibit about the women who made sweetgrass baskets. Then she had done all the research, taken photos of Aunt Ida and others, written the text, and built the backdrop. She'd even attached the Velcro strips that would hold the mounted photos in place. Of course, Victoria had reviewed each step of the project, but she had seemed pleased with Saluki's work.

She raised the small hammer and swung it at the tack, but instead hit her thumb.

"Owww." She stuck her thumb in her mouth, absorbing the sting with her tongue. Shoot, that worked for burns, not a misdirected hammer strike. She stomped her feet, trying to distract her mind from the pain in her thumb.

"Are you all right?" At the sound of Victoria's voice in the doorway, Saluki jumped and dropped the hammer.

She jerked her thumb out of her mouth and stuck her hand in her pocket. "Yeah. I'm fine. Just hit my thumb with the hammer." She gave a what-ya-gonna-do shrug.

"You want some ice? Let me look at it." Victoria rushed to her. The fragrance of lilacs reached Saluki's nose.

"Nah. Really, it'll be okay." Saluki showed her the red thumb. "These tacks are just so tiny, you know?"

Victoria laughed. "Tell me about it." She held out her left hand, waving polished nails. "I've lost more than one fingernail while building displays or remodeling houses. I had to start using acrylics."

Saluki didn't care much about her nails. She couldn't afford to get fake ones. Not yet, anyway.

The pain had subsided, so she bent to pick up the hammer and searched the floor until she found the tack she had dropped. Victoria moved to the boom box. "Mind if I turn this down so we can hear each other?"

"Oh, 'course not. Sorry about that. Since nobody else was down here …" As Saluki prepared to resume her work, Victoria returned to the display without a word and held the fabric in place. Carefully positioning the tack, Saluki hit it on the head the first time. She tapped it in. They repeated the process for a couple more tacks, and she grinned. "Thanks! That should do it."

"You're welcome. But I didn't come down here just to help you build this display."

"You didn't?" Of course, Victoria had more important work to do. Saluki turned to the table where she had stacked the mounted photos and captions she'd chosen for this exhibit. She wanted to see how all the pieces worked together before she moved the frame upstairs to the concourse. She chose one of the larger photos and placed it on the panel.

Victoria crossed her arms. "Mr. Danicourt just called me. He asked if you mentioned getting the letter from the academy."

Saluki jerked her head around. "Why'd he call you? Why not ask me himself?"

Victoria picked up one of the boards with text on it. "I guess he thought I should know. He told me the letters were supposed to be mailed yesterday. He sounded pretty anxious to find out what they said."

She took the board Victoria handed her and positioned it next to the photo. So Mr. D. didn't have the inside scoop on who had won scholarships. She picked up two more photo boards and placed them on the display.

"Well?" Victoria reached up to straighten one of the photos. "Did you get the letter or not?"

Saluki grabbed another piece of the exhibit from the stack on the table. "Yeah, it came today. But I haven't opened it."

"You haven't? Why not? Aren't you dying to know?"

"I'm not sure I want to win."

Victoria held an enlarged photo of Aunt Ida weaving a basket. "What are you saying? I thought you were excited about going to the academy."

She shook her head. "I've changed my mind." Not entirely the truth, but she was leaning in that direction.

"What happened?" Victoria placed the mounted photo in position and pressed it in place so the Velcro backing would grip the cloth display board.

Saluki handed her the next piece, a card with text describing the photo. "Nothing. I decided I'd rather graduate with my friends."

Victoria lined the piece up with the photo. "Hold on a minute." When she finished, she turned and grabbed Saluki's hands. "Now, listen to me. You're talking about one year compared to the rest of your life. Going to the academy gives you something you can't get at your school. An edge in life. Not to mention the money it will save you for college. Why would you give that up?"

Saluki didn't want to have this conversation. She had made up her mind. Victoria wouldn't understand. "I'd rather stay with my friends, that's all."

"It's not like you're leaving town. You can still see your friends on weekends, maybe even during the week sometimes."

No. They wouldn't even be her friends if she went to the academy. They had all but said so. "Wouldn't be the same. We've only got one more year to be together, and I want to go to classes with them, share all the big moments of senior year, you know?"

Victoria turned and paced the room. Here it came. The lecture from a big sister.

Victoria stopped in front of her and put her hands on Saluki's shoulders. Saluki was slightly taller, but she couldn't avoid being pinned by Victoria's gaze. "I understand how you feel. I remember how important all those senior moments seemed to me. They provide some precious memories."

Okay, so maybe Victoria could understand. A little.

"But believe me, Saluki, memories can't substitute for this incredible opportunity. And you'll make special memories wherever you go to school."

Saluki dropped onto a metal stool. The hard seat hurt but she didn't move. "My friends are already mad at me just 'cause I applied for the stupid scholarship. If I change schools now, I'll lose them." That probably sounded crazy to Victoria.

"Are you afraid that your friends will forget about you, like you think your dad did?"

She shouldn't have told Victoria about her dad. Now every decision she made would be connected to that. Although Victoria might be right. She was afraid her friends would forget her.

Saluki leaned over and propped her arms on her legs. "Majesty and I have been tight since third grade. We always hung out together. We just paired up with Dustin and TeeJay this year."

Victoria dragged another stool next to hers, the metal feet squeaking across the linoleum floor. "Okay. If Majesty has stuck by you all this time, why do you think she won't if you go to the academy?"

Saluki snorted. "Cause it's a foursome now. They'll find someone else to complete their group, and they won't need me anymore. That's what people do. They just quit on you."

"Hmmm." Victoria smoothed her short skirt then scooted onto the stool. "Sometimes people do that. I know."

"See? That's what I mean. It's like my dad leaving all over again." She couldn't keep the bitterness from her tone.

"I'm so sorry about your dad, Saluki. But it won't matter whether you change schools or not. If your friends care about you, they won't quit being your friends."

Saluki turned her face away to hide the tears that sprang to her eyes.

But Victoria had already seen. She reached for her face and turned it toward her. She pulled a folded tissue from her skirt pocket and offered it to her. "You think they'll be like your father, don't you?"

She took the tissue, wiped her eyes, then blew her nose. She nodded. "They said I would think I was too good for them. It feels like they're already pulling away from me."

Victoria wrapped her arms around Saluki, cocooning her in warmth. "I know it hurts. But if they would desert you because you go to another school, maybe they aren't really your friends. Or maybe they're jealous. But you can't let them determine the course of your life."

Now Victoria sounded like Aunt Ida. Saluki jumped up and began yanking the items off the display to get it ready to move upstairs. "If I stay, they won't have a reason to not be my friends."

"If they're true friends, they won't stop being your friends regardless. You need to decide based on what you want, not on what they might or might not do."

That made sense. Her friends just needed time to get used to the idea that she might go to a different school. She paused, clutching the stack of boards to her chest. "You think …?"

Victoria took the boards and set them carefully in a cardboard box. She turned back and gave her a quick hug. Her perfume brought more tears to Saluki's eyes—or maybe it was the hug. "I think you should open the letter and find out whether you're going to the academy next year."

Her fingers tingling, Saluki reached into her back pocket and pulled out the folded envelope. She slid her finger under the flap and ripped it open. With Victoria watching, she pulled out the single sheet of paper and read aloud, "We are pleased to inform you that you have been selected to receive a scholarship for full tuition—"

As the words sank in, she knew this was what she wanted. She looked at Victoria and screamed, "I got it!"

Victoria embraced her again. "I never had any doubt."

Chapter Twenty-Six

Victoria hated plaster dust. It coated her hair, her clothes, the floor. The white powder seeped under the closed door and floated throughout the rest of the house. Like the bitter undercurrent of resentment she felt at work, she couldn't escape it.

She stopped sanding the plaster wall and swiped her arm across her forehead above her goggles. She surveyed the parlor and shook her head. Two hours into the job and she was still sanding the first half of the front wall. At this rate, this room alone would take ten years to prepare for paint. Her bones ached and her muscles had grown accustomed to perpetual exhaustion.

Dong.

That pathetic doorbell again. She had to find someone to work on it. Maybe she should ask at the hardware store. She dropped the sanding block on the floor and brushed her hands on her faded jeans. Tugging the dust mask off her face, she let it drop below her chin but left her goggles in place. The plaster dust hanging in the air tickled her nose and made her sneeze.

The parlor door opened and Donna Grace's scarf-covered head appeared. "Yoo-hoo. Victoria, honey? Bless you." She entered and closed the door behind her. "Hope you don't mind, but I thought you might be in the middle of something and I'd save you the trouble of coming to the door." She pointed to her paint-stained jeans and frayed denim shirt. "As you can see, I came to help."

Victoria wanted to embrace her friend in gratitude, but that might make her seem desperate. In her family, adults hugged hurting children—or teenagers like Saluki—but not someone older who wasn't a relative. "You are just the ray of sunshine I need. I was getting ready to have a pity party."

"Well, then, let's get the party started." The woman's unending enthusiasm made Victoria laugh. "So what seems to be the problem and what are we working on today?"

Victoria swept her hand around the room. "This is the problem. It's a huge room. Between the cracked and chipped plaster and the old wallpaper paste, I don't think I'll ever get these walls smooth enough to paint."

"Uh-huh." Donna Grace meandered around the room, rubbing her hand across the walls. She studied a crack that stretched from the floor to the ten-foot ceiling. "Hmm." She turned to look at Victoria. "Are you a purist?"

"A what?"

"A purist. I mean, do you want to use only original materials? Do the walls have to be all plaster?"

Victoria glanced around at the original woodwork, the antique light fixture, the wavy glass windows. "No, I guess not. The house isn't a museum or anything. But what—"

Donna Grace came to stand in front of her. "Honey, with all your remodeling experience, I'm surprised at you. Don't you know that a little drywall compound will go a long way in covering up these cracks and rough spots? And it's a lot easier to sand smooth than this old plaster."

She felt as if she had tripped over a cement block. How could she have forgotten the times that Antonio had used the thin, doughy mixture to patch ceilings in those old houses? "Of course! Instead of sanding the plaster off, we put the mud on to make it smooth." This time she did hug Donna Grace, but in her excitement, she forgot the goggles were still in place and she hit her friend's head with them. "Oh, I'm so sorry." She pulled the offending equipment off and tossed it aside. "Did I hurt you?"

Donna Grace laughed. "I'm fine. I'm glad I could help.

Now, do you have any of that compound?"

She didn't, so they made a trip to the lumberyard for a five-gallon bucket, putty knives, joint tape, and two mud pans. After a detour to the Starbucks' drive-through, they returned to the house ready to tackle the no-longer daunting task.

As they worked, they shared stories about their week. Donna Grace had sold a two-million-dollar house and listed another one at three-point-five, amounts Victoria could barely comprehend. Sales like that happened rarely for Donna Grace, so she was happy for her friend.

Although Amelia had stayed out of Victoria's way all week, the atmosphere among the staff remained cloudy. "Most of the employees seem to be trying to decide which side to be on," Victoria said as she scooped more compound into her pan. "The thing is, they shouldn't have to choose."

"You're right about that, sweetie. One of these days, you're going to have to resolve the Amelia problem."

Victoria sighed and plopped a gob of compound on the wall. She spread it over a rough spot and feathered the edges to make it smooth. "I know. I'm trying to work with her. She has a lot of knowledge and could be a real asset if she'd stop trying to undermine me."

Working on the adjoining wall, Donna Grace spread a piece of tape over a crack and added some compound. "Sounds like you've done everything you can do, except for letting her go."

"Believe me, that has occurred to me. But if I let her go, I'm afraid it will cause even more resentment. She has lots of friends. And since she is Smith Alexander's niece, I don't think the Board will approve."

Donna Grace seemed to accept that and changed the subject. "Still seeing Randy Lee?"

"Yes. We went out to dinner Monday night."

"Hmmm."

"What is it?"

"I'm not sure that man can be trusted, from what I hear."

"What do you hear?"

She shrugged. "That he might be a womanizer. But mostly that he's a little shady in his business practices."

"That's just silly. How much could a carriage business cheat, anyway? It's all regulated."

For awhile, only the sound of their putty knives scraping on the wall broke the silence. Finally, Victoria said, "Randy Lee is kind and funny, and he pays attention to me. Unlike my first husband, Brian. First, he started ignoring me. Then he just walked out."

Donna Grace put down her putty knife and faced her. "Did it ever occur to you that Brian's the reason you choose men like Randy Lee?"

"What? Randy Lee's nothing like Brian."

"Exactly. You're trying to prove that Brian was wrong when he rejected you, but in your heart, you believe he was right. So you settle for the first man who looks at you."

Her face felt scorched. "He's not the first man to look at me."

Donna Grace picked up her knife and dunked it into the bucket of compound. "Of course not, sweetie. I'm sure lots of men would be interested. You're attractive and smart. You have a quality career, and you're a problem solver—except when it comes to your own life." She scooped mud from the bucket and dropped it in her pan. "From what you've told me, you've gone from one bad relationship right into another. I don't think you've given yourself a chance to just be you. No sense looking for a partner if you don't know who you are, and what you want."

"I told you. I'm not looking for marriage. Just companionship."

The look Donna Grace gave her could have melted an

iceberg. "Sure. But it's funny how a relationship can go somewhere we don't intend to go." She dipped the knife into the bucket again and eyed Victoria. "Especially if it's with the wrong person."

Victoria put her knife in the mud pan and set it on the floor. She hadn't asked for this lecture, and Donna Grace had no right to judge her. But she did want an answer to the question that had been burning in her since Brian walked out. "How do you know the difference between the wrong person and the right one?"

Donna Grace put the lid back on the bucket and pressed it down. "The right one will love you for all you're worth, treat you with respect, and be sincere and trustworthy. You'll feel like he would take care of you forever."

Victoria plopped onto the floor and leaned against the wall. "Brian did all those things. Until he didn't anymore."

Donna Grace dropped to her knees beside her and placed her hand on her shoulder. "Are you sure there weren't signs earlier? Before you got married? Some indication that he—I don't know—maybe he thought more about himself than he did you?"

That had been so long ago. Trying to remember made Victoria weary. She shook her head. "I don't know anymore."

"It doesn't really matter now, sweetie. You just need to give yourself time. Time to find out what you need and to eliminate anything that doesn't fit that need. You didn't deserve what Brian, or Antonio, or—was it Michael?—you didn't deserve the way they treated you. Now you need time to find out that you are worthy of better … And to learn that God loves you more than you can imagine."

Of course, she hadn't deserved the kind of treatment she'd received from her ex-husbands. But God hadn't come through for her, either. His love, if it existed, seemed far away. She wanted someone she could touch.

Maybe Randy Lee wasn't what Donna Grace expected in a man.

By the time Victoria reached her apartment that evening, her anger at her friend had cooled. She had to admit that she hadn't won any awards for her judgment in male companions.

But she had no one else. No one besides Randy Lee to take care of her. No other man in Charleston who really cared about her. Her eyes suddenly grew watery. She certainly had reason to feel sorry for herself. But what did her mother always say?

When life gives you lemons, make lemon meringue pie. She had tried to do that, and she would continue.

She picked up her cell phone from the table by the sofa and pressed "Favorites." She yearned for her mother's voice and listening ear, even if she had to hear, "I told you so."

Her mother picked up on the first ring.

"Hey, it's me." She couldn't keep the wavering out of her voice.

"Victoria! What's wrong?"

"Nothing, Mom. I'm just missing you … and Dad. How are you doing?"

"Oh, I miss him, too. Today was especially hard."

Today? Victoria looked at the date on her phone. How could she have missed that? This would have been her father's sixtieth birthday. She breathed deeply, grateful she had made the call tonight, even as weary as she was. Mom needed her tonight as much as she needed her mother.

Chapter Twenty-Seven

Time to make things clear. Fifteen minutes before the school bell rang Friday morning, Saluki met her friends outside the front entrance.

"We need to talk."

The four friends gathered as usual on the front steps. Saluki and Dustin perched on the concrete wall, and Majesty and TeeJay stood in front of them. "I've made a decision."

"Cool." Dustin wrapped his arm around her shoulders. "You're staying here next year, right, babe?"

She looked at him, touched his cheek. "Babe, staying here with you—" She turned to Majesty and TeeJay. "All of you, would be the best. Senior year together would be awesome."

"All right." TeeJay gave Dustin a high-five. "You were right, Dust. She came to her senses."

Majesty, who had always been tuned in to Saluki's thoughts, held back from the celebration. "I'm not sure y'all are listening to her. Let her finish."

"Thanks, Majesty. You know me well."

Dustin dropped his arm and turned to face her. "What are you saying? You're gonna do it? You're leaving us for the big time?"

Her entire body turned cold despite the sunny warmth of the May morning. She wanted Dustin, of all people, to understand why she had to take the scholarship. "I'm not leaving you. I'll still be around. We can see each other just like we do now. I just won't be in the same school."

She looked from his face to the others, where she saw the same disappointment and rejection. She jumped off the wall and stood straight, her shoulders back. "Listen, I'd really like you to be happy for me. But even if you're not, I hope you'll understand why I have to go to the academy. It's an opportunity I can't pass up. I'll be able to take more advanced classes and get college credit. That's huge, considering where I—where all of us—come from."

Majesty shifted her backpack from one shoulder to the other. "Yeah, we get that. It's just—well, it changes everything."

"How are we gonna hang out together when you're on the other side of town all day?" TeeJay hooked his thumbs in his belt loops and glared at her.

She would not back down now. She remembered something Victoria had said. "I know it will be different. But change is a part of life. This year, next year, it doesn't matter. Sooner or later, things would change anyway."

"But you're making them change sooner." Dustin's face reminded her of Tyler when he pouted because he didn't get ice cream when he wanted it. "You'll probably even find a new boyfriend at the academy." He emphasized the last word as if it were a poisonous snake. So much for her hopes that he might transfer, too.

"How can you even think that? You know we're meant to be together. We can make it work, even if I'm not here." She snuggled up to him.

"If you say so, babe." But his words left her wondering if he truly wanted to make it work.

The shrill siren of the five-minute warning bell echoed through the open doorway. Majesty tugged at TeeJay's arm. "Hey, we'd better get inside, or we'll be late."

Saluki picked up her backpack. "Listen, ya'll, this doesn't change our summer plans, right? We can still go to the beach and hang out together all summer."

TeeJay turned his head toward her. "Sure, Saluki. It'll be a great summer." But from his tone, she doubted that he meant it.

She turned to Dustin. "Are we okay?"

He pressed his lips together and nodded. "Yeah, babe. You do what you have to do. I'll deal with it."

Chapter Twenty-Eight

On the second Saturday morning in June, Victoria went to the storage shed to get the paint for the parlor. Today would be a good day, a milestone day. She would be able to cross the first room off her list by the end of the day.

Matt and his crew had completed their interior projects, except for the kitchen. They'd be installing the new cabinets next week. Her sweat equity would have to take care of the remainder, since she needed the rest of the bank loan to pay for scraping and painting the outside.

With Donna Grace's help, the parlor walls were ready for paint and, over the last few evenings, Victoria had varnished the woodwork. The excitement of almost finishing one room got the best of her, and she had determined to paint that room today.

Antonio would have insisted on sanding all the rooms first and painting everything at one time. But she needed one finished room to lift her spirits.

Even though most of the house still needed work, she had given notice on her apartment. This room would give her someplace to put her sparse belongings in two weeks. Easier to paint while the room remained empty.

She stretched, glorying in her backyard—her very own yard. After she finished the house, she would turn this space into a private retreat worthy of the Charleston Garden Club. New hedges and shrubs, some roses and crepe myrtles to go with the azalea bushes, maybe even a small pond with some fish. She could see it come to life as she stood on the back step, breathing in ideas along with the morning dew.

Sunlight streamers played peek-a-boo through the Spanish

moss hanging from the old live oak trees next to the shed. Somewhere down the block, a light breeze started a wind chime tinkling. When the breeze reached her yard, the branches swayed and bowed. Maybe she'd string a rope hammock between those two trees. A good place to spend a lazy summer afternoon—next year.

She turned to the lopsided storage building and saw that the rusty hasp that held the padlock hung uselessly from one bent nail. When had that happened? She yanked open the door and gasped. Yesterday, the shed had contained several thousand dollars' worth of lumber and paint. All that remained now were scraps of wood and two half-empty paint cans. She'd been robbed.

She yelled Antonio's favorite word, one she thought she'd never use herself. How could she afford to replace all those materials? She sank to her knees, and the knobby cement floor poked through her worn jeans into her skin. Tears streaming down her cheeks, she buried her face in her hands. The wind blew the door closed and she huddled in the empty gloom.

Chapter Twenty-Nine

Victoria still had lots of scraping and painting to do on the inside of her house, but she could get more done in the evenings after work if she didn't have the thirty-minute drive to North Charleston.

Moving to her new place could only speed things up for her. So, dressed in jeans and a faded UConn t-shirt, she scrubbed the toilets and the kitchen counter of the apartment. Then she picked up the last box full of cleaning supplies and locked the door for the final time. Her car was already packed with the rest of her belongings, a remake of her trip here five months ago.

She hadn't acquired anything since she'd come to Charleston. Until now. Now she owned a four-bedroom house. And a bed. She smiled at the thought of the brass bed she'd found at a resale store. Not one of the expensive antique stores on King Street, but a hole-in-the-wall junk store in West Ashley. The bed, though tarnished and bearing several dents, had been a find. With lots of elbow grease and polish, it would make a handsome start to her collection.

She had splurged on a good mattress set that would be delivered this afternoon. Boxes and suitcases would suffice as dressers for now. She would need to find a table and some chairs soon, though. She hated to eat standing up—or sitting on the floor cross-legged.

But the rehab fund was melting away faster than ice on the hot sidewalks. In order to replace the materials stolen from her shed, she'd had to cover the high insurance deductible. The police had given her no hope the thieves would be caught or any of the items recovered.

After letting herself into the house, she took the box of cleaning supplies into the kitchen and set it on the newly installed countertop. The extra cost of the dark green granite had been worth it; its rich color set off the warm tones of the cabinetry. Old and new cabinets matched perfectly, thanks to Matt's guidance on stain colors. The kitchen would definitely make the house a showplace.

But she had no time today to admire the progress. What should she do first? She looked up. Cobwebs in the corners. She needed to start at the top and work down. She'd been so busy refinishing the old cabinets that she had ignored the obvious.

As she retrieved the broom, mop and pail from her car, she noticed three teenagers watching her from the yard next door where they were smoking cigarettes. At least, she hoped they were just cigarettes. On one of her walks, she had met the man who lived there but hadn't seen these kids before. She waved and called, "Hello."

The girl said "Hey" and waved, but the two boys just jutted their chins at her in the way that teen boys seemed to think was cool. That was okay; there would be time to get to know them once she got settled.

Two hours later, she backed out of the last cabinet and dropped the sponge into the murky water in the pail. She could put food into the cabinets now that she had evicted the grime that had taken up residence there. At least the new cabinets had been easy to clean.

She added bug spray and shelf paper to her shopping list and thought of the remaining nine rooms. Cleaning the house would take forever, and she had barely scraped the surface of all the refinishing and painting it needed. The rehab loan required her to finish by the first of October. The project was too big for her, especially with preparations for the Lowcountry Festival taking up so much of her time. But she couldn't afford to pay someone else to do the work.

Her stomach growled. Why hadn't she thought to buy snacks? The yogurt she ate for breakfast didn't have enough calories for the kind of energy she needed today. At least she had brought some pop, and she pulled open a cold can of cream soda. She sipped the liquid, relishing the cool tingle on her tongue and throat.

She jumped when she heard a tap-tap at the front door, followed immediately by the door creaking open. "Yoo-hoo. Anybody here need some help?"

Donna Grace. She had promised to come, even though Saturday was a busy day for real estate sales.

Victoria pushed through the swinging door to the hallway and found Donna Grace holding a pail in one hand and a white Chick-Fil-A bag in the other. She wore Capri-length jeans and a paint-splattered cotton shirt. Her white hair was encased in a scarf. She waved the bag at Victoria. "Thought you might need some sustenance by now. Hope you like chicken biscuits."

Victoria grinned. "I'm so famished I could eat the bag and like it." She took the sack, opened it, and breathed in the aroma of warm chicken. "I am so glad to see you. I thought you might be too busy today."

"I told you I'd come, didn't I? I'd have been here sooner but the showing this morning took longer than I expected. This couple can't seem to make up their mind." She patted Victoria's arm. "Now, show me what you want me to do." She pushed open the door to the kitchen. "Oh, my. You've been busy. Looks like you're about finished in here."

"All that's left is to wash the floor," Victoria said. "I can do that if you want to start on the bathrooms."

"Why don't you eat? I'll finish in here. Just take your crumbs in the dining room so you don't mess up my clean floor."

By midafternoon, the two women had the main rooms

clean enough to move Victoria's things in from the car. Just as they carried the last two boxes upstairs, a horn honked out front.

"That should be Randy Lee with the bedframe." Victoria dropped a box of clothes she was carrying and ran down the stairs. Randy Lee had parked in front of the house and sat in his shiny monster of a truck, tapping out the beat of "Dixie" with the horn.

"Randy Lee," she called, but he couldn't hear her. She ran to the truck and yanked open the passenger door. "Randy Lee, stop that. You want the whole neighborhood mad at me?"

He looked at her and grinned, but he stopped tapping the horn. "Hey, sugar. You want to celebrate that you're moving in, don't you?" He slid across the seat and reached for her, planting a kiss on her lips. She backed away, and he hopped out of the truck.

"What kind of greeting is that for the man who has your bed?" He laughed at her discomfort then looked over her shoulder. "Oh, *she's* here."

She turned to see Donna Grace coming down the front steps. "Yes. She's been a big help today."

Donna Grace wiped her hand on her pants and stuck it out. "Hello, Randy Lee. Good of you to help Victoria."

He took her extended hand. "How could I not help when there are two southern beauties here?"

Donna Grace waved her hand. "You are a charmer."

"Sorry to interrupt this mutual admiration society." Victoria bounced on her toes. "But the people will be here with the mattress set any minute now. It would be nice to have the bed set up and ready before they come."

"Yes, ma'am." Randy Lee moved to the back of the truck and opened the tailgate. He pulled off the blue plastic tarp he had used to cover the pieces of the bed. Grabbing the two brass sections, he adjusted them under one arm. "I can take these if you ladies can bring the side rails and the slats."

Two long pieces of old angle-iron and three flat wooden boards remained in the bed of the pickup. Victoria took the rails and Donna Grace brought the boards, and they followed Randy Lee upstairs and into the largest bedroom.

Assembling the pieces took less than ten minutes. Randy Lee went back downstairs to wait for the delivery truck from the mattress store, and the two women began to polish the brass. Victoria soon realized bringing back the luster of the brass would take more elbow grease and polish than she had anticipated. Still, the knob-and-tube design fit the time period of the house perfectly.

They abandoned the polishing effort when Randy Lee announced that the rest of the bed had arrived. Once the delivery team left, Victoria removed the plastic from the mattress. Immediately, Randy Lee stretched out on top. "Ah, a good firm mattress. Just the way I like it." He patted the spot next to him and grabbed her arm. "Come on, sugar. Let's try it out."

Just as she swatted his hand away, Donna Grace walked in carrying three cans of pop. "I thought we could all use a drink." She came to a sudden stop and frowned, looking from Randy Lee to Victoria. "Did I interrupt something?"

"No, of course not." Victoria's face warmed. "Randy Lee's just kidding around. A drink sounds great." She took one of the cans, opened it, and gulped. "Thanks."

Randy Lee stood and took the can Donna Grace held out to him but didn't open it. "That's right nice of you, ma'am, but I've got some beer in the truck. I'll just put this back in the fridge for you."

Silence hung over the room until they heard the screen door downstairs slap shut. Donna Grace spoke first. "Well, I think I'll be going. Anything else you want help with before I leave?"

Victoria glanced around at the boxes that had taken over her bedroom. She grimaced. "No, I guess not. I need to find some sheets and make up the bed. Then I think I'll call it a day." She indicated the stacks of boxes. "I'll tackle this tomorrow. See if I can get organized before Monday."

"All right, then." Donna Grace nodded. "You won't want to cook tonight. You can come to my house for supper, if you'd like." Her voice sounded hopeful—because she wanted to get Victoria away from Randy Lee? Or because she wanted company? Victoria couldn't tell.

She shook her head. "Thanks, anyway, but I think Randy Lee's expecting to have dinner with me. We'll probably just grab some fast food tonight. I'm too tired for anything else."

Disappointment clouded Donna Grace's face. "I'll stop by one evening next week. Figure out what you want help with, okay?" She hugged Victoria and side-stepped as Randy Lee reentered the room, two beers in his hand. "Nice to see you again, Randy Lee." She scurried out as if unwilling to stay a moment longer.

"Something I said?" Randy Lee tipped his head toward her retreating back.

Victoria shrugged. "I don't think so. I guess she had things to do."

"Okay by me," he said. "Now we're alone." He offered her one of the beers, but she shook her head. He set it on the windowsill, popped the tab on the other one, and took a long drink.

Victoria found the box of linens and pulled out a set of flowered sheets. She moved to the bed and shook out the bottom sheet, letting it fall gracefully across the mattress. "Want to give me a hand?"

"Why, sugar, I thought you'd never ask." He set his beer down and moved to the other side of the bed, pulled the sheet over one corner, then the other, as she did the same on her side.

"Now that you've got this big old house, you might want somebody living here to keep you company." He winked at her.

She reached for the top sheet, searching for the right words. "I don't think so, Randy Lee. At least, not yet. I-I want to try it on my own for awhile."

He stepped back to the window and picked up his beer. Watching her, he sipped from the can. He wiped his mouth with his arm. "I hope you'll change your mind before too long. Neither of us is gettin' any younger."

The way her muscles ached from the day's physical labor, she hadn't needed that reminder.

Chapter Thirty

With only six weeks left before the Lowcountry Fall Festival, Victoria needed to show the Board of Directors that hiring her had not been a mistake.

For their monthly meeting, she provided printed promotional items along with tentative schedules for the week-long, multi-venue event. Victoria faced the chairman, Johnny Phillips, across the large conference table. The other members of the Board of Directors sat on either side of him. Next to her, Amelia fidgeted with her iPad.

As Victoria presented a summary of plans for the festival, the windowless conference room seemed to shrink. Despite gnats of worry flitting around her brain, she answered all their questions about logistics for parking, food vendors, and media coverage.

"Seems as though you've got things well in hand." Johnny closed his folder containing the plans. "Not that I'm surprised, of course."

The chairman's words blew a wisp of hope into her.

Smith Alexander, the bulky man next to Johnny, shifted in his chair. He stroked one thick, white eyebrow. "I have to admit, I am impressed. I didn't think you could pull it all together in such a short time."

She gripped the arms of her chair until her knuckles turned white. She felt, more than saw, Amelia trying to hide a smirk. Since the sabotaged campaign presentation, Victoria had been reluctant to include her in the regular briefings to the board. But sooner or later, the two of them had to start working in unison.

Victoria forced down the bile in her throat. "Amelia had

already done a lot of work before I came. Otherwise, I doubt we would be in such good shape." The color drained from Amelia's face. Good. Maybe giving her some credit would help thaw her attitude.

"Now, last year," Smith continued, "we didn't have enough porta-johns at Marion Square for the jazz concert. Have you made sure that doesn't happen again?"

"I saw the newspaper articles about that." She scanned her papers. "This year, we've ordered double the number as last year. That should prevent any problems."

"Good. I certainly don't want a repeat of that situation. Bad way to end a good festival."

"Smith, I'm sure you'll find something else to complain about." Lauren, on the other side of Johnny, softened her remark by leaning forward to smile at Smith. "I think Victoria has done a wonderful job. This should be the best Fall Festival yet."

"I agree." Johnny looked at a list in front of him. "Let's move on to the next topic—the Preservation Society's October house tour. Lauren, this is your item."

"That's right. I have a letter from the president of the Preservation Society." She opened a file folder and extracted several sheets of paper. She tapped them on the table and frowned. "It's not good news."

"All right, let's hear it," Johnny said.

"I'll spare you the formality. You can read it yourselves." She passed papers to the other two board members and handed copies across to Victoria and Amelia. "As you can see, the Preservation Society is expressing concerns about the tour. They only have half as many homes signed up as they did last year."

Smith scowled. "What seems to be the problem?"

"They're not sure if it's the economy or the cause they selected to share in the profits this year." Lauren held out her hands in the sign of surrender. "But they're thinking of canceling all together."

"Would that be such a bad thing? That would free up some of our budget for other things, wouldn't it?" Smith always seemed to be looking for ways to reduce expenses, as long as it didn't impact his favorite projects.

Johnny drummed his fingers on the table. "Maybe so, but the house tour is one of the major attractions between the Fall Festival and the Christmas season. I don't think the savings would offset the loss in prestige and potential visitors."

Lauren nodded. "That's right. Besides, they raise a lot of money for some very good causes."

Victoria watched the ping-pong discussion, unsure what her role was in this conversation. The Tourism Bureau had little involvement other than promoting the tour and providing seed money. She glanced at Amelia, but her assistant director seemed as puzzled as she did.

Smith picked up his coffee cup and leaned back in his chair. "Where do we fit in? There's not much we can do about it."

"Actually, there is. Maryann feels that four more homes would give them enough to make it worthwhile." Lauren looked pointedly at the two men. "I've offered to include my house, and I was hoping you gentlemen would agree to do the same. Then they would only need one more."

Coughing, Smith sat up straight and put down his cup. He cleared his throat and coughed again. "You know I can't sign up for that without checking with the war department."

Lauren jotted something on the notepad in front of her. "Fine. Why don't you call Lauraine right after the meeting? I'm sure she'll love the idea." She turned to Johnny and softened her voice. "What about you, Johnny? I know it's a hard season for you, but don't you think Ellie would have approved?"

Johnny bowed his head. When he looked up, his eyes glistened. "She had planned to sign up before … that last year, before she got the diagnosis. So, yes, in her honor, I'll do it."

Lauren leaned back and closed her folder. She gazed across the table. "Victoria, why don't you take the last spot?"

Victoria's stomach tightened. The tour was only two weeks after the bank's deadline, for which she had hoped to get an extension. "Me?" Her voice came out as a croak. She cleared her throat. "My house won't be finished. We can't possibly complete all the work in time."

"Your house is a fabulous example of the Charleston single house. It doesn't have to be finished. People will enjoy seeing the work-in-progress. Besides, it's for a good cause."

Victoria reminded herself to breathe. Lauren had been her chief cheerleader when she first came to Charleston. How could she turn her down? "What's the cause?"

"This year the proceeds are being shared with an organization that does Parkinson's research. The tour brings in over fifty thousand dollars."

Parkinson's. The cruel illness that had decimated her father and led to his early death. Of course she would help. Besides, being part of this tour could help her win acceptance with the city's leaders.

But she didn't want to show people a half-finished house, in spite of what Lauren said. She'd have to find a way to meet the already-tight deadline.

Chapter Thirty-One

Victoria had been warned about Charleston's summer humidity.

Sure enough, a series of steamy days forced her to close up the house and use the ancient window air conditioners. She couldn't accomplish much when she had to wipe perspiration off her face and neck every five minutes.

She needed to complete the downstairs rooms in order to draw more funds from the bank loan, and she'd had to postpone installation of the central air system until she could afford it.

After a busy week with meetings every evening, Saturday finally arrived. Donna Grace had planned to help paint, but yesterday, an out-of-town buyer had called her, wanting to spend the weekend looking for a home. Even without help, Victoria determined to get the dining room walls painted today. The sky blue color she had picked out matched the floral wallpaper she'd chosen for the entry hall.

She hauled the stepladder to the far corner of the room and set it up. She stirred the paint and poured some into a tray then wet the roller. The familiar latex odor assaulted her nose. As she prepared to start rolling, she realized she had forgotten a brush to trim the edges. Antonio always insisted that the trim work be done first.

After retrieving a brush from the closet where she now kept her paint supplies, she hefted the gallon can up the ladder. She dipped the brush in the paint and stroked it across the top of the wall in one smooth stroke, the way Antonio had taught her. She quickly became engrossed in the work, climbing down to move the ladder every few feet.

An hour later, she had nearly completed the circuit of the room. As she refilled her paintbrush, a horn honked next door. The sudden noise caught her off guard and she lost her balance. The paint can tumbled off the ladder. She grabbed for it but was too late. The quick movement threw her more off balance and she fell, landing hard on her knees in a puddle of blue paint.

Pain shot through her right leg and she cried out. Tears formed in her eyes and she spit out a curse. Just what she needed. A mess of paint and maybe a broken leg or something. And she had only trimmed out the walls. Not a single stroke with the roller.

Thank goodness she had spread plastic on the floor. That much paint would have ruined the wood floor, and she could have never scrubbed it all out. But at thirty-five dollars a gallon, she did need to salvage what paint she could and get it back into the can.

She tried to sit up but every movement of her leg shot sparks in front of her eyes. She swallowed the bile that rose in her throat. Michael had been right. She'd always been a wimp when she got hurt.

She needed help. Maybe the jerk who had honked his horn would hear her.

"Hello," she called out. But the windows were closed and the air conditioner was running. She summoned her strength and yelled, "Help! Help!" She stopped and listened. The revving of the car's engine mixed with the hum of the air conditioner. She was alone, with no one to hear her cry out.

Perhaps she could pull herself across the plastic-covered floor to the door. But when she tried, the pain shooting up her leg into her hip stopped her, and she screamed in agony. This was the result of her effort to move where no one knew about her past—no one knew her, period. No one cared enough to come check on her. She was alone once more.

When her scream subsided, she lay in the paint, alternately moaning and whimpering. Her mother would tell her to pray, but would it help? She had prayed when Brian left her, but it hadn't brought him back. She was on her own, as she always had been.

Only this time, she lay injured, unable to help herself.

Sometime later, Victoria thought she heard knocking. She couldn't tell how long she had been lying there, but the paint surrounding her had congealed on the plastic. The pain in her leg had finally subsided to a dull throb and she must have dozed off.

"It's open." Her voice sounded weak, far away. "Please, help me."

She heard the front door open.

"Victoria, it's Donna Grace. Where are you?"

"In here," she called. "The parlor. I fell."

"Oh, my gracious." Donna Grace rushed into the room where the overturned ladder and the puddle of blue paint running from the upended can told the story.

From where she lay sprawled on her side, Victoria croaked, "My leg. It hurts to move it."

Donna Grace knelt beside her, pulling out her cell phone. She grasped Victoria's hand and squeezed it. She smelled of powder and lilacs. Holding her phone in the other hand, she used her thumb to punch in the numbers. After reporting the situation and giving directions, she dropped the phone and placed her hand on Victoria's forehead.

Donna Grace closed her eyes. "Father, you're the Great Physician. You know what's going on. Please give Victoria relief from the pain until the ambulance gets here. And I ask you for her complete healing, in Jesus' name."

She stroked Victoria's head. "I'm so sorry, honey. I should have been here helping you."

Even though Victoria didn't think the prayer would make any difference, the words comforted her, and Donna Grace's presence reassured her. She wasn't alone, after all.

"You're here now. That's enough."

After hours at the hospital, Donna Grace insisted on taking Victoria home with her.

"You can't go up and down the stairs all the time," she said. "I'll fix you a cot at my house. It's not the most comfortable solution, but at least I can keep an eye on you."

Victoria appreciated the thought but she had work to do on her house. The deadline belonged to her, not to anyone else. However, with a broken kneecap and orders to keep weight off her leg for at least a week, she agreed. "Just for a couple of days."

Donna Grace helped Victoria into the house and onto the living room sofa. Propped against the arm of the couch with her leg cushioned by a decorative pillow, she leaned her head back and closed her eyes.

Donna Grace disappeared for a few minutes, returning with a green canvas-and-wood contraption.

She kept up a steady stream of chatter as she unfolded the military cot and set it up. "We have a couple of these old things. Al hated sleeping on one when we used to take the kids camping. But they belonged to his father, and I guess he felt like he had to use them."

The sound of her voice faded as the drugs Victoria received at the hospital pulled her into a haze. But worries about meeting her deadlines kept her from falling into a longed-for oblivion. Would the bank make concessions now that she would be laid up for a week? And what about the house tour? She had only two months, and she would need physical therapy—more time lost.

"Do you want to move to the cot now or stay on the sofa until bedtime?"

She forced open her eyes. Donna Grace stood over her.

Victoria squinted, saw that Donna Grace had found sheets and a pillow upstairs and attempted to make a neat bed on the cot. But the thought of moving again overwhelmed her.

"Stay here," she managed.

"All right, dear. Can I get you anything? Another pillow, something to drink?"

She realized her neck felt stiff. "Pillow."

Her friend retrieved the bed pillow from the cot and arranged it under Victoria's head and back, allowing her to recline more comfortably against the cushioned arm of the sofa.

"Thass better." She tried to smile then closed her eyes again. Donna Grace said something, but Victoria's mind couldn't focus on the words.

If her friend hadn't shown up today, she'd probably still be sprawled—she reached out a hand to touch her arm.

"Thanks for findin' me." Her hand dropped to her side and she fell asleep.

Sunlight streamed through the window and the fragrance of coffee tickled Victoria's nose, waking her to the beginnings of a throbbing ache in her leg as the painkiller began to wear off. She lifted her head and peered around. She lay on the couch in Donna Grace's living room. A cot with sheets tossed aside stood across from her.

She dropped her head back to the pillow. She remembered

falling off the ladder, the pain in her leg. Being all alone. But someone had come, had rescued her.

Donna Grace. And then she had stayed with her during the long wait at the emergency room. And she brought her here, helped her get comfortable on the couch. Beyond that, she remembered nothing.

She could hear footsteps in the hall, coming toward her. Donna Grace entered with a tray. She hoped that was coffee in the mug. She needed some. But she also needed something for the pain.

"Oh, good, you're awake." The woman's cheerful drawl soaked over Victoria like a cool mist on a hot day. "I fixed you some eggs."

She set the tray on the table and moved to help Victoria sit up, propping another pillow behind her back. "I thought you might want some more Tylenol, too. You want to keep enough in your system to keep the pain from getting too strong."

Victoria took two pills and the glass from her, sipped some water, and gulped the pills down. She had dreamed this exact scene—or maybe it had not been a dream. The realization hit her. "You slept on the cot?"

"Of course, sweetie. You seemed comfortable enough on the sofa, so I thought I'd leave you there. Unlike Al, I never minded sleeping on a cot." She rubbed her back. "Though my back isn't as flexible as it used to be." She picked up the tray and brought it to Victoria. "Here you go, dear. Try to eat something now."

Donna Grace pulled up a chair beside the couch and sat where Victoria could see her. "I used your phone to call Randy Lee. He's coming over. Do you mind if he stays with you while I go to church?"

Victoria took some eggs on her fork. "No, you go ahead. I'll be fine. Randy Lee can help me." She hoped her voice held more confidence than she felt. Randy Lee could be considerate most of the time. Surely he would help her now, when she needed him most.

Donna Grace nodded. "If you're sure. I don't have any showings scheduled tomorrow. I'll work from home so I can stay with you. You can't manage by yourself for a few days."

Tomorrow. She wouldn't be able to go to work. With only three weeks until the start of the Lowcountry Festival, how much damage would Amelia do while she was out?

The warm eggs tasted good, but after a few bites, the sleepiness returned. She pushed the tray across her lap. "I can't eat anymore."

Donna Grace took the tray and set it on the table, returning to help her get settled again. "Comfortable, dear?"

She nodded her head against the pillow. She tried to ask Donna Grace why she would do all this for her, but no words came out.

Whispered voices gradually pulled Victoria out of a snooze sometime later. When she opened her eyes, she found Randy Lee and Donna Grace facing each other, both unaware that she had woken.

"There's no need for that." Donna Grace, wearing a flowery cotton dress and heels, had apparently just returned from church. Standing with her arms outstretched, she looked like a mother tiger protecting her cubs. "She can stay here as long as she needs to."

"That's real nice of you, but I think she'll be more comfortable in her own house." Randy Lee towered over Donna Grace. "I can look after her and help work on the house at the same time."

Max jumped up on the sofa and stalked his way to Victoria's stomach. She reached out and stroked his back, and he began to purr.

They were making decisions for her. But Victoria's mouth tasted full of cotton, and she couldn't form any sound of protest.

Donna Grace's tone barely hid her disapproval. "I understand that, but what if she doesn't want you … moving in with her?"

Randy Lee's mouth tipped up in a half-smile. "Why don't we let her decide?"

Finally, Victoria managed to wet her lips and speak. "Let me decide what?" She tried to sit up but her body sank back into the cushioned sofa.

Donna Grace hurried to her side. "Let me help you there, sweetie." She put an arm around Victoria's shoulders and adjusted the pillows to provide support for her back. Max climbed down and skittered away. Victoria edged herself into a half-sitting position, leaning against the pillows.

From his position in the middle of the room, Randy Lee winked at her. "Mornin' there, beautiful. You took quite a tumble yesterday, didn't you?"

She must look anything but beautiful right now, but his grin sent heat waves through her body. "I guess I did. But what were you two talking about just now?"

Randy Lee strode to her and crouched beside the sofa. "I was tellin' Miz Donna Grace here that I could take you home and fix you up on your own couch. I can stay in the bedroom upstairs and look after you while you recuperate."

The brace immobilizing her knee seemed heavy and hot. She tried to move, but pain shot through her leg. She winced.

Donna Grace noticed and reached for the bottle of pills and glass of water on the table beside her. "Here you go. It's time for another pill." She shook out one tablet and handed it to Victoria then offered her the water.

Victoria took the medicine and considered Randy Lee's suggestion.

She didn't want to impose on Donna Grace much longer. But Randy Lee moving into her house? She'd been trying so hard not to let the relationship turn serious.

Randy Lee reached for her hand. "I'll help you get some of that painting done, sugar. And you won't have to be alone in that big house."

She groaned. The dining room must be a disaster after the fall she had taken. And she still had so much work to do. She couldn't get the house finished from Donna Grace's sofa.

She nodded. "That sounds good, Randy Lee. Thanks."

Donna Grace frowned. Victoria turned to her, felt the color flood her face as she realized what her friend must be thinking. But that shouldn't stop her from getting back into her own house. "Randy Lee's right, Donna Grace. It'll be easier if I'm right there to oversee the work. Besides, I don't want to be any more of a burden to you than I already have been."

"Honey, you aren't a burden. I enjoy being able to talk to someone besides my cat. You know you can stay here as long as you need."

Victoria reached out and squeezed her hand. "I appreciate everything you've done for me. Really I do. I just need to get back to some normalcy. And there are things I can work on at the house without being on my feet."

Donna Grace studied her then looked at Randy Lee. "Could I talk to Victoria alone for a few minutes?"

His brow wrinkled, but he nodded and rose. "Sure. I'll just go home and get some things together." He leaned over to give Victoria a peck on the cheek. "I'll be back for you in about an hour, sugar."

When he had gone, Donna Grace sat on the edge of the sofa next to Victoria. She stroked Victoria's forehead, brushing her hair off her face. "I know I sound like a mother now. But are you sure you want a man living with you?"

Randy Lee's teasing the day she had moved into the house flashed through Victoria's mind. But this was different. He knew it would be only temporary. And they would not be sleeping in the same room, much less the same bed. Her face flushed. "Don't be absurd. He's only doing it to help me. It's just for a week or so."

"I'm thinking about you. That big house will seem even lonelier once he leaves." Donna Grace squeezed her arm. "I just hope you don't regret this decision."

Chapter Thirty-Two

Already Victoria wondered if her friend had been right. She had been so anxious to get back to her own house that letting Randy Lee come take care of her seemed like the ideal solution.

After helping her get comfortable on the nearly new sofa she had found at a thrift store two weeks ago, he had returned to his truck. Even with her limited view into the hallway, she saw him carry in two suitcases, a duffel bag, and at least three cardboard boxes. How much stuff did he need to spend a few nights?

He thundered down the stairs and entered the room. "Can I get you a drink, sugar? Or something to eat? Got any food in the fridge?"

"I'm not sure what's there. But I could use something to drink. I need to take another pain pill. Maybe there's some iced tea or lemonade."

"You got it." He pivoted and left the room, returning a few minutes later carrying a glass of tea. He set it on the end table beside her, leaned down, and kissed her. From his pocket, he produced a brand-new bottle of ibuprofen. He peeled the protective plastic off the bottle and shook two pills into her hand. "There you go, pretty lady. What else you need?"

She sipped the tea and swallowed the medicine. This had been the right decision. Randy Lee would take care of her until she could get around on her own again. And she could get back to work on the house, instead of lying around on Donna Grace's couch all day.

Now, what could she do from a sitting position? She couldn't finish painting the dining room yet, but she could clean woodwork.

"Would you get some pillows and help me get situated in the hall? I could scrub the baseboard."

Randy Lee brought bed pillows from upstairs and helped her into position on the hall floor. Fifteen minutes later, after he poured varnish remover into the coffee can and retrieved her rubber gloves, goggles, and steel wool, she set to work. The position was awkward since she had to sit with her right leg propped on another pillow and twist her body to reach the baseboard, but at least she could accomplish something.

"Sugar, if you're all set, I'm going to go pick us up some food. There's not much in your fridge." Randy Lee stooped to kiss the top of her head. He stroked her cheek. "Okay?"

She could scoot along the floor on the pillow, and he wouldn't be gone long—she hoped. She nodded. "I should be fine for a little while. Thanks for doing this for me."

"No problem, pretty lady. I'm at your service for the next few weeks."

After he left, she attacked the woodwork with the wet steel wool. She had no intention of needing Randy Lee for "weeks," no matter how much she appreciated his attention. She had to get back on her feet, and back to her job. She had too much work to do, and too little time, before the Fall Festival, the bank's deadline, and the house tour.

A week later, Victoria saw the doctor again. An X-ray showed that her kneecap was healing properly. She had permission to return to work, as long as she continued to use the brace and crutches for a couple more weeks.

She would be limited in her activities, and would miss some work time for physical therapy, but at least she'd be in the office to oversee the final Festival preparations.

"Call me if you get tired, and I'll come get you." Randy Lee helped her into her desk chair late Monday morning after the appointment. He positioned a stool under her desk so she could keep her right leg elevated. "Take it easy, and let Jennetta get whatever you need."

He pecked her on the top of her head and left the office. He had been a huge help the previous week, finishing the painting in the dining room. He had promised to paint the laundry room today. She could get used to having his help all the time.

Now if preparations for the Festival were under control as well. She picked up the phone and dialed Amelia's number. "Can you come in and brief me on the Festival progress?"

A few minutes later, Amelia stood in her doorway, a frown on her usually impassive face.

Victoria waved her in. "Come on in and have a seat."

"Too bad about your leg, Victoria." Amelia dropped into a guest chair. "We didn't expect you back so soon."

"I'm just glad it wasn't worse. It was only a hairline fracture, and my doctor says it should heal quickly." She opened her file folder for the Festival. "The flowers from the staff were beautiful. I appreciate your sending them."

Amelia shrugged. "Sure."

Had Amelia's attitude thawed, or was she imagining it? "What can you tell me about the Festival?"

"It's all on track. Here's the status report." Amelia handed her the printed spreadsheet showing the tasks and what had been accomplished. "You'll see that we didn't miss a beat while you were out."

The attitude had returned. But from a quick glance at the report, it appeared that Amelia was correct. "This looks good. Let's review where we stand, and what needs to be done this week."

For the next half-hour, Victoria pried information from

Amelia, who seemed to regard each question as a challenge. When they had finished going through the list, she tucked the report into her folder. "Anything else that I should know about?"

Amelia rose. "Nope. Like I said, we managed just fine." She looked at her watch. "It's almost time for lunch, and I'll need to cover one of the stations at the information counter."

Victoria nodded. Meeting with Amelia always exhausted her, so she could use a break herself.

Jennetta offered to pick up a sandwich for her during her lunch break, and Victoria opened the most recent report on the advertising campaign.

The real proof, of course, would be hotel occupancy rates and attendance at Festival events. But so far, online impressions showed steady improvement. And "#LowcountryFestival" had been trending on social media. That was a great sign.

Around three in the afternoon, she felt her energy sagging. She phoned Randy Lee to come get her, but she got his voice mail.

"Hey, this is Randy Lee Johnson. You know what to do."

"I guess you're busy painting," Victoria said after the tone. "I'm ready to go home, so give me a call when you have a minute."

About fifteen minutes passed before her phone beeped. She punched the green button.

"Hey, sugar." His voice sounded tense. "Sorry I missed your call. I'll just need to clean up a little, then I'll come get you."

Sure. He would need to clean up the painting tools. "Thanks, Randy Lee. I'll be ready. No rush."

She had returned to work and found that all was well, while Randy Lee had painted. She called that a good day.

Chapter Thirty-Three

Clearly the Charleston Academy had been built by people with money. Although the three-story brick building was new, the columns and portico gave it the appearance of one of the elegant old homes south of Broad.

Saluki parked her faded pink Beetle in the far corner of the parking lot. Her mouth went dry at the sight of so many shiny Priuses and Mini-Coopers. The "Bug" had been cool at Central High where many students had no car. Maybe no one would notice her leaving it way out here.

Carefully trimmed shrubs lined the spotless sidewalks. Chrysanthemums in bright gold and red on the grassy hillside in front of the building formed a large "C" and "A." She had made it to the sidewalk along the side of the building when a girl jumped out of a parked blue Fiat as she passed.

She had darker skin than Saluki and wore her hair in a cute style with small tight braids ending in a mass of curls. Her teeth shown brilliantly in the middle of the biggest smile Saluki had ever seen. "Hi. I'm new here. Do you mind if I walk in with you?

Saluki stopped and shifted her backpack. "I don't mind, but I'm new, too. I won't be of much help."

"Okay, then we'll figure it out together." The girl joined her on the sidewalk. "I'm Julee, with two 'e's. I hate starting a new school my senior year." She had an unusual accent. British, maybe.

"Saluki. Me too."

Julee slipped her arms into her backpack and she and Saluki walked together toward the main entrance. "Saluki. That's a cool name."

Saluki grimaced. "It's a breed of dog."

"Really? I've never heard of it. It must be really rare. That's awesome that your parents wanted you to know you were special."

Rare. Special. She had thought the name degrading, like her dad thought she was no more important than a stray. "I guess so."

"So what's your story? I just moved to Charleston. How about you?"

Saluki shook her head. "I've lived here all my life."

"Then why are you starting a new school for senior year?"

She didn't want to admit that she was here on a scholarship. That would brand her immediately as lower income than everyone else. "My old school was … too easy, I guess. Here I can get college credit while I finish high school."

"So you're in the advanced track? Me too. Maybe we'll be in the same classes. That would be cool, wouldn't it?"

They reached the front steps and joined the stream of other students entering the building. Most were greeting friends and chattering about their summer. Saluki heard "beach" and "Europe" mentioned more than once. Although many of the girls showed off summer tans, Saluki felt as if she and Julee were two boll weevils invading a bale of cotton.

A tall blond boy wearing a navy blue jacket and tie held the door open for them. "Good morning, ladies. Welcome to another school year."

He looked sort of like Dustin and wore the same Axe cologne. Knowing that Dustin would not be here, the vacant spot in Saluki's heart burned.

"Thank you, kind sir." Julee led the way, and Saluki followed, nodding her thanks to the boy.

In the hall, Julee stopped and pointed to the main office. "I need to get my schedule. I didn't get registered until last Thursday, and they told me I'd have to pick up my schedule today."

Students flowed around them, some ignoring them and others giving them curious looks. Saluki pulled her schedule out of her pocket and then looked at the clock above the office door. "We've still got a few minutes. I'll go with you and find out if we have any classes together."

While they waited in the main office for a secretary to locate Julee's schedule, Saluki asked, "So where did you move from?"

"Seattle. My dad works for Boeing, and they moved him to help re-organize the plant here."

"Oh. I thought maybe you were from another country. England or something."

Julee laughed. "Actually, I'm from South Africa. We've only been in the U.S. for five years. My mum's a U.S. citizen, but my dad and I aren't. Yet."

The secretary returned and held out two sheets of paper. "Here's your schedule, Miss Foster. And here's a map of the school."

Julee laid the schedule on the counter. "Let's see yours. Are we in any of the same classes?"

Saluki unfolded her schedule and spread it out next to Julee's. "Look, we're in the same homeroom."

Julee ran her finger down the list. "And English, Math, Science, and Social Studies too! But you've got Art when I have Physical Education."

She touched Saluki's arm. "This is great. I'm so glad to have made a new friend already. We can even study together."

Saluki smiled. "Me, too. I was pretty nervous about coming here." She glanced at the room number for homeroom. "Three twelve. I think I remember where that is from the tour I got at registration. Let's go."

Somehow merging into the stream of kids rippling through the corridors seemed easier with a friend beside her. She could handle this new world after all.

Chapter Thirty-Four

Victoria heard the phone ringing but she couldn't find it. *Mother.* Her mother was calling her on the phone. Where was it? She had to answer. Mother needed her.

She forced herself to a sitting position. The phone continued to ring incessantly. *Don't give up, Mother. I'm coming.* Why did her right leg hurt? She couldn't move it.

Through the shadowy darkness, she could see that a sheet of some kind covered the window. But what was this room? And where was that phone?

She heard footsteps running down stairs.

"Victoria, come on." A sudden light exploded. She squeezed her eyelids shut. "Wake up, sugar. We've got to get out of here."

She eased one eye open. Randy Lee hovered over her. He handed her some crutches and lifted her to her feet. She nearly collapsed when she tried to put weight on her right leg, causing pain to shoot all the way to her hip.

The dream merged with the present and she tried to clear her mind. "What's going on? Why don't you answer that phone? Where are we going? Where's Mother?"

"It's not a phone, sugar." At her side, one arm on her back to steady her as she hobbled across the room, Randy Lee sounded worried, frantic. "It's the smoke alarm. There's a fire."

Fire. Now she understood. Her house! She would lose everything.

She halted in the hallway, leaned on the crutches, and looked toward the kitchen. A pungent electrical smell scratched her nose and throat. "We have to put it out." She adjusted her crutches and aimed toward the smoke. "We need buckets—"

"We can't, sweetheart." His strong hands on her shoulders shifted her, forced her to head for the front door. "I called 9-1-1. Fire department's on the way. We need to get out of the house."

Mutely she let him help her outside. Her mind went numb, helpless like her injured leg. He took the crutches from her and lifted her down the steps, carrying her away from the house until they reached the street. He set her back on her feet next to the light pole.

"Sugar, lean on this pole for support while I get your crutches, okay?"

The night air still carried the humidity of the previous day and she smelled wood burning in someone's fireplace.

No, not in a fireplace. In her house. In the structure itself.

As soon as Randy Lee returned, she grabbed the crutches and hobbled toward the corner of the house. She didn't want to watch, but she needed to see the damage for herself.

When she reached the driveway, she stared at the flames escaping the laundry room window, licking the side of the house. Her mouth felt swollen, her tongue thick and parched. Sirens screamed in the night, coming closer, turning on her street, just down the block.

But the blaze continued to eat away at her dreams, her future. Her eyes filled with tears. Randy Lee's arm came around her and she leaned into him, allowing him to take most of her weight. She felt like Scarlett O'Hara watching her city burn.

Victoria turned her face into Randy Lee's chest. Wetting his shirt with the tears streaming down her cheeks, she closed her eyes to this real-life nightmare.

Victoria could still taste the smoke as she sat in her living room waiting for the fire investigator to finish his tour of the house with Randy Lee.

With both hands, she hugged a paper cup in a cardboard sleeve, sipping the steaming coffee and trying to swallow the smoky grit that irritated her tongue. But she couldn't swallow the lump in her throat caused by this setback to her plans.

As if breaking her kneecap hadn't been enough to delay completion of work on her house, this disaster would surely keep her from meeting her deadline. She didn't even know yet how much damage the house had sustained.

Randy Lee had insisted that she wait here on the sofa, with her leg propped on a pillow. She was certain that electrical panel in the laundry room had been the cause of the fire. She should have heeded the electrician's warning.

Her leg throbbed from standing for hours as the firefighters battled the blaze. Randy Lee had persuaded her to sit awhile in her car, which he'd had to move down the block to make room for the firetrucks. But she hadn't been able to stay there. She had to know what was happening.

She'd crutch-hopped her way back to a vantage point in the street where she could watch the hoses spraying water onto the house, squelching the tongues of flame, then continuing to pour the saving liquid into the cavity until they were certain no sparks remained.

She had watched the streams of water flow down the side of the house, soaking the ground and running down the driveway. Dirty gray fluid eked out seams in the siding and around windows as hope eked out of her body.

But the house remained standing. Early this morning, the fire chief had even allowed them back inside. "I've taped off part of the second floor," he'd told her. "Don't go in that area until your contractor says it's okay."

Relief that she could stay in the house had overwhelmed her so that she couldn't even thank him. He'd removed the helmet with the "chief" label then flicked his blue eyes to her wrapped knee. "And ma'am, be careful from here on, you hear?" A smile twitched his lips. He swiped his forehead with his sleeve, replaced his helmet, and gave her a two-fingered salute.

Donna Grace appeared an hour later, bringing sympathy and Starbucks coffee. Randy Lee had called her, sensing that Victoria would need her presence. Now she waited with Victoria for the report from the inspector.

Heavy boots made their way down the stairs and Victoria tensed. From her nearby chair, Donna Grace reached over and patted her arm.

Randy Lee entered and stood opposite Victoria. The investigator filled the doorway then moved into the room.

"Miz Russo, Mrs. Collins." He nodded. "I can't tell you much just yet, but it looks like the fire originated at or near the electrical panel. It's pretty well unrecognizable now. Any idea who the manufacturer was?"

Victoria slumped against the back of the sofa and allowed Donna Grace to take the coffee cup out of her hands. She forced the name past her desert-dry lips, and the inspector nodded. "Thought it might have been. They're known for igniting spontaneously. Probably why the company went out of business. Somebody should have warned you."

"Somebody did," she muttered. "I was going to have it replaced next month."

The fireman whistled. "Bad timing. Sorry, ma'am."

Donna Grace showed him to the door, leaving Victoria staring at Randy Lee.

Overcoming her speechlessness, she moaned, "Your friend said it would be okay until he could get to it."

"Guess there's no way he could tell," he clipped. "But I'll help ya get it fixed."

"You'll have to." She gestured to her injured leg. "It's not like I can do much. But how will I pay for it?"

He shrugged. "You've got insurance, don't ya?"

"With a high deductible. I needed to keep the payments low."

"Well, then." He spread his arms wide. "You'll use the insurance money to buy materials and pay Matt, and I'll do some of the work to save you money."

She leaned back and sighed. She had few options. "Fine. But no more advice from your friends."

"Whatever you say, sugar."

Donna Grace returned and sat beside Victoria. "It could have been much worse, you know. It's a blessing that neither of you were hurt."

"She's right, Victoria. At least the alarm worked."

They were both right. But knowing they were safe didn't relieve her worry about restoring the house in time to meet her commitments.

Chapter Thirty-Five

"How long will it take to make the repairs?"

Victoria's voice sounded as irritated as her throat felt. She didn't mean to be impatient with Matt, but the fire damage increased her concerns about finishing the house on time. And the day was more than half over.

"I can't tell you yet." Matt's laconic drawl over the telephone aggravated her. She drummed her pen on her desk, waiting for him to explain.

"After I get over there and take a look, I'll call you back and tell you what the damage is. Have you called your insurance company?"

"Of course I did." Did he think she was an idiot? "They said an adjuster would be out this afternoon. But as long as we have photos, we don't have to wait to make the repairs. How soon can you get started?" Cell phone to her cheek, she adjusted her body in the desk chair.

Matt's crew had done craftsman-like work so far, but his work style seemed like that of a tortoise. Right now, she needed a rabbit's speed.

Even if the bank gave her an extension, she really wanted to be ready for the house tour—for her father. He had taken part in many Parkinson's studies to help find a cure, even though it wouldn't do him any good. This would be her way of helping, too.

But she had less than five weeks. Because her house was the only one of its style in this year's tour, the Preservation Society had billed it as one of the headliners for the event. She hoped showing off her restored house would gain her respect from the community. Besides, she didn't want to let down

Lauren.

"One of my crews was already scheduled to be there tomorrow." Matt's tone seemed a little sharper. "As soon as I can get there, I'll figure out whether to keep them going on the rooms upstairs or have them start repairing the fire damage."

She used her free hand to rub the knot forming in the back of her neck. She hadn't been sleeping well on the sofa, and the lack of sleep last night contributed to her irritability. She tried to bridle her impatience. "Okay, Matt. But—will you be able to work on the damaged areas and still finish the rest of the work?"

"Listen, I need to take a look. Then I'll figure out how to juggle my other jobs and put as many of my men on your place as I can. But 'til I get off the phone, I can't work all that out."

She held the phone away from her ear and studied it to see if it was steaming. He had never used such a heated tone with her. She put it back to her ear. "Okay, okay. I'll let you go. But call me as soon as you know something." She hesitated. "Please?"

"I will." His tone had softened. "I know you must be very upset. Sorry I spoke so rudely."

"That's all right. I don't mean to be so pushy, but I'm really worried about finishing everything on time."

"We'll do what we can. Call you later."

He clicked off, and she clutched the phone in her hand, rubbing the chipped finish of the green case. She had thought of replacing it, but between all the meetings and then her fall, she had put it off. Now it reminded her of the marred walls where the smoke had spread into the kitchen.

A quick rapping startled her. She looked up and found Lauren standing in the open doorway.

"Anybody home?" The tall blond, dressed in her usual Fashion-Avenue suit, crossed the six feet between them and bent to hug Victoria. "I'm so sorry about the fire, darlin'. I heard about it this morning. Are you okay?" She moved around the desk to sit in one of the two guest chairs. "Tell me what happened."

Victoria reached for her coffee mug and held it up. "Want some?"

Lauren shook her head. "Thanks, but I've had my quota already this morning."

Victoria sipped the lukewarm brew and wrinkled her nose. She set the cup back on the desk. She'd get a fresh cup after Lauren left. "The investigator thinks it was caused by a faulty electrical panel. Apparently that brand is known for starting fires."

"Oh, my goodness. You're lucky the thing didn't burn down with you in it. Were you asleep?"

Victoria's hand shook as she reached for her coffee again. The memory still frightened her. "I was dreaming … a nightmare really. I thought a telephone was ringing, but it was the smoke alarm. Thank goodness Randy Lee Johnson had been staying with me since I fell off the ladder. He called 9-1-1 before he woke me up and helped me out of the house."

Lauren smiled. "Thank God. You weren't hurt, then?"

She placed her mug back on the desk without drinking any. "A little smoke inhalation. My throat's sore today but nothing serious. But the house …" She shifted her leg on the low footstool under her desk, trying to find a more comfortable position. "I don't see how we can fix the damage and finish the other restoration work, Lauren. Not in time for the benefit tour."

"How bad's the damage? What's your contractor say?"

"I don't know." She looked up. "He's going over to look at it this morning. Said he'd call me when he knew."

"Don't you worry, honey. I'm sure the Preservation Society will understand."

She meant that Victoria should pull out of the tour. She

considered the idea, but it tasted like failure. She'd be letting down the tour organizers, ticket-buyers—and her father. She would not admit defeat. At least, not yet. "Maybe Matt can pull off a miracle."

Lauren pulled a folder out of her briefcase. "In the meantime, I've got something else to discuss with you."

Victoria didn't like her serious tone. What else could go wrong? "I could use something to take my mind off the fire, but I don't think I can handle any more bad news."

Lauren tapped the folder and cleared her throat. "I really hate to bring it up now, after all that you're dealing with, but … I think it's too important to put off."

Victoria's shoulders sagged. Had she offended someone, or had something happened while she was laid up? She leaned back in her chair and waited for Lauren to continue.

"I received this package yesterday. There was a note saying they sent it to me because you wouldn't do anything about it."

Victoria's skin crawled. She scratched her bare arm. "Who sent it to you? Why in the world would someone say a thing like that? I wouldn't do anything about what?"

Lauren frowned. "This evidence. It looks like fraud that you might be involved in."

Chapter Thirty-Six

"Fraud?"

The word caught in Victoria's throat. Heat rush to her face and the room whirled around her. She had done nothing wrong. Why would anyone think she had committed fraud?

Lauren nodded. "I'm sorry. I know this is bad timing. But—" She shook her head. "This is extremely serious." She handed the folder to Victoria.

She took the folder as if it were a hot potato. The first page was some sort of report. She couldn't make her eyes focus on the words. Something about carriage licenses. She turned to the next page. Photos of carriages. Blue with red fringe around their roofs, which bore the name of the company. Two Rivers Carriage Tours. Randy Lee's company.

She looked up at Lauren. "These are Randy Lee's. But what's the problem?"

Lauren leaned in and tapped her shiny coral fingernail on an enlarged photo of the carriage's license. "Look at that license." She flipped the page and pointed to a similar photo. "And that."

Victoria studied the two pictures side by side. It appeared to be the same carriage pulled by different horses. Er, mules. She couldn't see any other difference in the two photos. "So?"

"Look at the time stamps on the photos."

She forced her eyes to focus and compared the information printed on the bottom right corner of each photo. Same date, taken five minutes apart. She gave Lauren a questioning look.

"Both photos were taken as the carriages left the barn." Lauren paused, apparently expecting Victoria to see the significance.

The words swirled in her mind but wouldn't settle in any logical order. She tilted her head and squinted at the pages, trying to make sense of the photos.

"Victoria." The edge in Lauren's voice showed her frustration. "Two different carriages leaving the barn five minutes apart. With the same license number."

The meaning landed with a thud in her stomach. *Fraud.* Randy Lee's company had forged a duplicate license and put it on an extra carriage. She scrambled for an explanation. "Maybe—" Her voice sounded like an out-of-tune radio station. She cleared her throat and tried again. "Maybe something happened to the license plate and they hadn't had time to get a replacement—so they just did this as a temporary thing."

"There's more." Lauren reached across the desk and turned other pages in the folder. Page after page, side-by-side photos showed carriages with matching license numbers, taken a few minutes apart as they left the barn. "It looks like Randy Lee is running twice as many carriages as he purchased licenses for."

Victoria let the folder lay open on her desk. "I don't understand. How could he get around the lottery system?" She closed her eyes. "And why?"

Lauren stood and meandered around the office. "Why is the easy part. He avoids several hundred dollars in registration fees per year. More important, he can take in twice as much revenue and save thousands in tourism taxes since he only reports half of the carriage rides."

Victoria's stomach began to churn. "He's pocketing the tourism tax on the other half. And doubling the number of rides he sells." She did a quick mental calculation. "That could amount to a couple million dollars a year."

Lauren nodded and again took her seat. "Probably a

hundred thousand on the tourism tax alone. Not to mention the income taxes saved, since I would guess he doesn't report any of that income."

"But what about the lottery? Every carriage has to register at the booth and get an assigned route and a medallion. How could he avoid that?"

"I'm not sure. Someone has to be helping him. And, Victoria, that's the problem. The implication is that his help came from the top. From you."

"What?" She raised out of her chair but dropped back onto her seat, unable to stand up without taking her right leg off the stool. "How could I help him? Who said that I did?" She stared at Lauren, who met her gaze.

"I'm not saying I believe you did. That's why I'm here. The note was unsigned, of course, so I don't know who sent it. Though I have my suspicions. But it looks bad. Everyone knows you've been seeing each other since you started the job. And …" Her voice trailed off, and she looked as if she would rather be eating nails. "He applied for some licenses your first day. You signed off on them."

She lifted her injured leg from its resting place and rolled her chair back from the desk, putting distance between her and the accusations. Lauren didn't believe this nonsense. Did she?

That first meeting with Randy Lee replayed in her head. All she had done was sign a form. Everything looked in order. But she hadn't really known what she was signing. "No. I only signed the applications for four carriages."

Lauren rose and came to stand in front of her. "Whoever sent this package to me said you might have agreed to help him that day. Maybe even obtained the forged licenses for him."

"That's absurd! Why would I jeopardize my job when I had just started? I didn't even know the man then."

"That's the thing. The note suggested you knew him before you moved here. It seems … after you were here interviewing, Randy Lee made a trip to Connecticut. It looks suspicious, that's all. And … someone is trying to use it against you."

The temperature in the room seemed to be cooking her. She couldn't decide which made her angrier—the accusations against her, or the obvious fact that Randy Lee had used her. Had he gotten close to her in hopes of avoiding suspicion, or was he counting on her to look the other way? Either way, she had been blind—and stupid. Again.

She grabbed her crutches and struggled to her feet.

"Where are you going?"

She stopped and glared at Lauren. "I'm going to shut him down. Right now."

"No, Victoria. You have to let the city handle it. You can't let him know."

"If I'm responsible for approving licenses, I can unapprove them. And Randy Lee Johnson has just been unapproved."

Chapter Thirty-Seven

Victoria had to get to the carriage company barn.

It was only a few blocks away. No problem when she could walk but not a distance she wanted to attempt on crutches. Since Randy Lee had been driving her to work, she had no car available.

She took the elevator to the basement where she found Saluki mounting photos. Victoria asked if she was free to help her.

"Sure. What's up?"

"I need to deliver an official notice to Randy Lee Johnson. Would you mind taking me to his barn? I'll pay you for gas."

Saluki raised her eyebrows. "Of course."

When they reached the parking lot for the carriage company, Victoria hesitated. She didn't want the girl to see what could be an ugly scene. "Maybe you should wait for me here. I don't know how he'll respond to this notice." She patted the jacket pocket where she had placed the folded notice she had printed hurriedly from her computer.

"Can't be any worse than when my neighbors got evicted. Besides, you might need my help." She grinned.

Against her better judgment, Victoria agreed. They headed across the street and entered. The smell of hay and animals assaulted her. Country music blared throughout the large space. A man looked up from where he was raking straw. "Got tickets?"

Victoria shook her head. He pointed to the ticket office at the top of a short set of stairs. "You can buy 'em in there."

"No, we don't want a carriage ride. I'm looking for Randy Lee."

"He's gone out to the farm."

"Do you know when he'll be back?"

The man scratched his head then looked at the clock on the wall. "He's been gone a couple hours so I reckon anytime now. Guess you could wait up there if you want." He pointed to a small area next to the office where several crude benches lined the wall. A handful of customers waited for the next tour.

Victoria spotted a wheelchair ramp and Saluki helped her maneuver up it with her crutches. She found a seat between a family of three and an older couple. Saluki leaned against the handrail and watched something below her. After a few minutes, she turned to Victoria. "You should see these baby goats. They're so cute."

Most teenage girls went crazy over animals, especially baby ones. Victoria never had, and she had no desire to watch them now. Especially when the stench only made her think about Randy Lee. Did he really think he could take advantage of her and get away with it?

Saluki came to stand beside her. "Do you want anything?"

Victoria looked at the girl, grateful to have her with her. She should show her appreciation. "Would you like to go in the office and get something cold to drink?"

"Do you think they have a water fountain?" Saluki looked through the glass into the small shop.

"I doubt it." Victoria fished some currency out of her pocket. Since injuring her knee, she'd learned to carry money in her pants so she didn't have to manage a pocketbook in addition to the crutches. "Here, go buy something for yourself. And a bottled water for me."

A carriage pulled into the barn, discharged its passengers, and loaded most of the waiting tourists. A few minutes later, a different carriage came and went, heading out for another round of history and sightseeing. Which ones were legal and which ones weren't? It didn't matter, since she would be shutting down the entire business.

After about twenty minutes, Randy Lee sauntered through the large opening at the rear of the barn. Victoria stood, propping herself on one crutch. The movement caught his eye. She had never come to the barn before, and she could see the shock in his face when he saw her.

But his pasted-on smile never faded. He leaped onto the platform. "You're a sight for sore eyes, for sure. What brings you here today, lovely lady?"

He attempted to kiss her cheek, but she hopped backward. Men thought mushy actions could resolve any situation. She made her voice as icy as she knew how. "We need to talk."

He raised his eyebrows.

She glanced at the people waiting for tours. She didn't want to be the centerpiece of a public spectacle again. "Is there someplace private?"

He shoved his cowboy hat toward the back of his head. "Not really. We can talk in there." He nodded to the enclosed ticket office and store where Saluki was buying two bottles of water. Three other customers waited in line, but that was better than the dozen out here who were all watching them.

She grabbed her other crutch and headed for the door, fighting back tears. He probably wouldn't even apologize. Not for leading her on, making her think he cared for her. It had all been an act, a way to get close to her so she wouldn't look too closely at his operation. Once again, her loneliness had caused her to overlook the obvious signs. No more.

He hurried past her to hold the door open. Once inside, she hesitated, but the customers seemed preoccupied with their own business. Saluki came and stood by her but held onto the bottles of water. Randy Lee nodded to her. "Hey, there, Suki. You doing all right today?"

To her credit, Saluki didn't correct his pronunciation of her name. "Yes, thanks. Victoria, do you want your water?"

Her throat burned, but she shook her head. "Not right now."

Randy Lee shifted his feet, checked his watch, frowned. "What's this all about, sugar? I've got work to do."

"You took advantage of me, and you jeopardized my job! I thought you cared for me, but you only care for yourself. As of right now, your licenses to operate carriage tours are revoked." She pulled the folded cease-and-desist notice from her jacket pocket, unfolded it, and slapped it against his chest.

"What are you talking about, sugar?" He opened his arms as if to embrace her.

She held up her other hand to stop him. Nothing he could say or do would erase the humiliation. The new life she had tried to build here might still turn to ashes, if she couldn't prove her innocence. "You'll figure it out. You can only fool some of the people for so long before you get caught." She let go of the notice and the paper fluttered to the floor.

He ignored it and put his hand on her arm. "Can't we at least talk about this?" His eyes looked sad. Or perhaps worried. She didn't care. His pain couldn't begin to compare to her own.

"There's nothing to talk about." She shook off his hand and pointed to the people waiting in the barn for a carriage ride. "Refund their money and get your wagons off the street. You're finished."

Chapter Thirty-Eight

Between yesterday's sucker punch of Randy Lee's deception and the loneliness of the empty rooms, Victoria hadn't slept more than a couple hours.

A glow from the streetlamp reached through the window to the sofa where she had been trying to sleep. She held her watch up so she could read it in the sliver of light.

4:10. Less than an hour since she'd last checked.

With no one in the house to disturb, surely there was something she could work on. With an overwhelming burden of remodeling work remaining, she might as well get busy. How else would the big house be finished at all, much less on time?

Cicadas singing outside combined with an occasional squeak or thump. She knew these were typical sounds of the old house adjusting itself, settling down like an old woman whose bones squeak as she settles into bed. But for Victoria, the noises had become threats. Voices reminding her, *No one loves you. You'll always be alone. I never should have married you.*

She turned on the lamp next to the sofa and put her hands over her ears. She wouldn't listen. She pulled herself up, gingerly putting weight on her right leg. Then she limped to the CD player. Music would drown out the noises. And the voices.

The knee ached, but she could manage around the house without crutches. She would be seeing her doctor today, and she hoped to ditch the crutches and knee brace entirely. Which meant moving back upstairs.

What she really needed to do was get Randy Lee's things out of the upstairs bedroom. He had not come by to collect them last night, and she didn't want them cluttering up her space.

She waited until seven to call Donna Grace. Her friend's voice over the phone felt like a desperately needed embrace.

"Victoria, honey. How are you today?"

"To tell the truth, not so good. I need a ride to my doctor's appointment this morning."

"I'll be right over."

Donna Grace didn't ask for particulars. She just responded. By the time she arrived, Victoria had coffee ready.

They sat at the table and Donna Grace studied her. "You didn't sleep much."

Victoria grimaced. "Wasted my time putting on the makeup, huh?"

"No, no. You look fine to the average observer. It's just that I know you well." Donna Grace patted her hand. "Want to tell me what's going on?"

"I'm done with Randy Lee." She expected Donna Grace to smile or say, "Hooray." Instead, she looked at Victoria expectantly, compassion in her eyes.

Victoria told her about the photos and the showdown at the carriage barn. "I expected him to come by last night to get his things, but he didn't show. I'm glad, but now I've got to deal with all his stuff. I want to move back into my bedroom tonight."

Her appointment wasn't until nine, so they gathered some plastic bags from the kitchen. Then her friend helped her climb the stairs to pack up Randy Lee's belongings.

T-shirts and underwear formed a pile next to the open closet. Donna Grace pulled a green canvas duffel bag out of the closet and began to stuff the dirty laundry into it. "But tell me how you're doing, besides not getting much sleep."

"Lonely, I guess." Victoria dropped her crutches and limped to the dresser, gray Wal-Mart bag in hand. "It's not that

I'm afraid to be alone or anything. It's that I can't seem to get it right." She eyed the jumble of cologne bottles, hair gels and brushes, and belts that covered the dresser top. All belonging to Randy Lee. She scooped the entire lot into the bag

Donna Grace pulled an ancient brown suitcase out of the closet and thumped it on the floor. "My goodness. What in the world is so heavy?" She flipped open the metal latches, raised the lid, and gasped.

Victoria looked over at her. "What is it?"

Donna Grace shook her head. "You'd better come see."

Victoria hobbled to her side and stared down at clothes jumbled into the suitcase, cushioning a round, black object. "That-that looks like a cannonball. Why would Randy Lee have that in his suitcase?"

"Collectors will pay a few hundred for them, more if it has a special provenance." Donna Grace crouched down and fingered the metal object. "But I wonder why he brought it here."

A conversation with Randy Lee weeks earlier flashed into Victoria's mind. "He didn't bring it here. He found it here." Somehow, Randy Lee had managed to extract the cannonball from her attic rafter, either while she slept downstairs or when she was at work. "I told him about finding it in the attic, and that the Historical Society guy thought it might be worth a couple thousand dollars. But I never thought Randy Lee would try to steal it from under my nose."

She hobbled to the unmade bed and plopped on the edge of it. "Why do I keep getting stuck with these losers? What's wrong with me?"

Donna Grace closed the suitcase and latched it. "There's nothing wrong with you that's any different from the rest of us, honey. We all make mistakes, bad decisions. It goes all the way back to when Eve ate the forbidden fruit in the garden."

Sin. Victoria knew she'd done plenty of that. Even here,

where she had planned for things to be different. But she had failed. And this time, the cost might even be her career.

Donna Grace joined Victoria on the side of the bed. "Honey, there's a verse in the Bible that has helped me. It's from the Song of Solomon."

Victoria snickered. "The love song? That doesn't exactly fit now, does it?"

Donna Grace put her arm around Victoria's shoulders. "Hear me out. It says, 'You are all together beautiful, my darling. There is no flaw in you.' Now that doesn't mean we're perfect. None of us are. But it's God's way of telling us that He doesn't see our mistakes after He forgives them. But we have to ask for His forgiveness, and for His help not to repeat them."

Victoria didn't know how to avoid reliving her mistakes. She had proved that once again. No way God could see her as beautiful.

Chapter Thirty-Nine

The recorded music pounded in Saluki's ears as she entered the gym at Central High School where the annual "Back to School" dance was in full swing. Even though she was no longer a student there, Mr. D. had gotten her a pass to attend.

Her friends didn't even know she was coming, and she looked forward to surprising them. She had been busy with homework and her job, and she figured they had been just as busy. Dustin had made the football team. He'd had practice every day, so they hadn't talked all week.

She bounced to the beat and searched the crowd of dancers for Majesty or Dustin. Several other students waved to her or shouted "hello." It felt good to be back among familiar surroundings. She didn't mind the painted cardboard decorations and the paper streamers, although she suspected they wouldn't be good enough for a dance at the academy.

Across the room, Dustin's blond hair gleamed off the strobe lights as he gyrated with some girl she couldn't see amid all the pulsating bodies. Why hadn't he asked her to come with him? Then she wouldn't have needed the pass from Mr. D. She pushed that thought aside. He'd been busy all week, like she had.

She would wait until this song ended then she'd make her way over to him for the next dance.

"Saluki!" Majesty's excited voice in her ear startled her. She had been so intent on trying to see Dustin that she hadn't noticed her friend approaching. "What are you doing here?"

She turned to hug her. She had to shout over the music and laughter around them. "Mr. D. got me a pass. Isn't that great?"

Majesty pulled away. "Sure. Does Dustin know you're here?"

"Not yet. I just got here and—"

The music ended, and Saluki realized she was still shouting. She lowered her voice. "I see him on the other side of the room. I thought I'd go over now and surprise him."

"He'll be surprised, all right." Majesty tugged at the spaghetti straps on her sundress. "TeeJay's getting some punch. Why don't you come over and get some before you go see Dustin?" She grabbed her arm and pulled her away from the dance floor to the corner where the punch tables were set up.

"I don't want—" But Majesty held on tight until they reached the table where TeeJay held two cups. His mouth dropped open.

"Look who I found. She came to surprise Dustin."

"Hey, Saluki." He handed one punch cup to Majesty and held the other one out to her. "We didn't know you were coming. How'd you get in?"

Seeing they wouldn't let her go, she took the red plastic cup. "Mr. D. got a pass for me. He knew I'd enjoy getting together with my friends."

"Your old friends, you mean." He turned back to the table and picked up another cup. "You got new friends now, don't you?"

The punch in her mouth suddenly tasted vile, and she coughed, spitting it back into the cup. "I've made a couple of new friends, yeah, but you're still my friends."

TeeJay glanced at Majesty, doubt on his face.

"Look, Saluki," Majesty said. "It's probably better that you just leave."

Another song started, and she felt a headache coming on. What were they trying to tell her?

"There you are. We were looking for you. How come you

two aren't danc—" Dustin had come up behind her. When she turned, his face reddened. "Hey, Saluki. I didn't know you were coming."

He was holding hands with a girl she'd never seen before. White like him with blonde hair pulled into a ponytail, she exactly fit Saluki's idea of "perky."

"That seems to be the general consensus. I wanted to spend the evening with my good friends, and Mr. D. got me a pass." She stared at the girl as she spoke, but Blondie seemed oblivious. She kept tugging on Dustin's hand as though pulling him back to the dance floor.

Dustin seemed to remember his manners. "Oh, sorry. Saluki, this is Dawn. She's new this year. Dawn, Saluki used to go to Central, but she transferred to Charleston Academy."

She waited for him to explain that she was his girlfriend, but apparently she would be waiting a long time for that.

"Hi, Saluki. Nice to meet you." Dawn smiled at her but immediately turned her attention back to Dustin. "Are we going to dance some more or not? This song's almost over, and it's one of my favorites."

"Uh, yeah, okay." He looked at Saluki. "Excuse us. The girl's gotta dance." He gave a crooked smile and moved away, Dawn on his arm.

Heat climbed up Saluki's neck to the top of her head. Dustin had just dumped her without saying so. And only a few weeks ago, he'd told her he loved her. She looked around for the garbage can, found it at the end of the table, and tossed her cup into it. The punch splashed out onto her blouse.

"So that's why you didn't want me here." She stared at Majesty and TeeJay. "Because Dustin's moved on. I guess ya'll are a foursome now."

Majesty put one hand on her hip. "Now don't you go getting riled up at us. You're the one who left, remember. We stayed right where we've always been."

"Yeah. You're going to that fancy school now." TeeJay put his arm around Majesty's waist. "You won't be hanging around with us now that you got rich friends. You can't blame Dustin."

"Can't blame—" She sputtered. "The least he could do is tell me, not let me find out like this. I think I deserved that much." She shook her head. "Oh, never mind. I should be saying that to him, not to you."

She started to head for the exit when her words connected with her brain. Exactly. She needed to say it to his face. Just like Victoria had told off Mr. Randy Lee the other day.

She turned and searched the dance floor again. A slow song was playing now, and she spotted him with his arms around Dawn, his hands low on her hips. The taste of the punch rose in her throat again.

She turned back to the table and grabbed a full cup of the red stuff. Holding it carefully, she made her way through the dancers until she reached the couple. She tapped Dawn on the shoulder. "Excuse me a minute, Dawn." Her name might be appropriate, if she was good at washing things. When the girl stepped back, a puzzled look on her face, Saluki stepped up to Dustin.

"Thanks for telling me we were finished, Dustin. I guess that's how much love means to you."

She raised the cup and tossed its red contents into his face. He yelled and Dawn screamed. Punch ran down his Bruno Mars t-shirt and dribbled onto the polished basketball floor. Couples nearby stopped dancing to see what had happened, but Saluki ignored the rumble of questions and murmurs as she turned and stomped away.

She should have seen that Dustin cared more about having a good time than about her. Just like her dad.

Chapter Forty

Saluki's eyelashes stuck to her cheeks Saturday morning when she woke. She rubbed her eyes to get rid of the sandy feeling and pry open her eyelids. She squinted at the light glaring between the curtains.

What time was it? The aroma of cinnamon and apples tickled her nose. Mmm. Pancakes. Comfort food after the fiasco at the dance last night. She had cried herself to sleep. No wonder her face felt swollen and her nose raw.

She jumped out of bed. Who would be cooking? Mama had to work today, and Saluki should be watching the boys. They could burn themselves—or set the kitchen on fire.

Moaning, she pulled on sweatpants and a t-shirt. She rushed down the stairs, slipping on the bottom step. "Tyler, Isaiah, what are you up to? Are you trying to burn down the house? Why didn't—"

She burst into the kitchen and halted.

Mama turned, pancake spatula in hand. "Oh, good, you're up just in time. Pancakes are ready. Would you call your brothers for breakfast?"

"Mama? What are you doing home? You're supposed to be at work."

She gave her a crooked smile. "I called and told them I couldn't work today. Family emergency."

"What? What kind of emergency?" She looked around frantically. "Is one of the kids sick?"

Mama took four plates out of the cabinet and handed them to her. "No one is sick. We're going to have a special family day, that's all. Here, put these on the table, will you?"

She took the plates and clutched them to her chest. "But,

Mama, what's going on? You can't afford to lose that job."

"I know that, sweetie. My boss is understanding. It's not like I miss work a lot. Just the opposite, in fact."

Saluki shook her head. "But—?"

Mama patted her on the shoulder. "My family needs me today. That's all. Now, shoo. Set the table and call the younguns."

Breakfast took on an air of celebration. How long had it been since they'd all gathered around the table for a meal? Between school, her internship, and Mama's two jobs, they rarely got to eat as a family, especially in the mornings.

Saluki washed the dishes, and Mama hummed a tune as she rinsed and dried them.

"Want to talk about what happened last night?" Mama took a clean plate and held it under the scalding water streaming from the faucet. "You seemed pretty upset when you got home."

Her arms elbow-deep in suds, Saluki chewed on her lip. She hadn't thought about Dustin for a whole hour. Mama hadn't especially liked him. Would she understand the hole he had left in her heart? "I went to the back-to-school dance at Central."

"Mmm-hmm." Mama rinsed another plate and placed it in the drainer. "And it wasn't like it used to be."

Saluki grabbed the iron skillet and attacked it with a steel wool pad. "That's an understatement. My friends told me I had abandoned them, and Dustin had already moved on. He was with some new girl. Acting all huggy."

She steeled herself for the "I told you so." Instead, Mama tossed her dishtowel on the counter and put her arms around Saluki's waist from behind. "I'm sorry, sweetie. That hurts, doesn't it?"

She nodded, scrubbing harder. Mama gently took the cleaning pad from her. "You'll rub all the iron off that skillet if you're not careful." She turned her around to face her and put both hands on her face. They were the same height, so Mama's eyes looked right into hers. "Right now it feels like you won't ever get over him but, sweetie, you will. You just gotta take one day at a time. Trust me."

Mama couldn't know what this felt like. Could she? Besides, Saluki had not only lost her boyfriend, she had also lost her lifelong best friend. Her lips quivered.

"I know, sugar. You feel betrayed—not just by Dustin but by Majesty, right?" Mama always could read her thoughts. "You two have been friends forever. But I'm guessing if Majesty's the friend you think she is, that she'll come around."

"You think so?"

Mama nodded and picked up her dishtowel. "I do. And if she doesn't, then she's not worth frettin' over. Now let's finish these dishes and take the boys to the market."

They hadn't been to the old City Market for years. Saluki remembered when they would go as a family, back before Daddy left, and they wandered through the stalls, examining the various items for sale.

The last time, Daddy had given each of the three children a one-dollar bill and allowed them to pick out something special. She had found one of the many jewelry vendors and had selected a red-and-blue beaded bracelet. A couple weeks after Daddy left for good, the bracelet had broken and the beads had scattered all over her room. Several of them rolled into the furnace duct grate in the floor, and she dumped the remainder in the wastebasket.

The city had given the old brick buildings a face lift since then, but Mama had been too busy working to take them before today. At the end of the first market building, a boy about

Tyler's age hawked straw roses, calling out to passersby, "Roses, buy a rose? Only five dollar."

Nearby sat a wrinkle-faced woman in a multi-colored dress, weaving a sweetgrass basket. Letting the crowds swirl around them, Mama pulled Saluki and her two brothers into a tight knot and stopped to watch. Saluki thought of the basket she had found and repaired with her aunt's help. She should give it back to Victoria since it came from her house. Maybe next week.

They wandered into the middle building, which had been remodeled in recent years. Instead of wooden tables set up as temporary stalls in an open-air building like the first one, this building now boasted an air-conditioned space with permanent shops flowing one into the other. The smell of barbecue from one shop tempted them, but Mama reminded them it was too early for lunch. While Mama took the two boys to a toy store on one side of the wide aisle, Saluki stopped on the other side to look at a wall covered with hats.

She picked up a purple felt cloche and studied the price tag. She couldn't afford it, but she wanted to see how it would look on her. She tried it on, tilting it to one side, and studied herself in the mirror.

"That looks lovely, miss." The salesman had come to stand beside her, but when she saw his face in the mirror, her body turned cold. Was she dreaming? No, she could smell his Axe body spray.

His hair was thinner than she remembered, but this was the man who had played "horsey," letting her ride around the living room on his back. The man who used to take her to Folly Beach to hunt for seashells. Shock rippled through her, like the time she had jumped into the ocean water in March.

Did Mama know Daddy had moved back to town? Maybe he would try to put their family together again.

She turned and searched his face. Apparently he didn't

recognize her. "Daddy?"

Confusion flickered across his features. He looked away, seeming to study the display of hats.

"Daddy? It's me. Saluki."

He turned his gaze back to her. "Look at you. You're all grown up, aren't you?"

No hug. No "Nice to see you." Just unease. But what did she expect after eight years? "You're living here now?"

He reached for a wide-brimmed red straw hat. "Just moved back a couple months ago. Here, try this one." He held out the red hat.

He'd been back that long and hadn't even bothered to get in touch? She removed the purple hat and handed it back to him.

"I heard you're going to the academy this year."

She grabbed the red hat and set it on her head then turned to the mirror. "Really? I didn't know you kept up with me."

He adjusted the brim and tipped the hat to one side. "There. That's perfect for you. I saw the article in the paper about your scholarship."

"Oh." The article had been in the paper back in May. So he'd been around at least four months. Guess he had no plans to rejoin the family. She took the hat off and handed it back to him. "I can't."

"Don't you like it? Do you want to try a different style?"

He didn't want to talk about anything but hats. Nothing much had changed.

"No, I don't want a hat today, Daddy." She only wanted him to show some regret for having left them, for having missed out on her growing up, for not coming to see her when he came back to town. To offer to be part of her life from now on.

"Okay." He put the hats back on the display rack. "Well, you take care, you hear, Saluki?"

That was that. He moved off to help another customer. And she felt like her heart had ripped in two, just as it had when she had waited for him in the park and he hadn't come.

Chapter Forty-One

"I'm telling you, honey, there's a good man out there for you. You've just got to be patient and wait for God to reveal him to you."

Donna Grace handed Victoria a cup of cappuccino and turned to take her own cup of hot coffee from the server at the Starbucks drive-thru. Donna Grace had offered to spend Saturday morning showing her the best places to find bargains on furniture and other items. It was time to start decorating her house, now that several rooms were almost finished and the fire damage would soon be repaired.

"But why do I have such a hard time being patient? I promised myself when I moved here that I would not get involved with any man. I've been burned too many times. But I never seem to learn."

Donna Grace put the car into drive and pulled away from the window. As she eased into traffic on East Bay Street, she shook her head. "I know it's not easy to be patient, sweetie. Lord knows, it took me years to learn to be content with just God. And I couldn't have done it without his help."

Victoria sipped her drink and let the hot beverage scald her mouth and her throat. "I tell myself I am capable of living alone and managing life without a man. But I get so lonely. And then somebody like Randy Lee comes along …"

They turned onto a cobblestone alley that had never been paved over. The jarring action sloshed the liquid and Victoria quickly set hers in the cup holder before it could splash out the cover onto her hand.

"You won't be able—" Donna Grace's voice vibrated with each bump the car passed over. She held up her hand in the "wait" sign. She spotted an empty parking space at the end of the block and pulled into it. After backing into position, she shut off the engine. "Good. No parallel parking required."

She reached into the backseat for her purse but paused to gaze at Victoria. "I don't think you'll be satisfied until you find the one person whose love is always true."

How would she find someone like that? In the back of her mind, Victoria thought she'd heard the answer years ago, but she'd never understood it. Not then, and certainly not now.

She peered out the window at the crowded brick buildings along the street. "Where's the antique store?"

"It's more like a warehouse. Just two blocks down that way, by the river. You okay walking that far?"

"Sure. I just have to take it slow."

As they made their way carefully along the uneven sidewalk, Donna Grace told her about the large stone building where they were headed. "It was a cotton warehouse until the mid-1800s. After it fell into disrepair, the building was going to be torn down. But the father of the current owner bought it and restored it forty years ago."

Since then, she said, the family-owned restoration and antiques business had become well-known for the bargains to be found by someone willing to dig through the rooms of cast-offs in search of treasure.

"Just take your time and check out anything that appeals to you. We don't have to cover all three floors today. We can come back next Saturday."

Victoria shook her head as she followed Donna Grace up the brick steps. "I couldn't ask you to take another day off from work. I really appreciate your bringing me here today. I'll be able to find it on my own next time."

"You didn't ask me. I offered. I can schedule my house showings later in the day. If I have any next week. Business has been pretty slow lately." She pulled open the heavy metal door that bore only the word "Entrance."

Inside, the smell of old wood and dust greeted them. Heavy beams some twelve feet above them supported the next floor, and footsteps creaked across the wooden boards. From speakers hanging in the corner came the upbeat rhythm of oldies songs that locals called "Carolina beach music."

A middle-aged woman sat at an ancient wooden counter with a small laptop computer in front of her. "Good morning, ladies. Anything in particular you need help finding?"

"Thanks, Mazie, but no. My friend is looking for things to furnish the house she's restoring, but I think we'll just need to browse until we find something she likes."

The woman nodded. "If you need help, just ring one of the bells." She pointed down the long hallway, interrupted periodically by doorways. An old-fashioned dinner bell hung on the wall between every other doorway.

They proceeded toward the first opening and turned into a room where wooden doors of various sizes and conditions leaned against the walls. A narrow path led between the cast-offs to another opening. "I think windows are through there. You don't really need those, so we can skip these two rooms."

Donna Grace led the way to the next room. "As you can see, it's like a maze in here. I'll just let you look around, and if we get separated, just come back to the hallway here and I'll find you."

Victoria nodded. For the next half-hour, they wandered together, exclaiming over a marble fireplace mantel and studying some dusty Oriental rugs. Victoria decided on a carved wooden console table that would look lovely in her hallway and returned to the hall to ring the bell. By the time a man came and placed a "sold" tag on the table, Donna Grace had disappeared.

Victoria meandered on, stopping to examine an old stuffed wingback chair. But she decided it would need reupholstering, which she couldn't afford right now. She made her way past a couple of other customers and entered the next room then realized there was another room behind it. Donna Grace must have continued through there. She would catch up to her sooner or later. But this room, filled with old picture frames and paintings, captured her interest. Perhaps there would be some artwork here that she could afford.

She spotted a faded watercolor of mules pulling a wagon. Maybe she should buy it to remind her of Randy Lee. From the very first day she'd met him, her first day on the job, he had deceived her. He had sweet-talked her and wooed her, hoping she would never discover his ruse. How had she been so stupid?

You won't be satisfied living alone until you find the one person whose love is always true. Donna Grace's comment made no sense to her. If she could find someone whose love was true, she wouldn't need to live alone, would she?

Yet how could she tell? She hadn't done too well in the past. She had thought Brian's love was true, but he had left after only six months. And with Randy Lee, she had proven once more that she was not a good judge of character. And that she had no idea what true love looked like.

She forced herself to turn away from the farm scene. She definitely did not want a daily reminder like that. Weren't there any paintings here that would work in her house?

Some of the pictures leaned into other ones in haphazard stacks against the bookshelves that lined the wall. Others were piled on top of the shelves, with paper labels that identified each stack as "landscapes," "portraits," or "still-lifes."

Not sure what type of artwork she wanted, she spun around slowly, letting her gaze flick over the collection. As she turned all the way around, her breath caught at a life-size painting standing next to the door she'd entered.

The ornate gold-painted frame made her think that it must have come from an old church. A man in a white robe stood next to a stone well, both hands extended to a woman kneeling at His feet. Words lettered across the bottom of the painting read, "I am He."

From her growing-up years in Sunday school, Victoria knew that the man was Jesus, a Jew, who claimed to be the Son of God. The woman was a Samaritan, an outcast who had been married several times. More times even than Victoria. She had come to the well for water in the middle of the day, when no one else would be around.

But Jesus was there.

Mrs. White, Victoria's Sunday school teacher, had explained that Jews and Samaritans kept their distance, kind of like many blacks and whites in America. But Jesus talked to this woman. He even asked her for a drink of water. Then He offered to give her living water, which would never run out.

Victoria's eyes gravitated to the face of Jesus. He was looking at the woman in the painting, but she felt Him looking at *her*.

Jesus had known all about the Samaritan woman's life. Victoria grimaced. She had found it hard enough to tell Donna Grace about her failed marriages and the other poor choices she had made. She certainly wouldn't want a stranger to know everything about her.

But suddenly she wanted to confess everything to the man in the picture. Every bad choice, every hurtful word she had spoken, every vengeful thought she'd had. His face seemed so sympathetic.

No … sympathy was what she had gotten from her coworkers when Michael cheated on her. This was more like empathy—as if this man knew what it felt like to be betrayed—and compassion, as if He wanted to wrap her heart in His arms.

In His eyes, she saw love, love like she had felt from her father. Only more.

Victoria's heart almost skipped a beat. Could Jesus be the one true love that Donna Grace had spoken of? The one who could keep her from feeling lonely, who would comfort her during the long, dark nights?

Mrs. White had talked about a "personal" Jesus. One who let the little children come to Him, who wanted to know each of them, like a friend.

Suddenly, everything in the dusty room of the antique shop started to fade, as stories from Sunday school came flooding back. This Jesus, who had cried at the death of His friend Lazarus and then raised him to life again, who had turned water into wine for a wedding feast … He could fill the empty spot left in her heart when Brian abandoned her, when Antonio hit her, when Michael cheated on her, when her father died.

This was the same Jesus who had scattered the accusers of a woman caught in adultery then looked at the woman and said, "I don't condemn you. Go and sin no more."

Sin. Nobody liked to use that word anymore. But all it meant was poor choices. Mistakes. Doing things your way instead of God's way. And that's what Victoria had done for the last fifteen years. Hadn't she moved from New England to South Carolina, straight into the arms—and the deceit—of Randy Lee Johnson, even though she had promised herself that wouldn't happen?

Victoria ran her fingers along the folds of Jesus' robe as tears welled up in her eyes. She began to sob, uncontrollably, her body slumping to the floor near his feet. She was that Samaritan woman. She was the woman caught in adultery. And Jesus' hands were reaching down to her.

She tipped her head back and gazed into the eyes in the painting. Through the tears blurring her vision, Victoria saw in

His eyes a depth of understanding she had never seen before. She saw acceptance and forgiveness.

His eyes looked into her soul and loved her, despite the fact that she had stubbornly gone her own way. She thought of the woman in the Bible who brought the expensive perfume and used it to wash Jesus' feet. Then she had dried them with her hair. Victoria wanted to wash His feet, to kiss His hands, just to show Him that, like the woman in the Bible, she understood at last. And that she loved Him, too.

As a child she had thought she loved Him, but now she loved Him as more than a friend; He was her rescuer, her deliverer. She wanted to give Him control of her life, to trust Him completely.

Without thinking, she leaned into the painting. Her lips were on His feet, the sandaled feet of the Son of God whose love she had desperately needed all her life. Why had it taken her so long to realize her need for Him?

"I am He," the words from the bottom of the painting, filled the room. She could almost hear Him saying, "I am the one you are looking for." The love she had searched for filled her spirit, erasing all the years of insecurity and loneliness.

Chapter Forty-Two

The storm came up suddenly, bringing the fury of the ocean onto downtown Charleston.

The black sky darkened Saluki's mood even more as her family stepped out of the southern market building. They pushed back into the crowd of shoppers at the exit, all waiting for a break in the deluge.

Thunder rumbled through the market buildings and the downpour pounded the metal roofs. Vendors who kept the shutters open to allow breezes to flow through scrambled to close them as the wind threatened to blow the soaking rain all over their merchandise.

"Well, kids, we can make a run for the car, or we can go back to the hot dog stand, get lunch, and wait it out." Mama grinned, letting them know that she knew what the boys' choice would be.

"Hot dogs, please." Isaiah bounced on his feet, his short cornrow braids flying with the motion.

"All righty, then. Let's head that way."

They pushed through the people toward the other end of the building. Shoppers who had been caught outside had rushed for cover, filling the aisles beyond capacity. Saluki edged between a woman holding a poodle and a wooden table displaying necklaces and earrings. When they finally reached the opposite end of the building, they gathered with others waiting for a lull.

Saluki watched the downpour, sheets of rain appearing impenetrable. The water bounced off the pavement, rejected from its attempt to soak into the ground. Instead, it formed streams and little rivers that ran into the street and dropped through the grate into the storm sewer, lost in a larger flow headed for the ocean. She watched one raindrop until it disappeared among the million others.

"Saluki?" Mama's voice pierced her consciousness.

"Yes, Mama?"

"I said it's let up a little. Are you ready to go for it?"

"Sure. Let's go."

Mama led the way, holding a paper sack above her head as she jogged across the street between the buildings. Tyler and Isaiah followed, with Saluki last, making sure the two boys didn't lag too far behind.

When they were safely under the roof of the middle building, they jostled through the gaggle of people waiting to do the same thing in the opposite direction. Saluki brushed water off her shirt and wiped her hair with her hands. Tyler shook himself like a dog, sprinkling water onto Isaiah, who squealed in protest.

"Stop it, you two." Saluki caught Mama's questioning look and immediately regretted snapping at the boys. They weren't to blame for her bad mood. Thankfully, Mama just turned and led them through the door.

By the time they finished eating, the storm had passed, leaving behind a light sprinkle and puddle-filled streets. As they walked to the car, the boys ran ahead, jumping in puddles and splashing each other.

Mama held back to walk beside Saluki. "What happened back there?"

"Back where?"

"At the market. While we were in the toy store. You had started to relax, it seemed. But when you came back from the hat shop, you were as skittish as a cat hit by lightning."

"Oh." She scuffed her feet, deciding how much to say. Daddy had hurt Mama, too, leaving her with three children to raise alone. Did she already know he was back? "I saw Daddy.

He's working at the hat shop."

The intake of breath told her Mama hadn't known. "I'm sorry. What happened?"

Saluki shrugged. "Nothing, really. He showed me a couple of hats, said I looked good in them." She kicked at a wet paper on the sidewalk then bent and picked it up. A flyer for Two Rivers Carriages, the company that belonged to Victoria's friend. She crumpled it with one hand. "He read about my scholarship to the academy in the newspaper. That was about it."

Mama nodded. She pulled the keys from her pocketbook and jangled them. "Not the reunion you wanted, was it?"

She bit back tears. "Hardly. It was more like … seeing my first-grade teacher again after eleven years. He was surprised. And polite. But …"

Mama stopped at the car door and looked at her. "But what?"

She shook her head slowly. "He didn't seem glad to see me. Didn't care one way or the other. It was …" She swallowed, the words sticking in her throat. "Like I was just another customer."

"Kids, get in the car." Mama unlocked the door and shooed them inside then turned to her. "Saluki, sweetie, I know it hurts. But just remember, it's not you. It's him with the problem. Maybe he got a glimpse today of what he gave up, and he's afraid to admit he was wrong. He's been wrong for a long, looong time. He's missed out on seeing you grow into a sweet, smart, beautiful young woman. And don't you forget it."

Big sloppy raindrops started to pelt their heads. Mama laughed. "C'mon, let's get home and dry off."

As Mama maneuvered the car through the busy streets back to their neighborhood, Saluki gazed out the side window. As much as she didn't want to think about her dad, she couldn't help but wonder where he lived. And why he wanted nothing to do with her.

They passed from the posh manicured homes of the rich and famous, by the tree-covered College of Charleston campus with its elegant brick buildings, into their area of town where rundown, paint-deprived houses sat cheek-by-jowl with newly refurbished showplace homes. Someday Victoria's house would be one of those showplaces. Maybe her Mama's house could be, too. But not anytime soon.

Mama pulled the car into the driveway. The house looked like she felt—lonely and neglected. Yet she knew that love lived inside.

On the front porch, scrunched into a ball, sat a soaked figure, bare arms around the knees pulled to her chest. She looked up as the boys jumped out of the car.

Saluki caught her breath. Majesty! But why was she waiting on their porch, all wet?

"Hey." She stood up as Saluki approached. "I hoped you'd come home pretty soon."

Mama greeted Majesty and herded the two younger ones inside.

"What are you doing here? After last night, I thought—"

"That's why I came, Saluki. I felt awful about what happened. I've been waiting for you since about ten."

"You're all wet."

Majesty laughed, her voice tinkling up and down the scale. "You haven't lost your powers of observation. The wind was blowing way strong for awhile, and there was no place to get away from it."

"Why didn't you just go home?" She lived only three blocks away and could have run the distance in a few minutes.

She shook her head. "No way. I needed to be here when you got home."

"Why?"

"'Cause you're my best friend and always will be. I just

wanted you to know."

The varied shades of blue in the background of the old oil painting would fit perfectly with the main rooms of Victoria's house.

Upon finding her huddled on the floor in front of the picture and hearing her story, Donna Grace insisted on calling Matt to help bring it to the house and hang it for her.

"You can't not buy it, dear." Donna Grace held her cellphone to her ear. "It's priced cheaply because most people don't have room for such a large painting, or they think it's too religious. But it will fit perfectly in your parlor."

Victoria admitted she hated to leave it behind now that she had found it. Since it was short notice, she would pay whatever Matt asked.

Fortunately, the rain stopped by the time he arrived at the warehouse. Workers had wrapped yards of plastic around the piece and loaded it into Matt's pickup. Back at the house, Victoria and Donna Grace hefted one end while Matt, muscles in his arms rippling, managed the other end.

It took over an hour for Matt to install braces on the plaster wall to support the heavy frame and canvas. After the three of them maneuvered the painting into place between the two front windows, they stood back and admired it. The blue and white colors seemed to glow.

"It looks like He's right here in the room with you, Victoria," Matt said.

"That's right." She smiled. "I won't have to worry about being alone, will I?"

"You never did. But I reckon you didn't know that, did you?"

She shook her head slowly. "My parents always took me

to church, but I never understood how much Jesus loved me. Until today."

Matt started to pack up his tools. "Well, I sure am glad you figured it out. Does this mean you might come to church tomorrow?"

"I'll pick you up, if you'd like," Donna Grace added.

Except for her father's funeral, she hadn't been in church since Brian left her. But now, maybe it was time to try it again. She wanted to learn all she could about this new love she had found. "Thanks. That would be good."

Toolbox in hand, Matt headed for the door and she followed. "What do I owe you for this?"

"Not a cent. It was my privilege to help with this project. I'm glad Donna Grace called me."

"So am I." She held the door open for him. "I really appreciate it. I'll fix you dinner sometime to pay you back."

He grinned. "That's a deal, Victoria. A man gets tired of eating his own cooking."

She watched from the porch until he had pulled out onto the street then closed the door with a sigh. Why couldn't all men be like him, with no agenda? Just friendly and trustworthy.

After church Sunday, Victoria spent the afternoon scrubbing the stair handrail, removing decades of grime and built-up varnish.

Donna Grace's church had been nothing like she expected. But she had felt welcomed, and the sermon had been encouraging. Apparently, her judgment of church people in the "Holy City" had been misguided.

As she worked, she felt as though she was rubbing away years of mistakes and pain from her own life. When Brian had walked out on her, she had set out to prove that he was right—that she was unworthy to be loved by a really good man—if there was such a thing.

After several more failures, and the humiliating end of her third marriage, she came to Charleston determined to start over. At least that's what she had told herself. But she hadn't really worked at it, had she?

From the first day she met Randy Lee, she had let herself be used. By him, and by Amelia. The only positive step forward she had taken had been to buy this house. And she had almost ruined that by not replacing the electrical panel right away.

Fumes from the varnish remover made her light-headed. She dropped the steel wool in the can holding the liquid and climbed down the steps to open the front door. She breathed in the sultry August air.

Two boys rode by on bicycles, their legs churning like windmills as they raced to the end of the block. Determined yet carefree. She wanted to live like that.

Chapter Forty-Three

Victoria knew she had done the right thing. Still, heading to the city attorney's office Tuesday morning, she felt like she might be condemned to the electric chair.

She'd been here only seven months. Until she passed her one-year anniversary, she could be fired for any reason—or for no reason at all. If she lost her job, she'd have no way to make the payments on the rehab loan. And giving up her house would leave her no option but to return to Connecticut, where her past failures lurked around every turn.

She understood God's love now, and she didn't want to go back to her old life. Charleston represented a new beginning for her, in more ways than one. If she could prove her innocence in Randy Lee's scheme.

Wanting to make sure she looked her best for the informal hearing, she had dressed in her navy blue suit. She had wrestled to tie the new red, white, and blue scarf for the best effect, but that had put her behind schedule. An accident on King Street had backed up traffic, and she arrived with only minutes to spare.

When she rushed off the elevator on the third floor of City Hall, she nearly bumped into Randy Lee. He reached out his arms to steady her, but she stepped to the side.

What was he doing here? Surely he didn't expect to get his carriage licenses back. Not when the fraud was so blatant and the evidence so damning. Then there was his underhandedness in trying to take the cannonball.

"Hey, there, sugar. I was hoping we could talk before you go in there."

For the first time since she'd known him, Randy Lee wore

a suit—black pinstripes with a blue checked shirt and his usual bolo tie. Of course, he still wore his cowboy boots. But dark lines under his eyes made him look haunted. She wondered if he had slept since last Thursday, the day she shut him down.

"There's nothing for us to talk about. And don't call me 'sugar.'" She tried to proceed around him, but he stepped in front of her.

"Why, sure there is, sug—Victoria." He rubbed the back of his neck with his right hand. "You could put in a good word for me, can't you? I could pay a fine, license the extra mules, and we can forget this happened?"

She stared at him then shook her head. He had humiliated her, and his actions might yet cause her to lose her job. Did he really think she could forget? No more than she could forget how Brian walked out on her, how Antonio hit her, or how Michael cheated on her.

As she tried to brush past him, Randy Lee grabbed her arm. "Come on. After all I've done for you? Isn't there some way? I'll lose everything."

She glared at his hand on her arm, and he let go.

"Fraud, Randy Lee. Do you know the meaning of the word? You could go to jail. You implicated me by association. I could lose my job. On top of all that, you stole from me." She stormed past him, wondering how he even knew about this morning's meeting.

The receptionist showed her into the main office, a spacious room painted a sterile white. Framed certificates, no doubt from college and law school, decorated the wall behind the desk. The rumble of delivery trucks and honking horns filtered through large windows.

Mayor Stone and Smith Alexander, sipping coffee, sat on the prosecution side of a semicircle around the city attorney's desk. Only Lauren took the defendant's side, next to an empty chair meant for Victoria. She nodded and took her seat, folded her hands in her lap, and waited.

"You jeopardized the entire case when you shut down Two Rivers Carriage before we had a chance to investigate." Karen Sullivan toyed with a silver pen and looked around the room. She had assumed the top legal position for the city only a few months before Victoria had arrived. Now, in the role Victoria thought of as judge and jury, she seemed to be struggling for balance.

Lauren leaned forward in her chair. "Surely the photos would be enough evidence, Karen."

Mayor Stone, seated next to the attorney's massive desk, flipped through the photos. "These are clear evidence against Randy Lee, but they don't tell us who was helping him."

Victoria watched the volleys go back and forth and tried to swallow the thick mass growing in her mouth.

"Exactly right, Mayor." Karen laid down the pen and lifted her eyeglasses from where she had laid them on her desk, but she held them in her hand. "I was able to use the pictures to get a confession from Mr. Johnson."

So that was why Randy Lee had been here. The blockage in Victoria's throat shrank a little. But if he had already confessed, how did he expect her to help him? Besides, he could have lied about her involvement just to get even.

"I'm sure he cleared Victoria." Lauren leaned back and crossed her legs.

Smith Alexander, who had been observing until now, set his coffee cup on a side table. "What makes you so sure, Lauren?"

"Because I know Victoria, Smith. And so do you, if you'd just admit it. She's far more interested in helping the city than she is in helping herself … or helping a shady operator like Randy Lee Johnson."

Karen raised her hand to interrupt the discussion. "As a matter of fact, Mr. Johnson did not absolve Ms. Russo. But he did name the two individuals working at the carriage stand whom he paid off to provide him with fake tags and not record his extra trips. Both employees confessed. They've been terminated and have agreed to pay restitution, so we won't be filing charges against them."

Victoria barely heard the last part. Her mind stuck on the comment that Randy Lee had not absolved her. Yet he still thought she would allow him to continue operating? The man had some nerve.

"Ms. Russo." The attorney's voice got Victoria's attention. "Mr. Johnson would neither deny nor confirm your involvement. Do you have any idea why?"

At least he hadn't lied about her helping him. But what game was he playing? "I have no idea. Unless …" Of course. He would use his silence to get his way. She shifted in her chair. "He may be hoping to blackmail me into restoring his legitimate carriage licenses. He stopped me on the way in here this morning."

Lauren leaned forward. "Is he insane? He may go to jail, and he thinks we'll allow him to continue running his company? Not a chance."

Victoria focused on Karen. "I reminded him that he had committed fraud. There is no way I would let him start the tours back up. And I assure you that I knew nothing about what he was doing until Lauren brought those photos to me last week."

Karen put her glasses on and studied the papers in her file. "Without proof that you were involved, we have no reason to charge you as an accessory. However, if evidence should come to light …"

Victoria's shoulders slumped. The city attorney didn't believe her. This cloud of doubt would hang over her unless Randy Lee cleared her name. Like that would happen.

"We will be bringing charges against Mr. Johnson," Karen

continued. "That's the only legal action, for now."

"The media is all over this scandal." Mayor Stone blotted his forehead with a handkerchief. "It makes the whole system look bad."

"Absolutely, Jimbo." Smith pulled a newspaper from the briefcase next to his chair. "It was inevitable that the media would notice after Ms. Russo closed the carriage company. That left a lot of angry people without rides and overtaxed the other companies."

"That's not Victoria's fault." Lauren uncrossed her legs and crossed them the other way. "I believe the fact that she took quick action to shut him down demonstrates that she didn't know what he was doing."

Victoria nodded. She couldn't open her mouth for fear of spewing out something unpleasant.

Karen put her glasses on and looked at Victoria. "I agree. I find nothing to indicate that you were aware of, much less involved in, Mr. Johnson's fraud. Your quick action at least prevented further illegal operations."

Victoria felt the tension leave her body. She swallowed and the lump in her mouth dissolved. "Thank you for your faith in me."

The attorney cleared her throat. "The final decision, of course, is up to the mayor and city council, but I'm recommending no action be taken against you for thirty days. At that point, the council can review your situation and decide whether further action is warranted."

Thirty days. She just had to get through the Lowcountry Festival, then she would worry about what the council would do. With a successful festival, maybe she could keep her job.

Karen handed Victoria several sheets of paper. "I have put together this memo that outlines the procedures you should take if anything like this occurs again. We would not want a repeat of this scenario."

"Of course not." Victoria took the papers without looking at them. She would wait until she was alone in her office to read them.

"Mayor Stone, what do you think?" Karen looked at the mayor.

"I think it was an unfortunate situation." He shifted in his chair. "If no new information comes to light, I'll recommend that the council take no action against Victoria."

Victoria allowed herself to relax, for now. But she knew the cloud of doubt would remain over her unless she could find a way to clear her name.

Chapter Forty-Four

The festival had been a success. So far. Attendance at most of the events had increased ten percent or more over last year. Media coverage had been positive, and Victoria had received congratulations and thanks from business owners and two of the board members.

At the craft fair yesterday at Hampton Park, Smith Alexander's only remark had been, "Haven't heard of any complaints yet, Ms. Russo." Not quite a compliment but she hadn't expected to hear any praise from him.

Only one event to go—the Labor Day finale. Jazz at Marion Square. As she lay in bed, wide awake at four in the morning, she reviewed her mental list. Stage set up, check. Scaffolding for lights and sound, check. Technicians would be setting up the equipment starting this morning.

Musicians all in town and housed in local hotels, check. Mayor prepared to emcee, check. Weather? Who was she kidding? She had no control over that. Still, she reached for her phone and pulled up the weather app, smiling when she saw the column of suns until dark, and after that, only wispy clouds over the moon. High of eighty-four. Perfect.

What else? Porta-Potties. They should have been delivered last night. Fifty of the ugly blue beauties. With an expected crowd of five thousand, that should be enough. Without a repeat of last year's problem, Smith Alexander would not be able to find fault with her planning abilities.

She rolled over and punched her pillow back into position, pulled the sheet up around her neck, and closed her eyes. Everything was in order. She could use a little more rest. The concert wouldn't end until late, and she intended to make sure the equipment was all removed and the majority of the trash picked up before she left. She surely wouldn't get home until long after midnight. She tried breathing deeply, relaxing, willing herself back to sleep.

It didn't work. She threw off the sheet and sat up. No use kidding herself. Today was too important. No way would she be able to stop her mind from going a hundred miles an hour. She may as well start the day. She'd just swing by the park to make sure nothing had happened overnight.

Since it was a holiday, she didn't have to go into the office, though she probably would stop by. But she could dress comfortably for this long day. After showering, she decided on jeans and a red button-up shirt. Relaxed but not too casual.

Starbucks wouldn't be open this early, so she fixed herself a travel cup of coffee and headed out. Ten minutes later, as she approached the park, she finally loosened her grip on the steering wheel when she caught sight of the scaffolding, secured by guy wires. People had been killed at other events when heavily loaded scaffolding blew over in gusty winds.

No sign of the lighting and sound techs yet, but the sun also had yet to appear. The crews would be here in another hour or so. She cruised slowly down the block, nodding in approval at the row of blue stalls lined up side-by-side. Delivered last evening as promised.

In the dark, she couldn't see the ones on the other side of the park, but there should be three different sets of fifteen, and one set of five. Just to be sure, she counted the first row of portable toilets as she passed.

Eight. Nine. Ten. She braked. Had she miscounted? Maybe.

She checked up and down the street. No traffic. She put the car in reverse and backed up to the beginning of the row then drove forward, counting more slowly. Only ten.

Maybe there had been a misunderstanding, and the other

five from this set had been positioned across the park. That wouldn't be so bad. She turned the corner, peering through her headlights where they pierced the darkness. The streetlamps were no help, located so far apart. But where were the Porta-Potties? She reached the end of the block. Nothing.

Impossible. Her heartbeat accelerated, and her fingers gripping the steering wheel became moist. Deep breath. They had to be here somewhere. She squinted, searching frantically along the third side of the park for some indication that the missing facilities had been simply misplaced.

There. She spotted the shadows of more toilets mid-block and turned the car quickly up the one-way street. But as she drew nearer, she banged her fist on the steering wheel. She could already tell there weren't enough units. That only left the area behind the stage, the least convenient location of all. Who would be idiotic enough to put most of them there?

She counted this group. Ten, the same as on the opposite side. That would mean thirty Porta-Potties would need to be moved as soon as possible. At least the owner of the company had given her his mobile number for emergencies. She checked the clock on the dash. Five-thirty. She probably shouldn't call him until seven; that would still give him plenty of time to re-position the units.

But when she turned the final corner and saw the grassy space behind the staging, she stopped the car in the middle of the street. Clearly, the other thirty were not there. She jumped out, leaving her door wide open, and ran to the set of portable toilets.

"No, no, no, no!" She pounded on the door of one, as though someone might be in there who could help. Only five of the units had been located here. That meant they had delivered the exact same number as last year. Last year's fiasco would be repeated unless she could fix this, and fast.

Maybe they'd been stolen. She checked the grass in the

area, but saw no sign that anything heavy had been set there recently. Besides, who would steal Porta-Potties in the middle of the night? Or anytime, for that matter?

No, the company had screwed up. She had signed the rental order for fifty, but somehow they had only delivered twenty-five.

She had to call the owner right now. He would have to act fast to get the proper number delivered, and he'd need every minute to get it done. Besides, this was an emergency if she'd ever had one.

She returned to her car and moved it to the curb, then pulled out her phone. After several rings, she heard a sleepy voice. "Yeah?"

"Mr. Philips? This is Victoria Russo with the Tourism Bureau. Where are the rest of my Porta-Potties?"

He cleared his throat. "What do you mean, the rest of them? Aren't they at the park where we put them last night?"

"If you did, someone stole them overnight. There are only twenty-five here."

"That's what you ordered, ma'am."

"No. I ordered fifty."

"You did, but yesterday someone called and said there had been a change of plans and you were going back to the configuration you used last year. Two sets of ten and one set of five. I thought it was strange, given all the commotion last year, but—"

"Someone called? Who?"

"What? Oh, I don't know if we got her name. She said she was calling for you, so I figured you must know what you were doing."

Amelia. Sabotaging her again. It had to be, but she'd never be able to prove it. Right now, she just had to salvage the situation.

"I hate to tell you this, but I did not ask anyone to make

that call. What can you do to fix this? We need twenty-five more delivered as soon as possible."

"So someone played a prank on you? Got us, too, I suppose. I'm real sorry about that. Let me make some calls and see what I can do."

As she clicked off, Victoria realized this was a good time to pray if there ever was one. She needed God to help Mr. Philips get the additional toilets delivered, or she would be looking for a new job.

Chapter Forty-Five

Victoria completed her fifth cycle of the park's perimeter as the Philips' Porta-Potties truck delivered the final units under the noon sun. Fifty portable toilets, just as ordered, were now in place.

Walking the boundary of the park had helped to calm her while she waited. The audio technicians were starting their sound checks with the musicians, and food vendors were firing up their portable kitchens. Hot oil and cinnamon for fried pastries mixed with the aroma of seafood brought in for the Lowcountry Boil. She wanted to try some of that local specialty tonight, if her roiling stomach didn't rebel.

She continued her fast pace, detouring to follow the sidewalk that cut diagonally across the square park. In a few hours, throngs of jazz lovers would fill the grassy areas. Now that the blue containers had arrived, she could relax.

Actually, she wouldn't be able to relax until after the concert ended tonight. Or maybe after she confronted Amelia tomorrow. If she showed up today, Victoria would struggle to watch her words. She still could not believe the woman's jealousy had caused her to jeopardize one of the biggest events of the year.

"You look like you could use some lemonade." Victoria hadn't even noticed Donna Grace approaching across the grass. Her friend held out a paper cup with a plastic cover and straw stuck in it.

"How did you know?" She stopped walking and took the cup. "You're just what I needed. The lemonade is a bonus."

"Uh-oh. I thought that was some ferocious walking you were doing." Donna Grace sipped from her own cup. "Want to walk and talk or sit over there?" She motioned to a park bench a few feet away.

Victoria wanted to continue observing, to assure herself that everything was in order. "Let's walk—slowly though. I think I've overdone it with my knee, waiting for those portable toilets to be delivered."

Donna Grace took up position next to her, and they strolled toward the temporary stage. "Why on earth were you speeding around the park like that? I didn't think I would ever catch up with you. It looks like everything is ready, so what's going on?"

Victoria stepped over several cables strung across the sidewalk. She called to a gaffer working at a speaker nearby. "You'll make sure these cables are covered, right?"

The young bearded man looked up. "Yes, ma'am, as soon as I finish connecting them here, I'll take care of it."

"Thanks." She turned back to Donna Grace. "We almost had a total failure. You know about the lack of toilets last year, right?"

"Mercy, yes. It was a disaster. The media didn't stop talking about it for two weeks. I heard it was one of the main reasons the previous director left."

Victoria sucked on her straw. "I never heard that, but it doesn't surprise me." She pointed to the nearest row of Porta-Potties. "I had fifty ordered, but someone called and cut the number in half. Fortunately, I discovered it before dawn this morning, and the vendor just finished delivering the rest."

"Oh, my," Donna Grace said. "Any idea what happened?"

"I can't prove it, but I suspect Amelia is the one who called."

"What are you going to do about it?"

She turned to face Donna Grace. "What can I do? I can't accuse her of making the phone call without evidence. She'll complain to her uncle, and I'll be the one with no leg to stand on. Smith Alexander doesn't need much reason to fire me."

"I wouldn't be so sure about that." Donna Grace grasped her arm. "He may have had doubts, but he knows good work when he sees it. And you're doing good work." She gestured across the square where workers continued to check technical arrangements for the evening concert. "After this concert is over, Smith will have to acknowledge that you were the right person for the job. But you can't continue to let Amelia undermine you."

A gust of wind brushed Victoria's hair, and she turned her face up to catch the cooling effect. She pulled a tissue from her pocket and wiped the perspiration off her forehead. "I should have let her go weeks ago, when she messed with the slides in my presentation."

"Maybe. But you wanted to give her a chance to work with you."

"Right. I thought I could win her over. And … I know what it's like to be discarded like a used dishcloth."

They strolled in silence as Donna Grace appeared to be considering that. She stopped at a hibiscus shrub covered with orange-colored blossoms. She plucked a dead bloom off and held it between her fingers. "Do you remember last Sunday's sermon about the vine and the fruit?"

"You mean about pruning the branches that don't produce fruit?"

"Exactly. When Jesus prunes us, it is for our own good. He removes things from our life that are not fruitful. And I think sometimes, the best thing we can do for someone else is to prune the bad. By being truthful with Amelia and making her face the consequences for her actions, you could actually help her to grow. Hopefully she'll learn something that she will take with her to the next job."

"So you think I should fire her? But what about proof?"

"Oh, honey, you know she's given you reasons. She's

been uncooperative from the beginning. And didn't you warn her once before?"

"I did, but …"

"I'm sure if you write up all the struggles you've had with her, HR will back you up. You're the manager. You need to act like it."

She might be the manager, but firing Amelia without proof seemed so drastic. After all, the city had given her the benefit of the doubt on the fraud charges—so far, at least. Could she do less?

The final sad notes of the jazz music echoed in Victoria's head as she moved upstream against the crowds leaving the concert. Almost eleven o'clock and her knee ached, but she'd be here another couple of hours. She wouldn't go home until every last scrap of trash had been picked up.

By the time Charlestonians headed to work tomorrow, the only evidence of tonight's concert would be the blue Porta-Potties, which Mr. Philips had guaranteed would be removed no later than nine in the morning. When public venues were used for events, returning them to pristine condition as quickly as possible showed attention to detail and avoided criticism. She had learned that lesson in Waterbury early in her career.

"Thanks for helping. Want to trade bags?" She handed an empty trash bag to a short bald man who had been picking up trash and took his nearly full bag. She wanted to encourage the volunteers, mostly Rotary Club members, who had come out at this late hour to help with the cleanup.

Carrying the full trash bag toward the stage, which the contractors were quickly disassembling, she stopped to speak to other volunteers along the way. When she reached the dumpster behind the stage, the large green container reeked from the stale food and beer cups that had already been collected. Good thing it would be picked up in a few hours, before the garbage got too ripe.

"Hey, Victoria." Smith Alexander joined her at the dumpster and threw a full bag of garbage on top of the brimming container. He dusted his hands off. "I have to admit, the concert went smoothly. In fact, I haven't heard any complaints about any of the festival events."

"Of course not, Smith." Lauren headed toward them, shining a flashlight across the grass in front of her. "I told you Victoria knew what she was doing." She put her arm around Victoria's shoulder. "She was definitely the right choice for the job. This concert was wonderful, and the entire festival was a success."

Victoria glowed from her head to her toes, whether from Lauren's praise or from Smith's begrudging acceptance, she didn't know. Still, the knowledge that she had passed a major test reassured her, especially considering Amelia's treachery. Dealing with her assistant was a roadblock she still had to break through.

Should she mention the incident to Lauren and Smith? No. That would only sound like whining. She needed to handle personnel issues on her own. As long as she documented her reasons, even Smith would not be able to find fault with her actions.

Still, she recoiled at the thought of having to confront Amelia. That would not be an easy discussion, and she still wasn't sure what to say.

When she finally arrived home around one-thirty in the morning, she was too keyed up to sleep. She crawled into bed with a devotional book based on Proverbs that Donna Grace had given her. She turned to the reading for the previous day:

A wise person's heart controls his speech,

and what he says helps others learn.
Pleasant words are like honey from a honeycomb—
sweet to the spirit and healthy for the body.

How did she reconcile the Bible's advice about "pleasant words" with the idea of firing Amelia?

She read the author's comments about the passage, about choosing words from a heart of love, so that others might learn and grow.

Victoria grasped that. Every day, the truth of God's love amazed her. She understood that Jesus had forgiven her, even though she had chosen to walk away from Him, to live on her own terms. She had betrayed His love, and yet He had still loved her.

But hadn't she been betrayed as well? First by Brian then by other men in her life. And now by Amelia. How could she set aside her own feelings of betrayal when she confronted Amelia?

She re-read the last part of the devotional:

Tough love carried out with God's grace and in God's power can be transformative. It calls the other person to a higher standard, challenges her to turn away from sin and to the One who loves her as much as He loves you.

That was the answer, wasn't it? Amelia needed to be held accountable for her actions, but Victoria could act in love and grace.

Chapter Forty-Six

Victoria arrived at work at six-thirty Tuesday morning, her stomach churning like it had the day she started the job. But today would be different. Today, she would take charge.

She left a note on Amelia's office door asking to see her at once. Then she booted up her computer and searched the office intranet until she found what she wanted. She began preparing the forms.

After her long talk with God, she understood. What she was about to do might be hurtful to Amelia in the short-term, but in the greater scheme of things, it was the right thing to do.

Sometimes it didn't matter if words—or actions—hurt or not. What mattered was whether they were truthful and loving. Being honest with Amelia meant forcing her to live with the consequences of what she'd done. If firing Amelia cost Victoria her job, so be it.

So intent was Victoria on writing out her explanations for terminating Amelia that she hardly noticed when the clock in the concourse downstairs chimed eight times and the buzz of activity increased. Another hour passed before she finished and sent the e-mail to the human resources manager. Then she printed two copies. As she removed the pages from the printer on the credenza behind her desk, the clock struck nine.

Five minutes later, a knock was followed immediately by the door being opened. "You wanted to see me?" Amelia's sultry voice conveyed the usual dislike and lack of curiosity.

"Come in and close the door."

The woman sauntered in, pushed the door, and let it swing closed with a bang. She wore a two-piece purple dress that stretched tightly across her hips. When she plopped herself in one of the guest chairs, Victoria caught a whiff of her cheap cologne. Amelia sat back and crossed her arms.

She was making it clear that she didn't want to be here, and she was about to get her wish. Only she'd be leaving the organization, not just Victoria's office.

Victoria silently said a quick prayer and squared her shoulders, then she handed Amelia three sheets of paper. She kept the other set for herself. "I think this is self-explanatory."

Amelia scanned the top sheet. Her eyes opened wide, and she sat up straight. "You—you can't do this."

"I can and I am. I've already informed HR. You'll note that it's effective today."

"But—but …" She sputtered. "Uncle Smith—Mr. Alexander won't let you get away with this."

Victoria shrugged, refusing to acknowledge that she had the same concern. "We'll see what he thinks when he learns how you've behaved."

Amelia's leg twitched, as if she wanted to stomp her foot like a five-year-old. "You can't run this place without me. You got no idea what you're doing."

"That's where you've been wrong all along, Amelia. Not only do I know what I'm doing, but I know what you've tried to do as well. You have tried to sabotage my leadership at every turn. But no more. That is why you are being terminated."

"You can't prove—"

She held up a hand. "It doesn't matter what I can and can't prove. You have failed to cooperate with me in running this bureau. I tried to work with you but you resisted. You were determined to get rid of me and get the job for yourself. But it didn't work, did it?"

"But I've got twenty years here. I've got rights."

Victoria had anticipated that. But she had documented Amelia's infractions with dates and details. She had the high ground, even if Amelia's uncle defended her.

"Unfortunately, your years of experience didn't help you learn respect for authority. You were passed over for this job. You blamed me for that, but you have only yourself and your poor attitude to blame for your dismissal."

"What about my family? How will I take care of them?"

This was Victoria's one regret. But she knew she had made the right decision. She had to trust that God would show Amelia how to provide for her family. And that He would draw her to Himself, changing her attitude about future employment.

"I want you to know that I am sorry. You should have considered that before you tried to sabotage yesterday's concert. You claim to care about Charleston, yet your actions jeopardized the success of the festival. I won't allow you to have any more opportunities to ruin tourism for the city. You'll need to clear out your office within the hour."

Victoria rose and walked to the door, willing her weak knee to support her.

Amelia jerked to her feet and tossed her head, shaking loose a section of her poufy hairdo. She gave Victoria a glare that could have melted butter. "You won't get away with this, Ms. Yankee."

Victoria opened the door and waited for Amelia to walk through it. "It's already done, Amelia. Good-bye."

She closed the door and collapsed against it, tension leaving her body. As difficult as the conversation had been, Victoria knew she had finally found her footing here in her new city.

Saluki knew something was up when she entered the employee break room Tuesday afternoon. The usual buzz was more of a whisper.

"Hey, John, what's going on?" She sat down with the older man, whom she had helped post new signs directing visitors to the tour bus waiting area a couple weeks ago.

He looked around, but the room had emptied out quickly. "Amelia's gone." His deep voice rumbled with uncertainty. "Nobody knows what happened. She packed her stuff in a box and stormed outta here this morning."

He rose and dumped his coffee in the sink. "Everybody's wondering who's next. But so far, no one else has been called upstairs. I'd tread lightly if I were you."

Saluki smiled. "Sure. You, too."

So Victoria had finally done it. What she needed to do several months ago, Saluki figured.

She locked up her purse and practically skipped up the stairs. Victoria's door was closed so she went into the secretary's office. "Hey, Miss Jennetta. How's it going today?"

Jennetta didn't even look up. "Lordy, Saluki. I got no time to chat with you today. Victoria's taking charge, and she's uprooting everything. I can sure use your help, though."

She scurried to the desk. "Sure, what can I do?"

Jennetta pointed at a foot-high stack of folders. "I need you to take those to the workroom and shred everything in them. Save the folders, though. We're gonna need them."

"Shred—everything?"

"That's what I said. Director's orders. She's cleaning house, and that stuff is five years old. She said that's the old way and from now on, we gonna do things the new way."

Saluki scooped up the pile and headed out. "This is a good thing, right, Jennetta?" She looked over her shoulder.

Jennetta smiled at her. "It sure is, honey. It sure is."

Twenty minutes later, she returned the empty folders to Jennetta's office, but the woman wasn't there. Saluki hesitated by the door leading into Victoria's office. It opened and Jennetta came out. "Oh, there you are, Saluki. Victoria wants to see you."

"Hey,what's going on?"

"Come on in. I'm finally doing what I should have done six months ago. I'm organizing things the way I want to. Sit down. I could use a break."

"I heard Amelia left." Saluki picked up some folders from one of the chairs and sat. "But she wasn't happy about it."

Victoria took the folders from her. "Yes, she's gone."

"You fired her?" She lifted her eyebrows. "Seriously?"

Victoria set the folders on the one empty corner of her desk and dropped into her chair. "I can't really talk about it. It's a personnel issue. But you and I haven't had a chance to visit for a couple weeks. Tell me how you're doing."

Saluki's stomach plummeted. Victoria had known she was going to the dance. She would rather hear about Amelia leaving than tell Victoria what she'd done. "The back-to-school dance was a disaster." She crossed her arms and slumped in the chair.

"What happened?" Victoria leaned across the desk and held out the candy jar.

She took a miniature peanut butter cup and began to unwrap it slowly. "My friends didn't want me there. They said I had abandoned them. And Dustin was dancing with some new girl named Dawn. Like the dish soap. I don't think I'll be going to any more dances there." She popped the candy into her mouth.

Victoria helped herself to a Dove chocolate. "So Dustin was a jerk. Maybe your friends were trying to protect you. That doesn't mean you shouldn't go back for dances. You could try talking to them, explain again why you went to the academy."

She nodded. "Actually, I don't think the school will let me back in. I sort of made a scene."

"Saluki! What did you do?"

"I threw a cup of punch all over Dustin. Red punch."

Victoria gaped. "You didn't!" She let a laugh escape. "I'd

have loved to see that."

"Yeah, I guess it was pretty funny. Majesty said Dustin was spittin' mad. And Dawn acted like they were all a bunch of goons."

"Majesty? So you have talked to her since then?"

"Yeah, she came over the next day to apologize. Waited four hours for us to get back from the Market and got soaked in the process." She smiled at the memory.

"She's a good friend to do that."

"Yeah, she is. But there's more."

Victoria offered her more candy, but she shook her head. She didn't want to use chocolate for comfort food. She knew what problems that would cause.

"What else happened?"

"At the Market, with Mama and the kids. I saw my daddy."

She explained how she had felt snubbed by his actions.

When she finished, Victoria nodded. "I can see how that would ruin your day." She smoothed out her Dove wrapper. "I like the sayings they put in these, don't you? This one says, 'You are in charge of your own life.'" She pushed it across the desk toward Saluki. "I think you need to keep this. I've already started to take charge of my life."

Saluki picked up the wrapper and studied it. "I thought you already were in charge." She creased the wrapper neatly and pushed it into her jeans pocket.

Victoria waved her hand around the office. "I've been passive ever since I arrived in Charleston. But not anymore. I know how to run a tourism bureau, no matter where it's located. I may not be able to prove that I didn't know about Randy Lee's fraud, but as long as I'm here, I'm going to do my job and get this office into shape. You need to do the same thing with your life."

Saluki nodded. "You mean like what I did to Dustin?"

"That was a start. Not necessarily the best way to handle the situation, though I guess you got your point across. But I'm not just talking about Dustin."

"What else, then? I already started at the academy, even when my friends didn't want me to."

Victoria leaned across the desk. "You did, and that was a very good thing. But I'm thinking about your dad."

He'd left Saluki's family, and she couldn't do anything about it. He made it clear that day at the Market that he had no time for her. She folded her arms and slumped in the chair.

"You know the way he acts has nothing to do with you, don't you?" Victoria stood and came around the desk to sit in the chair next to Saluki. "I don't know your dad, but I'm guessing he's got his own demons. Whatever they are, he thinks he has to keep his distance from you and your family."

"Then why'd he come back to Charleston? It was better when I didn't have to worry about running into him somewhere by chance."

Victoria touched her shoulder. "Maybe so. But he's here now. What you can do, though, is the same thing you'll do when you see Dustin. You can be polite, but you get to choose whether to let him hurt you again or not. Does that make sense?"

Saluki tilted her head to the side. "I shouldn't get my hopes up? If I don't expect anything from him, I won't be disappointed."

"Exactly. Choose to think and react in a way that guards your heart."

Maybe she could do that. But it wouldn't be easy.

Chapter Forty-Seven

"What do you think about this one? Right after school started, I was trying to get to know the city and taking pictures of the buildings. I think we could use it."

Julee turned her laptop to show Saluki another video clip. The girls were camped out in Julee's dining room Sunday afternoon with notes and papers scattered across the polished tabletop. They had already spent three hours working on their joint senior project.

Saluki's eyes burned from viewing too many videos. "Okay, but this is the last one for today. We've still got three weeks before the project's due."

She peered at the computer screen and watched one more street scene in downtown Charleston. Since Saluki loved history and Julee wanted to become an architect, the girls had decided to make a mini-documentary on the city's historic architecture. Julee had the newest cell phone with a high-quality camera, so she had done most of the filming. Saluki had researched the history of the buildings. Together, they were selecting the most compelling segments, then they would write a script and record the narration.

Saluki watched as the camera focused on an iron gate then zoomed into the courtyard of a hotel. Their goal had been to visually show how buildings affected the lives of people, but that had proven harder than they expected. Julee had taken over twenty hours of video, but they didn't yet have enough to portray the story they wanted to tell.

"This has possibilities. See how intimate that spot is?" Julee leaned over Saluki's shoulder to point at the screen. A man and woman stood in shadow, nearly hidden in a niche in the courtyard wall. The ideal place for a romantic meeting—or, in this case, an argument.

Saluki could tell that the two were yelling at each other. That's the kind of stuff they wanted, where the structure might influence actions. She leaned in for a closer look, and her mouth gaped open.

"Whoa, wait a minute." She fumbled for the mouse and clicked on rewind. Then she played the video in slow motion, putting her nose almost on the laptop screen. "Are you kidding me? Are you kidding me!" She turned to Julee, who had taken a step away from her. "When did you take this?"

"The date's right there." Julee pointed to the corner of the monitor screen. "What is it? What's the big deal?"

Saluki paused the playback. "Do you know who that is?"

Julee shook her head. "No. Should I?"

Saluki leaned back in her chair. "That's Randy Lee Johnson and Ms. Amelia. You know, the woman Victoria fired? And, let's see, it had to be a few days after Victoria shut down his business." She started the video again but kept it in slow motion. "I wonder what they were arguing about."

Perching on the edge of the dining room table, Julee crossed her arms. "Looks to me like he's really angry with her. But listen, it doesn't matter that you know them, does it? I mean, we can still use the video for our project, right?"

"Have you got a thumb drive you can spare? I need to copy this." Saluki continued to study the pair on the screen as they argued, until Amelia stalked away and the recording ended.

Julee dug in her computer case and pulled out a USB drive. "Here, you can use this. But what are you going to do with it?"

"I'm going to show this video to Victoria. It's pretty obvious that Randy Lee was upset with Amelia. It has to be related to the whole fraud thing. Maybe it'll help clear

Victoria's name."

She told Julee how Victoria had confronted Randy Lee, and how Victoria was suspected of helping him commit fraud. With only a couple weeks left before the council made a decision, Saluki knew Victoria would want to see this film.

The next afternoon, Saluki went to Victoria's office as soon as she got to work. She tapped on the open door. "You got a minute? I've got something to show you."

Victoria waved her in. "Of course. What is it?"

"It's a video my friend Julee shot a few weeks ago. I think it'll surprise you."

She handed the memory stick to Victoria, who held it in her palm. "What's it about?"

"She was just fooling around downtown taking pictures. When she showed this to me yesterday, I knew you'd want to see it."

Victoria wrinkled her forehead. "You've got my curiosity up now." She turned her chair and inserted the device into her computer. When the list of files appeared on the screen, Saluki pointed to the only video format in the list.

"That one."

Victoria clicked on the file, and the video began playing. Like Saluki had, she watched casually for a couple of minutes. "So? What's so interesting about this argu—" She caught her breath. "Randy Lee? He's yelling at Amelia."

"And she's yelling back, I'd say." Saluki crossed her arms and waited until the five-minute clip ended. "Wouldn't you love to know what they were fighting about?"

"Sure." Victoria clicked the mouse and watched the video again. "I wish I could read lips."

Saluki plopped into one of the guest chairs. "You wanna know what I think?"

With her eyes riveted to the screen, Victoria nodded. "What do you think?"

"I think Miz Amelia was really the one who conspired with Randy Lee. Maybe she sent the photos just to make you look bad. She had wanted your job. He probably blamed her for his business getting shut down."

Victoria rotated her chair to face Saluki. "That makes sense, Saluki. But this video doesn't prove any of that." She put her elbows on the desk and rubbed her temples. "Maybe it doesn't have anything to do with the fraud. We don't know what they're saying, and we'll probably never know."

"But—but aren't you going to give it to the city attorney? At least it shows that the two of them were—I don't know. They were meeting, and they argued about something!" Saluki's reasoning sounded lame even to her.

Victoria ejected the device from her computer. "I'll pass it on to Lauren. I appreciate you bringing it to me. But I don't think it will make any difference. Even though there's no evidence that I helped Randy Lee commit fraud, the doubt is still there. And I'm afraid this video will do nothing to erase that doubt."

"You were wrong, Victoria."

Victoria looked up from her computer and her shoulders sank when she saw that the unexpected comment came from Lauren. Standing in Victoria's office doorway, Lauren waited to be invited in. A rose-colored scarf looped around her neck and accentuated her gray pantsuit, emphasizing her model-like appearance.

Victoria stood and crossed the room to greet her. It had been a week since she had seen Lauren, the day she gave her the video Julee had shot. She had no idea what she'd done wrong now, but she hated that she had disappointed her strongest supporter. Again. "What do you mean, Lauren? I was wrong about what?" She returned to her desk chair.

Lauren glided into a guest chair, placing a leather briefcase beside her feet. "I took your video to the city attorney. You were wrong when you told me it wouldn't prove anything."

Victoria leaned her elbows on her desk. "You mean it did prove that I wasn't involved? But what … how?" She had prayed that God would absolve her, but she wasn't sure it could really happen.

"Turns out the mayor has a friend in D.C. who can read lips. Because of the distance and the lighting, he couldn't make out everything that was said. But he was able to enhance it and pick up part of the conversation. Enough to convince everyone that you were not guilty of any fraud. Your case won't even be on the council's agenda next week."

Victoria let the words wash over her. *Not guilty*. Once again she felt peace. Not only had God forgotten her past, but now Charleston's officials knew she was innocent in Randy Lee's scheme.

"And, by the way, Victoria. Smith Alexander won't mention it, but he thinks you did the right thing in getting rid of his niece. It seems he knew all along that Amelia had been undermining you. He was just waiting for you to show some courage."

So that was the reason she had not been reprimanded after firing Amelia. Having a relative on the board didn't guarantee the woman a job she didn't deserve. Victoria had been as wrong in fearing the repercussions as Smith Alexander had been in his opinion of her.

Now at last she could focus on her job without the shadow of suspicion clouding every decision she made.

Chapter Forty-Eight

Two weeks later, Saluki called Majesty after work and asked if they could get together for pizza Friday night.

"Victoria wants us to come to her house for sort of a preview for the house tour. She says she wants to practice on us. The house tour is still a few weeks away, but there's a lot of work to finish up, and she wants to get an idea of how it's going to play out. Would you ask TeeJay and the others to come, too?"

"What about Dustin?"

Saluki swallowed hard. "Dustin, too. Even his new girlfriend."

"Are you sure?"

"No. But—yeah, I'm sure."

Majesty laughed. "Okay, girl. He's pretty steamed at you, but I'll see if I can get him to come." She paused. "I'll probably have to promise there won't be any red punch."

Saluki laughed at the memory of Dustin's face covered in red liquid. "You can promise him that. I got it out of my system."

The next day at school, she invited Julee and another classmate she had gotten to know. "It's nothing fancy, ya'll. Just pizza and soda. And … just so you know, it's not my house. It belongs to my boss."

Julee nodded. "That's pretty cool that she would let you give a party at her place."

"Oh, it's her party. But she wanted me to invite my friends. So …"

She crossed her fingers that this would work—mixing her two worlds. Old friends and new.

By Saturday afternoon, she had gnawed her fingernail tips off. As she and Victoria made last minute preparations, Victoria caught her chewing on her pinky nail. "Here, make yourself busy and stop worrying." She handed her a stack of napkins and paper plates to put on the table.

Victoria had decorated as she would for the house tour, complete with a lace tablecloth and an arrangement of mixed cut flowers on the dining room table.

"The house looks real pretty." Saluki arranged the paper products at the end of the table next to the plastic forks. The pizza would be served buffet-style. "I've got to get something from my car. I'll be right back."

She retrieved the sweetgrass basket from the backseat and hugged it to her chest. Mama had helped her fill it with fresh flowers and wrap it in pink tissue paper. Aunt Ida assured her it was now almost as good as new. She hoped Victoria would love it as much as she did.

When she walked into the kitchen, Victoria's eyes grew round. "What in the world?"

"It's sort of a housewarming gift."

"Oh, Saluki. You didn't have to get me anything."

She handed it to her. "I wanted to do this. I hope you like it."

Victoria untied the ribbon that held the paper in place and gasped. She lifted the basketful of flowers and twirled it slowly. "It's beautiful. Is this the basket you found in the closet?"

"Yes, ma'am. My aunt taught me how to fix it."

"You did an amazing job. I can't even tell that it had been damaged. But don't you want to keep it?"

She shuffled her feet. "It sort of belongs here, in your house, where it came from."

Victoria studied her. "I have the perfect spot for it. Come on." She led Saluki to the hallway where she placed the basket on the console table she had positioned against the stairway wall. She moved two candlesticks from the center so that they flanked the basket. "That's lovely. And look how well the flowers match the candlesticks." She turned and hugged Saluki. "Thank you so much. I will treasure that basket."

The doorbell rang and Victoria opened the door to admit Julee and Sue Ellen from the academy. They chatted for a few minutes, and Victoria led them into the dining room. "The pizzas should be here in about fifteen minutes. Meanwhile, help yourself to some pop."

The next group to arrive included Majesty, TeeJay, and Dustin. Saluki greeted them at the door. "Hey. Come on in." She led them into the dining room. "I want you to meet some of my friends from the academy. Julee, Sue Ellen, these are friends from my old school."

This was the moment she had worried about. Would her new friends act superior, or would her old friends be insulted that she had invited her new friends? She breathed a sigh of relief when Julee and Sue Ellen acted like the others were just friends they hadn't met yet. Minutes later, they were all chatting about schools, cars, and sports.

She didn't talk to Dustin except to offer him a drink, but when she went into the kitchen to get more ice, he followed her. "Saluki, thanks for inviting me. I—you didn't have to. I wouldn't have blamed you—"

"I didn't know if you'd come after what I did to you at the dance." She scooped ice into the ice bucket. "Majesty told you Dawn was invited, too, right?"

He gave her a lopsided grin. "She, uh, didn't know about you and me before that. And I didn't invite her. I was hoping maybe you'd forgive me. You know, nothing's changed between you and me. I still care for you."

She stared at him, her fingers frozen to the metal ice bucket. He couldn't believe that. "Really? Nothing's changed.

We'll still go to college together and get married after we graduate?"

He smiled. "Yeah. Just like we planned."

She shook her head slowly. "I thought you were smarter than that, Dustin."

"Smarter?"

"Look, I hope we can still be friends. I mean, the four of us together were great. But everything's changed with you and me. It's over, Dustin. I don't need a boyfriend I can't trust. I've seen what that's like with the way my daddy treated my mama. I deserve better."

She pushed past him into the dining room and let the door swing back in his face, not caring whether it hit him or not. She wouldn't let him hurt her again.

Lonely nights seemed less lonely now.

When the shadows threatened to obscure her joy, Victoria played a CD of contemporary Christian music that Matt had brought over. The words to the songs, and the oil painting in her parlor, helped her remember the love of God and chase away the loneliness.

She lay in bed reviewing her progress on this Saturday morning, the second day of October. She had worked until midnight to paint the upstairs hall. Yesterday had been her original deadline to complete the remodeling work. Even though the bank had given her a month's extension, she had pushed herself to finish one more project, her own private celebration of how far she had come.

Matt's crew had restored the laundry room and kitchen, as well as the exterior siding. The unknowing visitor would never realize there had been a fire.

Surprisingly, even after finishing the work he had

contracted to do, Matt had stopped by at least once a week to check on her progress. He'd even offered to help her paint, but he had been her contractor, which made him her employee. Not her friend, no matter what Donna Grace said.

Besides, she didn't want to take advantage of his generous nature. Just because he always seemed glad to see her at church on Sunday didn't mean she should impose on him to help.

Victoria had spent every Saturday and nearly every evening since the festival stripping and refinishing woodwork throughout the house. She only hoped she could get the remaining projects done in time for the house tour in two weeks. She still needed to paint two of the guest bedrooms and clean everything until it shone.

Around seven thirty, she rolled out of bed, went downstairs to the kitchen, filled the coffeepot with water, and flipped the switch to start it brewing. Just as she dropped into a chair to wait for the coffee to finish, the doorbell rang—a pleasant chime that made her smile. The elderly man at the hardware store had known exactly how to fix it.

She wanted to ignore the bell. Probably Randy Lee here to beg again for forgiveness. Forget it. He had come by three times in the past month. His sweet talk no longer had any effect on her. But it was beginning to look like he would not give up unless she threatened to call the police.

As she approached the door, he began pounding on it.

"Victoria? Are you okay?"

But it wasn't Randy Lee. That was a girl's voice. Saluki? Why would she be here, especially so early on a Saturday morning?

She hurried to the door. "I'm fine, Saluki." She unlocked the door and pulled it open. "I was in the kitch—" Not only Saluki stood there, but several of her friends who had come to the party the night before. All dressed in cutoff jeans and faded t-shirts, even Julee and Sue Ellen.

Saluki grinned at her, while the others held back. "Victoria, my friends and I want to help you get your house ready for the tour."

Speechless, Victoria nodded and backed up so she could swing the door open wide. They might be young and inexperienced, but she needed all the help she could get.

She led the way to the kitchen and offered them coffee. Only Julee accepted. Victoria couldn't believe Saluki had brought friends. It wasn't like remodeling projects were easy. Or fun. But working together, maybe they could have a good time.

She assigned Saluki and Majesty to painting one of the bedrooms, and provided sponges and buckets of hot, soapy water to the others. Julee and TeeJay went outside, and Sue Ellen and Dustin started cleaning the bathrooms.

Two hours later, Donna Grace showed up. "I thought maybe you could use some help getting things ready, but I saw some kids outside washing windows."

Victoria smiled. "They were way ahead of you this morning. I think we just might make this deadline after all."

"Are you saying you don't need me?" Donna Grace pouted, pretending to have hurt feelings.

"Not at all. I need you to supervise the final touches. With your experience selling houses, I'm sure you'll know just what's needed to make it pop."

"All right, then. Let's inspect what you've done so far."

Donna Grace began making notes of where Victoria needed accessories, and Victoria joined Saluki and Majesty in painting. Matt showed up after lunch.

Holding a wet paint roller, Victoria went to the top of the stairs to greet him as Donna Grace let him in the front door. Victoria's mouth gaped open as he stepped into the foyer carrying an object that appeared to be three stakes tied together with a leather strap.

"What in the world is that?"

Matt looked up at her, a grin spread across his face. "Call it a housewarming surprise."

"But, what's it for?"

Donna Grace closed the door. "Don't make him stand there holding it, dear. Come on, Matt. I know the perfect spot." She led him into the dining room.

Victoria returned the paint roller to the tray, then scurried down the stairs. In the dining room, Matt and Donna Grace were stationed in front of the bay window where they had positioned the polished wooden object.

Matt turned to her. "Now then, where's that cannonball?"

Victoria stared at him. "What?"

Donna Grace laid a hand on her arm. "The cannonball, dear. Matt found this lovely antique stand that will be perfect to display your treasure."

Of course. Donna Grace had probably suggested this. Victoria smiled at the pair's collaboration. She led the way to the hall closet where she had stored the Civil War relic until she decided what to do with it. "It's in here."

Matt ducked into the space under the stairs and retrieved the cannonball. He grasped the artifact to his chest and carried it into the dining room. "As heavy as this is, Randy Lee sort of did me a favor by removing it from the attic. I'm just glad he didn't leave too much of a mess for me to repair." He placed the iron ball gingerly on the stand.

Victoria watched him, grateful he didn't look at her. The reminder of Randy Lee's deceit still caused heat to rush to her face. Matt's thoughtfulness with this gift emphasized the contrast between the two men. "I-I don't know how to thank you, Matt."

He turned and held his hands in front of him, palms up. "No need. I just want to help. Put me to work. What's left to do?"

This time, Victoria accepted his offer. By five o'clock all the upstairs rooms had been painted. A little more decorating, cleaning, and washing the bedroom windows and the house would be ready to show off.

Everyone but Donna Grace left, with the teens promising to return the following Saturday—the day before the house tour.

Victoria and Donna Grace sat on the porch swing enjoying the spring evening. "They're good kids." Donna Grace sipped her lemonade. "Reminds me of when my boys were that age."

"I was so surprised they came. Why would they give up a Saturday to help me?"

"Why not? Saluki's your friend, isn't she? And they're her friends. Friends help each other."

Victoria pushed her feet to start gently swinging. "I didn't think I would ever have friends like that here in Charleston. Or like you. I'm grateful."

"Honey, you've been a good friend to Saluki. And to me. That's all it takes to make friends, no matter where you live."

"I guess you're right." She sighed. "At night, by myself in this big house, I don't feel so—alone, like I did before."

Donna Grace placed one hand over hers on her lap. "I'm glad you found out that you're never alone. God is always with you."

Victoria nodded. The evening breeze brought with it the scent of a neighbor's outdoor grill along with the comfort she had felt when she first saw the painting of Jesus in the antique store.

Chapter Forty-Nine

As promised, Saluki and her friends returned to Victoria's house the following Saturday. Saluki looked forward to helping Victoria and Donna Grace arrange furniture, put up curtains, and finish the cleaning.

About mid-morning, Dustin found Saluki washing the inside of the windows in one of the upstairs bedrooms. He brought a roll of paper towels and a rag and dropped them on the floor, then brandished a spray bottle of Windex. "Want some help?"

"No, I got it. I haven't been in the front bedroom, if you want to do that one." She didn't want to be too close to him. His cologne still made her tingle.

Instead of picking up his supplies, he set the spray bottle next to them. "Actually, I was hoping we could talk."

She kept her own spray window cleaner in one hand and squirted more on the windowpane. "What about? Football?"

"Come on, Saluki. Not about football. About us."

She rubbed the glass until it squeaked. "There is no us, Dustin. We're just friends now, remember?"

"I remember." He rubbed his hand over his short blond hair. "That's what you said. But I can't believe you don't still have feelings for me. Like I do for you."

She saw a spot on the upper window but the lower sash was in the way. She tried to push it down but it wouldn't budge. She beat on the top part of the frame with her fists, then the pain caused her to regret that action.

Dustin nudged her aside and lowered the sash while she rubbed the side of her hand.

"I don't know what kind of feelings cause a guy to cheat

on his girlfriend." She attacked the insect remains on the glass, squirting cleaner on it then scrubbing with a paper towel. "But whatever feelings I had for you were quashed that night at the dance. I told you that already."

Dustin grabbed her arm and pulled her around to face him. "Come on, babe. I made a mistake. Can't you forgive me?"

Her heart pounded with his nearness, and she felt herself falling into the depths of his dark eyes. Her lips burned with the memory of his kisses. He leaned his head over hers and their lips touched gently.

She let the tension flow out through her toes and relaxed against him. She had missed this. She allowed him to take the bottle of glass cleaner and the wadded-up paper from her, and she locked her hands around his neck like she used to do. She might never find another guy who cared for her like Dustin did. She belonged here, in his arms.

"That's my girl. See what you've been missing?" His hands started to roam down her back. "Let's get away from here for awhile. We could go to my house. Nobody's home."

What was he saying? "We promised Victoria we'd help her today."

"Yeah, but everything's almost done." He kissed her neck, her ear. "They won't miss us for a little while. I just want you all to myself."

He really did love her. He had just made a mistake. "I don't think we should go to your house if no one's there. You know I want to be a virgin when we get married."

"Come on, babe. Since we're gonna get married anyway, it doesn't really matter, does it?" He kissed her again, sweet and tender and long.

She broke the kiss. "It matters to me."

"But a guy's got needs." He brushed his lips against her curls and fingered her hair at the back of her neck. She longed to spend the rest of the day like this. "That's the only reason I started seeing Dawn, babe, 'cause you weren't ready for this. But you are now, aren't you?"

An alarm rang in her ears. She shook her head and pulled away from him. "What? You—you went out with Dawn because she would sleep with you?"

He held out his arms toward her, like he could coax her back to him. "It didn't mean anything. It's you I want."

A chill encircled her, and she shivered. How had she not realized Dustin was that kind of guy? "Get. Away. From. Me."

His face contorted into a question, then his jaw hardened. "So. You're the same old prude you were before. I thought you would get some sense at that other school."

She picked up the bottle of spray and pointed the nozzle at him. "I have developed some sense. Sense enough to know that I deserve better than this. Better than you."

He backed away. "Hey, don't point that at me. You could blind me or something."

"Get out. Out of this room. Out of this house. And out of my life. I was wrong. We cannot still be friends. Friends respect each other. Obviously, you don't respect me. And I certainly don't respect you."

Genuine or not, the hurt on Dustin's face showed that he finally understood she meant what she said. And Saluki knew that she had spoken truth.

Chapter Fifty

Victoria's house looked amazing. Woodwork gleamed and plush rugs accented the polished wood floors. Saluki knew how carefully Victoria had selected the minimal furnishings to keep the focus on the house itself.

Someday, Saluki told herself, she would own a house like this. She just had to apply herself in college, find a good job, and work hard. Victoria believed she could do it, and Saluki believed her. But all in due time.

Right now, she needed to help make the appetizers. She and Julee had offered to serve refreshments during the tour.

As she strolled through the hall, she stopped to admire the flower arrangement on the console table. The woodsy scent of chrysanthemums reminded her of Aunt Ida's autumn soup. She put her hand on the basket, touching one of the spots she had repaired. Her fingers knew exactly where each hole had been, and she swelled with pride that the repair felt exactly like the woven areas around it.

"Beautiful, isn't it?" Victoria's voice made her jump, and she dropped her hand, tucking it behind her back as if she had something to hide.

"Yes, ma'am. These flowers look great. Did you arrange them?"

"I did." Victoria stepped up to her. "But I'm not talking about the flowers. I meant the basket. It's lovely. You have a right to be proud of it."

Her face flushed. "Thanks. I'm glad you like it."

"Come on. We've got a hundred pinwheels to make."

In the kitchen, Julee had just finished chopping green and red peppers in the food processor. Victoria asked Saluki to get out the tortillas while she stirred the peppers into the cream cheese mixture. They formed an assembly line. Victoria covered the tortilla shells with the spread, and Saluki arranged deli-sliced ham and turkey on top. Julee rolled each one up and sliced across it to make pinwheels. The colorful peppers gave them a festive look.

An hour later, they had finished arranging the appetizers on borrowed silver trays and had covered each tray with plastic wrap. "The punch is in the fridge. Can I count on you girls to get it out just before the tours start?"

Julee nodded. "Sure, Ms. Russo."

"I told you to call me Victoria. Now let's go get changed."

The two girls had brought dresses with them, and Victoria led them to one of the bedrooms upstairs. The girls quickly shed their jeans and t-shirts. Saluki pulled on the jewel blue dress that Julee had helped her find at a thrift store, and Julee zipped the back for her. The wide ruffle at the v-neck made her feel elegant, and she loved the fashionable style of the hemline—above her knees in front but dropping to mid-calf in back.

Julee insisted she twirl to show it off. "It's gorgeous. You look great."

Saluki turned and hugged her friend. "Thank you so much for helping me find it. I could never have afforded a new dress this nice."

Julee shrugged. "Who cares whether it's new or not? Nobody knows, and it makes sense to stretch your money as far as you can."

"Turn around. Let me zip you up now." Saluki tugged on the zipper pull of Julee's high-waisted dress. The multi-colored stripes made her look taller. "You don't have to worry about money, though."

Julee peeked over her shoulder. "Are you kidding me? My dad gives me a pretty nice allowance, but I have to buy all my own clothes and pay my own way for movies or pizza, whatever." She turned and studied herself in the full-length mirror Victoria had leaned against the wall. "I don't mind though. Someday I'll be on my own, and I'll need to know how to manage money. It's a life skill, like my dad says."

Saluki was surprised by this. She'd thought Julee's dad paid for whatever she wanted. She was about to ask why he didn't when Victoria knocked and entered.

Wearing a print dress with a high collar, Victoria looked like she had just stepped out of a Victorian family portrait. She smiled and rotated one finger in a circle. "Turn around, let me see." They did so. "You both look lovely. Beautiful dresses."

They glanced at each other and grinned.

Victoria checked her watch. "We've got about ten minutes, but we have a problem."

Saluki glanced at Julee, then back at Victoria. "What kind of problem? Did we forget something for the food?"

"No." Victoria took a deep breath. "One of the women who was supposed to take groups through the house just called. Her son's got some kind of bug. She hoped her husband would be home from a business trip in time, but he missed a connecting flight. She tried to find a babysitter, but no one wants to watch a sick child."

Saluki's heart sank. One of them would need to miss the tour. She wouldn't ask Julee to go. She was used to taking care of sick kids; Julee, an only child, wasn't. "I'll go watch the boy. Help me with this zipper so I can change." She turned her back to Julee.

Victoria held up her hand. "No, that's not what I meant. She lives in Mount Pleasant. There isn't time for you to get there and her to get back here."

Saluki tilted her head. "What're you going to do, then? Without her, you'll never get all the groups through in four hours."

"I was hoping you would help with the tours. You know as much about the house and the work we've done as I do."

Saluki thought a boa constrictor had taken up residence in her intestines. "Me? I can't ..." Ten people were scheduled in each group. Ten people she didn't know. She would be fine serving food or punch, smiling and speaking one-on-one to the guests. But giving tours? That would be like public speaking, like the scholarship committee meeting. Only repeated eight times in four hours.

Victoria's eyes pleaded. "I know you hate speaking in public, Saluki. I'd ask Julee, but she doesn't know the house like you do. I really need your help."

Julee spoke up. "You can do it. I'll stay with you the first few times, for moral support. We can just put the refreshments out and let the guests help themselves."

Victoria reached into her pocket and pulled out a small stack of index cards. "Here. I made these up for the tour guides. You know all the stuff on them, but they might help you stay focused. Please do this? For me?"

Saluki reached out and took the cards. She hoped the perspiration on her hand wouldn't smear the ink and cause it to run all over her dress.

When the last tour group had left, Victoria stepped onto the front porch to enjoy the quiet.

A handful of visitors chatted in small groups scattered across the yard. Lauren broke away from one of the groups, women dressed as if going to an old-fashioned Easter parade.

She joined Victoria on the porch. "They love your house. You've made quite an impression."

The compliment pleased Victoria, but it didn't compare to the satisfaction of simply completing the project.

Lauren lowered her voice to just above a whisper. "Those three are on the board of WCS, and they're thinking of asking you to join."

WCS. The Women of Charleston Society. An elite group of ambitious, well-off, and influential women. Women she admired, like Lauren. Victoria chuckled. A few months ago, she'd have given up her inheritance to be invited. But now? The prestige didn't seem important, not if it took her away from friends like Donna Grace and Saluki.

"No offense, Lauren. But I'm not sure I'd be interested."

"It's your call, of course. But give it some thought, okay?"

"I will. I'd be flattered, and I know you have some important projects. But I'm ready for some quiet time." She bent to pick up a scrap of paper that someone had dropped on the porch. "How did the tour go at the other houses?"

"Good, from what I saw. People at my house seemed pleased with the homes they had already visited. And the society president said ticket sales were double last year's."

Victoria wadded the paper scrap into a ball and rolled it in her hand. "That's wonderful."

"Yes. The proceeds will cover their annual budget and provide a sizable donation to Parkinson's research."

Victoria's heart warmed. Her father had wanted to help future victims of the disease, even though the research came too late for him. He would have been pleased that her efforts had contributed to the cause.

She would phone her mother and tell her. She also needed to tell her about finding Jesus. God could help with Mother's loneliness, too. She was sure of it.

But that call would wait until tonight. Right now, she had to clean up.

Lauren said good-bye, and Victoria went in search of Saluki and Julee. She found the girls in the kitchen, snacking on the leftover food.

Saluki seemed as bubbly as foaming punch when sherbet was added to it. "That was so much fun, Victoria. Thanks for asking me to give the tours."

"She did great." Julee handed Victoria a tray with a few pinwheels remaining. "After a couple times through, she didn't even need me to help."

Victoria placed the leftover appetizers in a small plastic storage container. "I think it went very well. Lauren Redmond—you know she's the one who asked me to be part of the tour—came by near the end. She said the event was really successful. The Preservation Society raised twice as much money as last year."

Saluki took the plastic container from her and put the lid on it. "So everybody's happy, huh?"

"I think so, from what Lauren said."

Victoria finally felt like she belonged in Charleston. Not because of this house but because of the people she now counted as friends.

Chapter Fifty-One

After work Monday, Victoria went to the Market and bought a large bunch of cut flowers.

Now that the tour was over, she had made a decision. She understood how much Saluki longed for the love of her father. Nothing Victoria could do about him, but she could share the new love she had found. God could make a difference in Saluki's life, as he had in her own.

She kept the car window down as she navigated the streets of Saluki's neighborhood. No sense in missing a second of the eighty-degree temperatures in October, not when Mother was already complaining about the cold weather up north.

She grabbed the loosely wrapped package from the backseat and headed up the walk. The sweet fragrance of the flowers pleased her as she rang the bell. Sounds of a video game sifted through the screen door as she waited on the front porch.

"Victoria?" Saluki appeared at the door. "What are you doing here?" She pushed open the screen door. "You want to come in?"

She hesitated. She didn't want to intrude. "I can't stay. I just wanted to bring this back to you." She extended the package, its shape obvious beneath the tissue paper.

Saluki's eyes widened. "The basket? You were supposed to keep that."

"No, I want you to have it back."

Her face drooped. "I guess it doesn't really fit your fine house."

"No, no, Saluki. It's beautiful. I was proud to display it yesterday. It fit perfectly. But … you worked so hard to repair it, and since your aunt used to make them. Who knows? Maybe she made this very basket. I think you should keep it. To remind you of her … and me."

The girl's eyes watered. "You're not leaving, are you?"

"Leaving? You mean leave Charleston? Not a chance! This is my home now."

"But you said to remind me of you …"

"You're the one who will leave, Saluki. You'll go to college and have a career and a wonderful life. I know that's not until next fall, but I figure you can use the basket in the meantime."

Saluki threw her arms around her. "Oh, wow." She had to juggle the basket with one arm to keep it from being crushed between them. "Thank you so much! How did you know how much this basket meant to me?"

She shrugged and smiled. "I just guessed. Now do you want to take it inside and give the flowers some water, or are you going to leave it out here and let them wilt?"

Saluki widened her eyes. "Oh, my gosh. You should come on in. Mama just got home. She's been wanting to meet you."

"I'd like to meet her, too. But I can't stay long." Saluki stepped back and Victoria followed her into the small living room. A patterned sofa and overstuffed chairs had obviously seen years, perhaps generations, of the family's life. A boy sat cross-legged on the floor in front of a bulky TV, fingers speeding over the buttons of a game controller. Their entrance didn't distract him from the exploding robots on the screen.

"Mama," Saluki called toward the back of the house. "Miss Victoria's here."

"Goodness gracious." The words floated from the other room seconds ahead of Saluki's mother. As she entered, she wiped her hands on the red-and-white checked apron tied around her waist. Her face looked nearly as worn as the furniture, but her smile assured Victoria that she was welcome.

"I been hearing so much about you, but I begun to think Saluki was making you up."

When Victoria extended her hand, Saluki's mother took it with both of hers and squeezed. "I sure do thank you for all you done for my Saluki. I work so much it's hard for me to give her the guidance she needs. But she listens to what you say."

"Mrs. Franklin, you're doing fine. Saluki is a good worker and a responsible young lady. I enjoy having her around."

Saluki shifted her feet. "Mama, look. Victoria brought back the basket that Aunt Ida helped me fix. She said I could keep it."

"That's mighty nice. You worked hard on it, didn't you?"

Crashing noises from the other end of the room rose over her words. The boy flopped backward onto the floor and groaned.

"Isaiah, we have company. Turn off that game now, and come meet Saluki's boss." He whined but stood up and went to the television set to shut it off. She turned back to Victoria. "My other son, Tyler, isn't home from basketball practice." She grabbed the boy's shoulder as he tried to slip past them. "Shake hands with Miss Victoria."

"Yes, ma'am." He stuck out his hand and Victoria took it. "Nice to meet you. My name is Isaiah. I'm eleven." He looked at his mother. "Can I go now?"

She smiled. "You got homework?"

"Done."

"Good. How about setting the table for supper then?"

He moaned but headed down the hall, untied sneakers dragging across the bare wood floor.

"Will you stay for supper?" The question caught Victoria by surprise. This family couldn't afford to feed another person.

"No, thank you. I need to be going. But I wanted to ask you—that is, if she wants to—" She nodded at Saluki. "If Saluki could go to church with me next Sunday."

Mrs. Franklin's shoulders stiffened. "I take my kids to church whenever I can."

"Yes, of course. I didn't mean to imply …" Victoria swallowed and tried again. "It's just that, well, I grew up going to church, but I found out that wasn't enough. It took me three marriages and several other, um, relationships, but I see now that those men weren't what I needed. It was God that I needed all along. And this church I'm going to—"

She paused to catch her breath. This wasn't going as well as she had hoped. She looked at Saluki, and their eyes locked. She knew Jesus could help fill the void in Saluki's life left by her father. "Well, I'm learning how to rely on God instead of myself or some other person."

The other woman pursed her lips then nodded. "If Saluki wants to go, it's okay by me. I would take her regular, if I didn't work most Sundays."

Victoria smiled. "I know you would." She turned to Saluki. "What do you say? Will you come?"

She nodded. "You bet. Sounds cool."

"Okay, then. I'll plan to pick you up at ten next Sunday."

Chapter Fifty-Two

"You've done a fabulous job with this house, Victoria." Matt accepted the glass of lemonade Victoria offered him and took a long swig.

The Saturday after the house tour, she had finally honored her promise to make dinner for him. She'd prepared lasagna from scratch the way she had learned from her mother, and watching him enjoy it had been worth the effort.

He had told funny stories from his "coming up" years, as he called them. When she talked about her father's illness and death, he had listened, responding to her hurting heart with care. Now they had moved to the front porch to enjoy the gift of another warm October evening.

"You know I couldn't have done it without you." She set her own glass down on the painted white iron table and joined him in the porch swing. "The way you and your men fixed everything and got it all done on schedule. That was a real blessing." She was starting to talk like Donna Grace. That made her smile.

"Maybe so, but your design skills certainly helped. You have a real eye for color." He casually laid his arm along the back of the swing.

Her heart pounded. In between her husbands, she might have flirted with him, teased him until he kissed her—or more. Matt was truly one of those "good men" that she had been convinced did not exist. If only she had met him sixteen years ago. Before she married Brian.

He moved his foot and the swing started moving gently back and forth. "Sure is a good night to be sitting here on a swing watching the world go by."

She felt comfortable with Matt. She relaxed and let her head rest against his arm. "It is. I'm ready for some watching for awhile. The last few months have been pretty hectic." His cologne smelled like the Old Spice her dad had always used.

He laid his hand on her shoulder in a brotherly way. Or was it more? "I'm hoping you'll still let me come around, even though I'm not working for you."

She sat up straight. She knew Matt was a gentleman, and she could enjoy his companionship. But she needed to be on her own for awhile. To live on her terms, trusting Jesus instead of the flavor-of-the-month. "Matt, I like you. A lot. And I do want you to come around—occasionally."

His questioning eyes felt like a knife piercing her skin. She stood and stepped to the porch railing, studying the new crape myrtle bush she had planted at the front corner.

"But I need some time. I told you I had been married." She turned to face him, leaned against the railing. "The truth is—I've been married three times. And ... since I turned eighteen, I haven't been on my own for even a full six months at a time."

She expected to see shock in his face. Instead, a slight grin started and edged its way into a full-blown smile. "You're different now. I can see that, even from when I first met you. You're not so wary. It's finding faith, isn't it?"

She nodded. "Yes, that has made all the difference. I never knew how real it could be."

He studied his hands. "All right, so you need time. You're not ready for a serious relationship. I can wait. We'll see each other at church but that's all." He stood, looked into her eyes. "For now."

She breathed a sigh of relief. "Thank you for understanding. I would like to get to know you but right now, I need to get to know me."

"So is six months long enough? I'd like to share spring in

Charleston with you."

She heard his teasing tone, but rather than tease him back, she shook her head. "I really don't know. We'll have to wait and see, okay?"

He nodded, bent over and kissed her cheek, and strode down the steps to his pickup.

She watched until the taillights on his truck disappeared at the corner where he turned. She went inside and picked up her phone.

"Donna Grace, this is Victoria. Do you want to come over? I feel like playing a game of Scrabble."

The Outcast

No clouds floated across the Samaritan sky to relieve the heat as Leah trudged to the well outside the village walls, her water jug balanced on one shoulder. The small outline of her shape, cast by the sun directly overhead, tried to escape her sandals with each step she took. Even her shadow didn't want to be near her.

As she approached the community well, she stopped to set down her burden and wipe the perspiration from her forehead. She had no choice but to come for water in the middle of the day, despite the scorching sun. The other women shunned her if she tried to join them in the morning or evening. At least she could drink some of the cool water before she headed home with her full jug.

She lifted the jug again and moved forward, then halted. A man sat on the ground, his back against the stones, his hood partially covering his face, his head against his knees as if he were sleeping. Logical, given the temperature and time of day, but why did he have to choose this place for his rest? Would he send her away without letting her draw the water she needed for the day?

She stepped forward, trying not to make a sound. If he were asleep, perhaps she could fill her jug and leave without disturbing him. She whispered a small prayer to Yahweh, even though she didn't deserve to be heard. If she returned without water, she would receive a tongue-lashing from the man who would be waiting at home for his noon meal.

Moving slowly, she made her way to the opposite side of the well. But as she prepared to lower her jug, the man stirred. He coughed, then asked, "Would you give me a drink of water?"

She flinched with surprise, nearly dropping her vessel into the well. He spoke with the cadence of a Galilean, but Jews avoided contact with Samaritans. They rarely even traveled this way, and a Jewish man would never talk to a Samaritan woman. If this man knew her reputation, the reason she came to the well at the noon hour, he would consider himself defiled.

"You are a Jew. How can you even ask me, a Samaritan woman, for a drink of water?"

His soft answer barely reached her ears, but his tone caused her heart to pound. "If you knew who it was asking for a drink, you would ask him for a drink instead. And he would give you living water."

Leah studied the stranger more closely. He must be someone important. But if he were so powerful, why did he have no servants with him? With no servants and no water vessel, how could he give her a drink?

"Sir, you don't have anything to use to get water, and the well is deep." She set down her water jug and stepped closer to the man. The hood of his robe kept his face partially hidden. "So where are you going to get this living water?"

When he didn't answer, she grew bolder. "You're not more important than our ancestor Jacob, are you? He gave us this well. He and his sons and his animals drank water from it."

The man stood then and motioned to the well. "Everyone who drinks this water will become thirsty again. But anyone who drinks the water I give them will never become thirsty again. In fact, the water I will give them will become a spring that gushes up to eternal life."

Never be thirsty again? She wanted that. "Sir, give me this water!" she pleaded. "Then I won't have to come here every day in this heat."

"Go get your husband, and bring him here," the man said.

Startled by this change in topic, Leah stammered, "I-I don't have a husband."

The man turned to face her and his eyes looked into her heart. "You're telling the truth." His voice, void of condemnation, soothed her pounding pulse. "You've had five husbands, but the man you're living with now isn't your husband."

Stunned that this visitor to her country knew about her life, Leah searched for words. She fought to keep her voice from cracking in fear—or awe. "So you're a prophet!" Maybe he could explain things she had wondered about. "Our ancestors worshiped on this mountain. But you Jews say that we must go to Jerusalem to worship. What difference does it make?"

"The time is here," he said, "when true worshipers will worship in spirit and truth. The Father is looking for people like that to worship him."

More confused than before, Leah shifted her feet. "I know the Messiah is coming. When he comes, he will tell us everything."

"I am he, speaking to you now."

Several other men approached the well, but stopped several feet away. Leah glanced toward them and saw curiosity on their faces, yet they said nothing. The man's words suddenly pierced the haze in her mind and she understood. Her breath caught in her throat and she completely forgot the errand that had brought her to Jacob's well. She had been talking with the Messiah!

She had to tell someone. Abruptly, Leah lifted the bottom of her robe and ran toward town, abandoning her water vessel.

The hour of rest had ended and commerce had begun once more. She hurried up to some men and women gathered in front of a small shop.

Ignoring their haughty stares, she interrupted the silversmith in mid-sentence. "You have to come with me," she gasped. "This man I met at the well—he told me everything

I've ever done. He knew all about my shameful life. But he promised me living water, and said that I'd never be thirsty again."

All speaking at once, they threw questions at her. She caught her breath and told them what had happened. Hearing the excitement, passersby stopped and merchants came out of nearby shops to join those listening. She had to start from the beginning twice, but when she concluded, Leah looked at the faces around her.

"Could this be the Messiah?" she asked.

The people murmured to each other, and then one man shoved through the crowd and hurried toward the well. Others followed him, some running eagerly, some shaking their heads skeptically. Soon the entire crowd headed out of the city to see this man who claimed to be their Savior.

The long-awaited Messiah chose a broken, fallen woman to spread the word that He had come at last. Because she shared what this man meant to her, an entire village met Jesus. And had the opportunity to drink Living Water.

Questions for Thought and Discussion

How does Victoria's story parallel the biblical story of the Samaritan woman at the well (see the Book of John, Chapter 4)? How does it differ?

In what ways can you identify with Victoria's feelings of rejection?

How did Victoria's decision to restore the old house parallel her move to Charleston?

How could Amelia have responded differently to Victoria? Vice versa?

Victoria determined to use only positive words. Was she successful? Why or why not?

What does Proverbs 16:24 say about the power of words? How do you reconcile that with the lesson that Victoria learned?

Why did Saluki and Victoria become friends? What did they have in common? How were they different?

What changes in Saluki's life did the sweetgrass basket represent? Did the basket have significance in Victoria's life? In what ways did the restoration of the basket differ from what happened in their lives?

Was there anything supernatural about the painting of Jesus that Victoria found? Why did it have such a profound effect on her?

Have you ever been affected deeply by a painting or other creative work? Did it change your understanding of God or your life?

About the Author

Marie Wells Coutu, a debut novelist, has written for business, government, and nonprofit organizations, including the Billy Graham Evangelistic Association for fifteen years. The author or editor of five published nonfiction books and hundreds of newspaper and magazine articles, she has edited devotionals and other books published by the Billy Graham Evangelistic Association. She manages an inspirational website, mended-vessels.com, where she and others blog, review books, and offer inspiration and encouragement.

She has been a finalist in the 2009 ACFW Genesis Contest, 2010 Women of Faith Writing Contest, and placed as a Bronze Medalist in the 2011 and 2012 Frasier Awards sponsored by My Book Therapy.

A graduate of the 2005 and 2008 She Speaks conferences sponsored by Proverbs 31 Ministries, she has spoken to church, ministry, and non-religious groups ranging in size from twenty to three hundred. She presents dramatic readings to church groups, and has been interviewed for newspapers, radio, and television.

She holds BA and MA degrees in journalism from Murray State University (Kentucky), and taught journalism and mass communications at St. Cloud State University (Minnesota). She and her husband divide their time between Iowa and Florida. They have two children and four grandchildren.

Marie is a member of American Christian Fiction Writers, and served as president of the local chapter, Carolina Christian Writers. She has held various leadership roles for government communicators' associations and the local historical commission.

You can find Marie on the Web:

www.Mended-Vessels.com
www.MarieWellsCoutu.com
Marie Wells Coutu Facebook
Twitter: @MWCoutu

Other Books by the Author

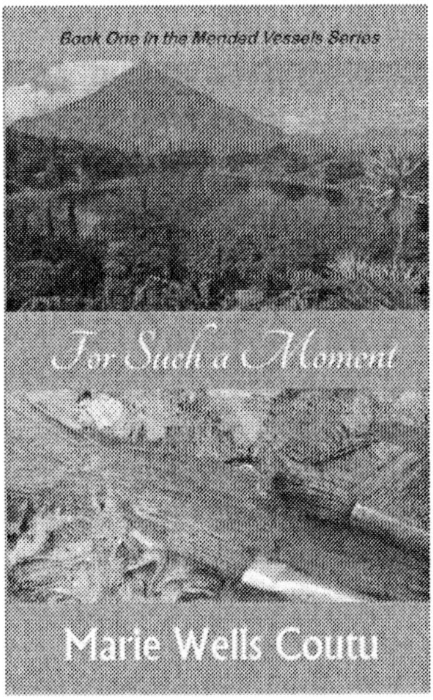

"If I don't do this, I might as well perish ..."

Revealing her secret could save lives … or change hers forever. In this book that re-imagines the story of Queen Esther in a contemporary setting, Ellen Neilson enjoys her comfortable life as the wife of an American CEO. Having lived in America since the age of ten, she has forsaken her mixed heritage and kept aspects of her childhood secret. Her husband has become engrossed in his job, and she believes having a child will salvage their troubled marriage.

When her cousin Manuel, whom she hasn't seen for twenty years, shows up as one of her husband's managers, Ellen fears that her past will be revealed. The company buys a banana plantation in her native country of Guatemala, and Manuel informs her that illegal pesticides have poisoned the water. People are dying, but she doesn't know who's to blame for the cover-up.

For Such a Moment

Available on Amazon, Kindle, and
from your favorite bookseller by request.

Look for other books

published by

Write Integrity Press

www.WriteIntegrity.com

and

Pix-N-Pens

Pix-N-Pens Publishing

www.PixNPens.com